PRAISE FOR

THE KISS QUOTIENT

"This is such a fun read, and it's also quite original and sexy and sensitive." —*New York Times* bestselling author Roxane Gay

"*The Kiss Quotient* is the perfect balm for any reading slump and a wonderful palate cleanser for the summer. It also might just be the best book you read all year." —*Bookpage*

"Hoang's witty debut proves that feelings are greater than numbers, no matter how you add things up." —*People*

"Hoang knocks it out of the park with this stellar debut." —*Publishers Weekly* (starred review)

"A riveting, compulsively readable romance that brims with feeling and warmth." —*Entertainment Weekly*

"Hoang's debut novel is unputdownable, exceptional, and leaves a strong impression that won't wane anytime soon." —NPR.org

"An absolute delight—charming, sexy, and centered on a protagonist you love rooting for." —Buzzfeed

"A vividly romantic tale filled with depth, humor and a universal sense of humanity." —#1 *New York Times* bestselling author Emily Giffin

PRAISE FOR HELEN HOANG

"Hoang's writing has a sharp, quirky, emotional edge that will resonate with anyone who has ever tried to navigate the complicated world of modern relationships."

—Jayne Ann Krentz, *New York Times* bestselling author

"Compulsively readable." —*Library Journal* (starred review)

"Hoang's writing bursts from the page." —Buzzfeed

"Hoang mixes sexy and tender with panache." —NPR.org

THE
Bride
TEST

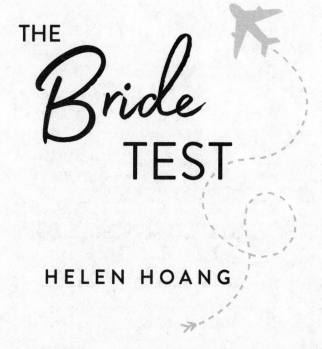

HELEN HOANG

JOVE
NEW YORK

A JOVE BOOK
Published by Berkley
An imprint of Penguin Random House LLC
1745 Broadway, New York, NY 10019

LIBRARY OF CONGRESS CATALOGING-IN-PUBLICATION DATA

Names: Hoang, Helen, author.
Title: The bride test / Helen Hoang.
Description: First Edition. | New York : Jove, 2019.
Identifiers: LCCN 2018053953| ISBN 9780451490827 (paperback) | ISBN 9780451490834 (ebook)
Subjects: LCSH: Romance fiction. | BISAC: FICTION / Romance / Contemporary. |
FICTION / Contemporary Women.
Classification: LCC PS3608.O1775 B75 2019 | DDC 813/.6—dc23
LC record available at https://lccn.loc.gov/2018053953

First Edition: May 2019

Printed in the United States of America

11th Printing

Cover design and illustration by Colleen Reinhart
Book design by Kristin del Rosario

Dedicated to

Me
Thank you for loving me and teaching me
how to chase my dreams.
I'm proud to be yours.

And

Johnny
I still miss you, but especially at weddings.
Love, always.

Acknowledgments

First of all, I need to thank *you*, dear reader. I'm honored that you've chosen to spend time with my words and I hope that something here resonates with you, makes you think, or makes you feel.

This book was extremely difficult to write for a variety of reasons, and I'm so thankful for the people who supported me during the process. Suzanne Park, you are the most considerate, hardest-working person I know. You inspire me. Gwynne Jackson, thank you for your kindness and patience and for always being genuine. It means more than I can say. A. R. Lucas, I'll forever associate rainbows with you. Thank you for being there when things are rough. Roselle Lim, how is it that we only just met this year? It feels like we've been friends forever.

Thank you, ReLynn Vaughn, Jen DeLuca, Shannon Caldwell, and my fantastic Pitch Wars mentor, Brighton Walsh, for reading early drafts of this book. Thanks to Brighton's Bs for always being welcoming: Melissa Marino, Anniston Jory, Elizabeth Leis, Ellis Leigh, Esher Hogan, Laura Elizabeth, and Suzanne Baltzar.

Thank you to the sensitivity readers who provided alternate perspectives on the diversity involved. I'm grateful for your valuable input.

Mom, thank you for leading by example and being you. I wouldn't be where I am without you. Many thanks to the rest of my family for putting up with me as I wrote this book, especially when I was antisocial and wrote through all of our vacations. I love you all. Because I made the grievous mistake of not mentioning my nieces and nephew last time: Sylvers, you are super-super-duper awesome. And Ava, Elena, Anja, and Henry, too.

No acknowledgments would be complete without my amazing agent, Kim Lionetti. I couldn't have asked for a better partner for this publishing journey we're on. You make this even more special, and I can't thank you enough.

Finally, thank you to the incredible publishing team at Berkley: Cindy Hwang, Kristine Swartz, Angela Kim, Megha Jain, Jessica Brock, Fareeda Bullert, Tawanna Sullivan, Colleen Reinhart, and others. This was an ambitious project for me, and you've all surprised me with how supportive you've been. I'm proud to work with you.

PROLOGUE

Ten years ago
San Jose, California

Khai was supposed to be crying. He knew he was supposed to be crying. Everyone else was.

But his eyes were dry.

If they stung, it was due to the heavy incense fogging the funeral parlor's reception room. Was he sad? He thought he was sad. But he should be *sadder*. When your best friend died like this, you were supposed to be destroyed. If this were a Vietnamese opera, his tears would be forming rivers and drowning everyone.

Why was his mind clear? Why was he thinking about the homework assignment that was due tomorrow? Why was he still functioning?

His cousin Sara had sobbed so hard she'd needed to rush to the bathroom to vomit. She was still there now—he suspected—being sick over and over. Her mom, Dì Mai, sat stiffly in the front row, palms flat together and head bowed. Khai's mom patted her back from time to time, but she remained unresponsive. Like Khai, she shed no tears, but that was because she'd cried them all out days before. The family was worried about her. She'd withered down to her skeleton since they'd gotten the call.

Rows of Buddhist monks in yellow robes blocked his view of the open casket, but that was a good thing. Though the morticians had done their best, the body looked misshapen and wrong. That was not the sixteen-year-old boy who used to be Khai's friend and favorite cousin. That was not Andy.

Andy was gone.

The only parts of him that survived were the memories in Khai's head. Stick fights and sword fights, wrestling matches that Khai never won but refused to lose. Khai would rather break both of his own arms than call Andy his daddy. Andy said Khai was pathologically stubborn. Khai insisted he merely had principles. He still remembered their long walks home, when the weight of the sun was heavier than their book-filled backpacks, and the conversations that had taken place during those walks.

Even now, he could hear his cousin scoffing at him. The specific circumstances eluded him, but the words remained.

Nothing gets to you. It's like your heart is made of stone.

He hadn't understood Andy then. He was beginning to now.

The droning of Buddhist chants filled the room, low, off-key syllables spoken in a language no one understood. It flowed over and around him and vibrated in his head, and he couldn't stop shaking his leg even though people had given him looks. A furtive glance at his watch confirmed that, yes, this had been going on for hours. He wanted the noise to stop. He could almost envision himself crawling into the coffin and shutting the lid to block the sound. But then he'd be stuck in a tight space with a corpse, and he wasn't sure if that would be an improvement over his current predicament.

If Andy were here—*alive* and here—they'd escape together and find something to do, even if it was just going outside to kick rocks around the parking lot. Andy was good that way. He was always there when you needed him. Except for now.

Khai's big brother sat beside him, but he knew Quan wouldn't want to leave early. Funerals existed for people like Quan. He needed the closure or whatever it was people got from them. With his intimidating build and the new tattoos on his neck and arms, Quan looked like one badass motherfucker, but his eyes were rimmed red. From time to time, he discreetly brushed the moisture from his cheeks. Just like always, Khai wished he could be more like his brother.

A metal bowl rang, and the chanting stopped. Relief was instant and dizzying, like an enormous pressure had suddenly dissolved. The monks worked with the pallbearers to close the casket, and soon a procession filed sedately down the center aisle. Because he disliked standing in lines and the claustrophobic press of bodies, Khai stayed seated as Quan got to his feet, squeezed Khai's shoulder once, and joined the exodus.

He watched as relatives trudged past. Some cried openly. Others were more stoic, but their sadness was obvious even to him. Aunts, uncles, cousins, distant relations, and friends of the family all supported one another, joined together by this thing called grief. As usual, Khai was not a part of it.

A group of older women that consisted of his mom, Dì Mai, and two of his other aunts brought up the end of the line because of a near-fainting spell, sticking close in adulthood just like everyone said they had as young girls. If it weren't for the fact that they all wore black, they could have been attending a wedding. Diamonds and jade hung from their ears, throats, and fingers, and he could smell their makeup and perfume through the haze of the incense.

As they passed his row, he stood and straightened the hand-me-down suit coat from Quan. He had a lot of growing to do if he was ever going to fill the thing out. And pull-ups. Thousands of pull-ups. He'd start those tonight.

When he looked up, he discovered the ladies had all paused next to him. Dì Mai reached a hand toward his cheek but stopped before touching him.

She searched his face with solemn eyes. "I thought you two were close. Don't you care that he's gone?"

His heart jumped and started beating so fast it hurt. When he tried to speak, nothing came out. His throat was swollen shut.

"Of course they were close," his mom chided her sister before tugging on her arm. "Come, Mai, let's go. They're waiting for us."

With his feet frozen to the floor, he watched as they disappeared through the doorway. Logically, he knew he was standing in place, but he felt like he was falling. Down, down, down.

I thought you two were close.

Ever since his elementary school teacher insisted his parents take him to a psychologist, he'd known he was different. The majority of his family, however, had discounted the resulting diagnosis, saying he was merely "a little strange." There was no such thing as autism or Asperger's syndrome in the countryside of Vietnam. Besides, he didn't get into trouble and did well in school. What did it matter?

I thought you two were close.

The words wouldn't stop echoing in his head, bringing him to an unwelcome self-realization: He was different, yes, but in a *bad* way.

I thought you two were close.

Andy hadn't just been his best friend. He'd been his *only* friend. Andy was as close as close got for Khai. If he couldn't grieve for Andy, that meant he couldn't grieve at all. And if he couldn't grieve, the flip side also had to be true.

He couldn't love.

Andy had been right. Khai's heart really was made of metaphorical stone.

The knowledge spread over him like petroleum in an oil spill. He didn't like it, but there was nothing to do but accept it. This wasn't something you could change. He was what he was.

I thought you two were close.

He was . . . bad.

He unfisted his hands, worked the fingers. His legs moved when he commanded them. His lungs drew breath. He saw, he heard, he experienced. And it struck him as being incredibly unfair. This was not what he would have chosen. If he could have chosen who went in that casket.

The chanting started again, signaling the funeral was nearing its end. Time to join the others as they said their final good-byes. No one seemed to understand it wasn't *good*-bye unless Andy said it back. For his part, Khai would say nothing.

CHAPTER ONE

Two months ago
T.P. Hồ Chí Minh, Việt Nam

Scrubbing toilets wasn't usually this interesting. Mỹ had done it so many times she had a streamlined routine by now. Spray with poison everywhere. Pour poison inside. Scrub, scrub, scrub, scrub, scrub. Wipe, wipe, wipe. Flush. Done in less than two minutes. If they had a toilet-cleaning contest, Mỹ would be a top contender. Not today, though. The noises in the next stall kept distracting her.

She was pretty sure the girl in there was crying. Either that or exercising. There was lots of heavy breathing going on. What kind of workout could you do in a bathroom stall? Knee-ups maybe.

A strangled sound issued, followed by a high-pitched whimper, and Mỹ let go of her toilet brush. That was definitely crying. Leaning her temple against the side of the stall, she cleared her throat and asked, "Miss, is something wrong?"

"No, nothing's wrong," the girl said, but her cries got louder before they stopped abruptly, replaced by more muffled heavy breathing.

"I work in this hotel." As a janitor/maid. "If someone treated you badly, I can help." She'd try to, anyway. Nothing rankled her like a bully. She couldn't afford to lose this job, though.

"No, I'm fine." The door latch rattled, and shoes clacked against the marble floor.

Mỹ stuck her head out of her stall in time to see a pretty girl saunter toward the sinks. She wore the highest, scariest heels Mỹ had ever seen and a skintight red dress that ended right beneath her butt. If you believed anything Mỹ's grandma said, that girl would get pregnant the second she stepped foot on the street. She was probably pregnant already—from the potency of a man's child-giving stare.

For her part, Mỹ had gotten pregnant by messing around with a playboy from school, no skimpy dress and scary heels needed. She'd resisted him in the beginning. Her mom and grandma had been clear that studies came first, but he'd pursued her until she'd caved, thinking it was love. Instead of marrying her when she'd told him about the baby, however, he'd grudgingly offered to keep her as his secret mistress. She wasn't the kind of girl he could introduce to his upper-class family, and, surprise, he was engaged and planned to go through with the wedding. Obviously, Mỹ had turned him down, which had been both a relief and a shock for him, that son of a dog. Her family, on the other hand, had been heartbroken with disappointment—they'd pinned so many hopes on her. But as she'd known they would, they'd supported her and her baby.

The girl in the red dress washed her hands and dabbed at her mascara-streaked cheeks before tossing her hand towel on the counter and leaving the bathroom. Mỹ's yellow rubber gloves squeaked as she fisted her hands. The towel basket was *right there*. Grumbling to herself, she stalked to the sinks, wiped off the counter with the girl's hand towel, and launched it into the towel basket. A quick inspection of the sink, counter, mirror, and neatly rolled stack of towels confirmed everything was acceptable, and she started back toward the last toilet.

The bathroom door swung open, and another girl rushed inside. With her waist-length black hair, skinny body, long legs, and danger heels, she looked a lot like the previous girl. Only her dress was white. Was the hotel having some kind of pageant? And why was this girl crying, too?

"Miss, are you okay?" Mỹ asked as she took a tentative step toward her.

The girl splashed water on her face. "I'm fine." She braced her wet hands on the granite countertop, making more mess for Mỹ to clean up, and stared at her reflection in the mirror as she took deep breaths. "I thought she was going to pick me. I was so sure. Why ask that question if she doesn't want that answer? She's a sneaky woman."

Mỹ tore her gaze away from the fresh water drops on the counter and focused on the girl's face. "What woman? Pick you for what?"

The girl raked a certain look over Mỹ's hotel uniform and rolled her eyes. "You wouldn't understand."

Mỹ's back stiffened, and her skin flushed with embarrassed heat. She'd gotten that look and tone of voice before. She knew what they meant. Before she could come up with a suitable response, the girl was gone. And, forget the girl's grandpa and all her other ancestors, too, another crumpled towel lay on the counter.

Mỹ stomped to the sink, wiped up the girl's mess, and threw the towel into the basket. Well, she meant to. Her aim was off, and it landed on the floor. Huffing in frustration, she went to pick it up.

Just as her gloved fingers closed around the towel, the door swung open yet again. She looked heavenward. If it was another crying spoiled girl, she was leaving for a bathroom on the other side of the hotel.

But it wasn't. A tired-looking older woman padded to the sitting room on the far end of the bathroom and sat on one of the velvet-upholstered love seats. Mỹ knew at first glance the lady was a Việt *kiều*. It was a combination of things that gave it away: her genuine granddaddy-sized Louis Vuitton handbag, her expensive clothes, and her feet. Manicured and perfectly uncalloused, those sandaled feet had to belong to an overseas Vietnamese. Those people tipped *really* well, for everything. Money practically poured out of them. Maybe today was Mỹ's lucky day.

She tossed the hand towel in the basket and approached the woman. "Miss, can I get you anything?"

The lady waved at her dismissively.

"Just let me know, miss. Enjoy your time in here. It's a very nice bathroom." She winced, wishing she could retract the last words, and turned back toward her toilets. Why they had a sitting room in here was beyond her. Sure, it was a nice room, but why relax where you could hear people doing bathroom stuff?

She finished her work, set her bucket of cleaning supplies on the floor by the sinks, and performed one last inspection of the bathroom. One of the hand towels had partially unrolled, so she shook it out, rerolled it, and set it on the stack with the others. Then she repositioned the tissue box. There. Everything was presentable.

She bent to pick up her bucket, but before her fingers could close around the handle, the lady said, "Why did you fix the box of Kleenex like that?"

Mỹ straightened, looked at the tissue box, and then tilted her head at the lady. "Because that's how the hotel likes it, miss."

A thinking expression crossed the lady's face, and after a second, she beckoned Mỹ toward her and patted the space next to her on the sofa. "Come talk to me for a minute. Call me Cô Nga."

Mỹ smiled in puzzlement but did as she was bid, sitting down next to the lady and keeping her back straight, her hands folded, and her knees pressed together like the virginest virgin. Her grandma would have been proud.

Sharp eyes in a pale powdered face assessed her much like Mỹ had just done to the bathroom counter, and Mỹ pressed her feet together awkwardly and beamed her best smile at the lady.

After reading her name tag, the lady said, "So your name is Trần Ngọc Mỹ."

"Yes, miss."

"You clean the bathrooms here? What else do you do?"

Mỹ's smile threatened to fade, and she kept it up with effort. "I also clean the guests' rooms, so that's more bathrooms, changing sheets, making beds, vacuuming. Those kinds of things." It wasn't what she'd dreamed of doing when she was younger, but it paid, and she made sure she did good work.

"Ah, that is— You have mixed blood." Leaning forward, the lady clasped Mỹ's chin and angled her face upward. "Your eyes are *green*."

Mỹ held her breath and tried to figure out the lady's opinion on this. Sometimes it was a good thing. Most of the time it wasn't. It was much better to be mixed race when you had money.

The lady frowned. "But how? There haven't been American soldiers here since the war."

Mỹ shrugged. "My mom says he was a businessman. I've never met him." As the story went, her mom had been his housekeeper— and something else on the side—and their affair had ended when his work project finished and he left the country. It wasn't until afterward that her mom discovered she was pregnant, and by then it was too late. She hadn't known how to find him. She'd had no choice but to move back home to live with her family. Mỹ had always thought she'd do better than her mom, but she'd managed to follow in her footsteps almost exactly.

The lady nodded and squeezed her arm once. "Did you just move to the city? You don't seem like you're from around here."

Mỹ averted her eyes, and her smile fell. She'd grown up with very little money, but it wasn't until she'd come to the big city that she'd learned just how poor she really was. "We moved a couple months ago because I got the job here. Is it that easy to tell?"

The lady patted Mỹ's cheek in an oddly affectionate manner. "You're still naïve like a country girl. Where are you from?"

"A village close to Mỹ Tho, by the water."

A wide grin stretched over the lady's face. "I knew I liked you. Places make people. I grew up there. I named my restaurant Mỹ Tho Noodles. It's a very good restaurant in California. They talk about it on TV and in magazines. I guess you wouldn't have heard about it here, though." She sighed to herself before her eyes sharpened and she asked, "How old are you?"

"Twenty-three."

"You look younger than that," Cô Nga said with a laugh. "But that's a good age."

A good age for what? But Mỹ didn't ask. Tip or no tip, she was ready for this conversation to end. Maybe a real city girl would have left already. Toilets didn't scrub themselves.

"Have you ever thought of coming to America?" Cô Nga asked.

Mỹ shook her head, but that was a lie. As a child, she'd fantasized about living in a place where she didn't stick out and maybe meeting her green-eyed dad. But there was more than an ocean separating Việt Nam and America, and the older she'd grown, the larger the distance had become.

"Are you married?" the lady asked. "Do you have a boyfriend?"

"No, no husband, no boyfriend." She smoothed her hands over her thighs and gripped her knees. What did this woman want? She'd heard the horror stories about strangers. Was this sweet-looking woman trying to trick her and sell her into prostitution in Cambodia?

"Don't look so worried. I have good intentions. Here, let me show you something." The lady dug through her giant Louis Vuitton purse until she found a manila file. Then she pulled out a photograph and handed it to Mỹ. "This is my Diệp Khải, my youngest son. He's handsome, ha?"

Mỹ didn't want to look—she honestly didn't care about this unknown man who lived in the paradise of California—but she decided to humor the woman. She'd look at the picture and make all the appropriate noises. She'd tell Cô Nga her son looked like a movie star, and then she'd find some excuse to leave.

When she glanced at the photograph, however, her body went still, just like the sky immediately before a rainstorm.

He *did* look like a movie star, a man-beautiful one, with sexy wind-tossed hair and strong, clean features. Most captivating of all, however, was the quiet intensity that emanated from him. A shadow of a smile touched his lips as he focused on something to the side, and she found herself leaning toward the photo. If he were an actor, all the aloof dangerous hero roles would be his, like a bodyguard or a kung fu master. He made you wonder: What was he thinking about so intently? What was his story? Why didn't he smile for real?

"Ah, so Mỹ approves. I told you he was handsome," Cô Nga said with a knowing smile.

Mỹ blinked like she was coming out of a trance and handed the picture back to the lady. "Yes, he is." He'd make a lucky girl even luckier someday, and they'd live a long, lucky life together. She hoped they experienced food poisoning at least once. Nothing life-threatening, of course. Just inconvenient—make that *very* inconvenient. And mildly painful. Embarrassing, too.

"He's also smart and talented. He went to graduate school."

Mỹ worked up a smile. "That's impressive. I would be very proud if I had a son like him." Her mom, on the other hand, had a toilet cleaner for a daughter. She pushed her bitterness away and reminded herself to keep her head down and go about her own business. Jealousy wouldn't get her anything but misery. But she wished him extra incidences of food poisoning anyway. There had to be some fairness in the world.

"I am very proud of him," Cô Nga said. "He's why I'm here, actually. To find him a wife."

"Oh." Mỹ frowned. "I didn't know Americans did that." It seemed horribly old-fashioned to her.

"They don't do it, and Khải would be angry if he knew. But I have to do something. His older brother is too good with women—I don't need to worry about him—but Khải is twenty-six and still hasn't had a girlfriend. When I set up dates for him, he doesn't go. When girls call him, he hangs up. This coming summer, there are three weddings in our family, *three*, but is one his? No. Since he doesn't know how to find himself a wife, I decided to do it for him. I've been interviewing candidates all day. None of them fit my expectations."

Her jaw fell. "All the crying girls . . ."

Cô Nga waved her comment away. "They're crying because they're ashamed of themselves. They'll recover. I had to know if they were serious about marrying my son. None of them were."

"They seemed very serious." They hadn't been fake crying in the bathroom—that was for sure.

"How about you?" Cô Nga fixed that assessing stare on her again.

"What about me?"

"Are you interested in marrying my Khải?"

Mỹ looked behind herself before pointing at her own chest. *"Me?"*

Cô Nga nodded. "Yes, you. You've caught my attention."

Her eyes widened. *How?*

As if she could read Mỹ's mind, Cô Nga said, "You're a good, hardworking girl and pretty in an unusual way. I think I could trust you with my Khải."

All Mỹ could do was stare. Had the fumes from the cleaning chemicals finally damaged her brain? "You want me to marry your son? But we've never met. *You* might like me..." She shook her head, still unable to wrap her mind around that. She *cleaned toilets* for a living. "But your son probably won't. He sounds picky, and I'm not—"

"Oh, no, no," Cô Nga interrupted. "He's not picky. He's *shy.* And stubborn. He thinks he doesn't want a family. He needs a girl who is more stubborn. You'd have to make him change his mind."

"How would I—"

"Oi, you know. You dress up, take care of him, cook the things he likes, do the things he likes..."

Mỹ couldn't help grimacing, and Cô Nga surprised her by laughing.

"This is why I like you. You can't help but be yourself. What do you think? I could give you a summer in America to see if you two fit. If you don't, no problem, you go home. At the very least, you'll go to all our family weddings and have some food and fun. How's that?"

"I—I—I . . ." She didn't know what to say. It was too much to take in.

"One more thing." Cô Nga's gaze turned measuring, and there was a heavy pause before she said, "He doesn't want children. But I am determined to have grandchildren. If you manage to get pregnant, I know he'll do the right thing and marry you, regardless of how you get along. I'll even give you money. Twenty thousand American dollars. Will you do this for me?"

The breath seeped from Mỹ's lungs, and her skin went cold. Cô Nga wanted her to steal a baby from her son and force him into marriage. Disappointment and futility crushed her. For a moment, she'd thought this lady saw something special in her, but Cô Nga had judged her based on things she couldn't control, just like the girls in the skimpy dresses had.

"The other girls all said no, didn't they? You thought I'd say yes because . . ." She indicated her uniform with an open palm.

Cô Nga said nothing, her gaze steady.

Mỹ pushed up from the sofa, went to collect her bucket of cleaning supplies, opened the door, and paused in the doorway. With her eyes trained straight ahead, she said, "My answer is no."

She didn't have money, connections, or skills, but she could still be as hardheaded and foolish as she wanted. She hoped her refusal stung. Without a backward glance, she left.

That evening, after the hour-long walk home—the same one she did twice a day every day—Mỹ tiptoed into their one-room house and collapsed onto the section of floor mat where she slept at night. She needed to get ready for bed, but first, she wanted to do nothing for a few moments. Just nothing. Nothing was such a luxury.

Her pocket buzzed, ruining her nothing. With a frustrated sigh, she dug her phone out of her pocket.

Unfamiliar phone number.

She debated not answering it, but something had her hitting the talk button and pressing the phone to her ear. "Hello?"

"Mỹ, is this you?"

Mỹ puzzled over the voice. It was slightly familiar, but she couldn't place it. "Yes. Who's this?"

"It's me, Cô Nga. No, don't hang up," the lady added quickly. "I got your number from the hotel supervisor. I wanted to talk to you."

Her fingers tightened on the phone, and she sat upright. "I don't have anything left to say."

"You won't change your mind?"

She resisted the urge to throw her phone at the wall. "No."

"Good," Cô Nga said.

Frowning, Mỹ lowered her phone and stared at it. What did she mean *good*?

She returned the phone to her ear in time to hear Cô Nga say, "It was a test. I don't want you to trick my son into having a baby, but I needed to know what kind of person you are."

"So that means . . . ?"

"That means you're the one I want, Mỹ. Come to America to see my son. I'll give you the entire summer to win him and go to his cousins' weddings. You'll need the time. It'll be work to figure him out, but it'll be worth it. He's good stuff. If anyone can do it, I think it's you. If you want to. Do you?"

Her head began spinning. "I don't know. I need to think."

"Then think and call me back. But don't take too long. I need to arrange your visa and plane ticket," Cô Nga said. "I'll be waiting to hear from you." With that, the call disconnected.

A lamp on the other side of the room clicked on, illuminating the tight, cluttered space with soft, golden light. Clothes and kitchen paraphernalia hung from the walls, covering every square centimeter of crumbling brick not taken up by the old electric stove, tiny refrigerator, and miniature TV they used to watch kung fu sagas and bootleg American films. The center floor space was occupied by the sleeping bodies of her daughter, Ngọc Anh, and her grandma.

Her mom lay between Grandma and the stove, her hand on the lamp's switch. A fan blew humid air at them on the highest setting.

"Who was that?" her mom whispered.

"A Việt *kiều*," Mỹ said, barely believing her own words. "She wants me to come to America and marry her son."

Her mom propped herself up on an elbow, and her hair fell in a silken curtain over her shoulder. Bedtime was the only time she let her hair loose, and it made her look ten years younger. "Is he older than your grandpa? Does he look like a skunk? What's wrong with him?"

At that moment, Mỹ's phone buzzed with a message from Cô Nga.

To help you think.

Another buzz, and the photograph of Khải covered the screen—the same one from before. She handed her phone to her mom wordlessly.

"*This* is him?" her mom asked with wide eyes.

"His name is Diệp Khải."

Her mom stared at the picture for the longest time, quiet save for the soft sighing of her breathing. Finally, she handed the phone back. "You have no choice. You have to do it."

"But he doesn't want to get married. I'm supposed to chase him and change his mind. I don't know how to—"

"Just do it. Do whatever you have to. It's *America*, Mỹ. You have to do it for this one." Her mom reached over Grandma's thin sleeping form and pulled Ngọc Anh's thin blanket up to her throat. "If I had the opportunity, I would have done the same for you. For her future. She doesn't fit in here. And she needs a dad."

Mỹ clenched her teeth as childhood memories tried to spill from the corner of her mind where she trapped them. She could still hear the children singing *Mixed girl with the twelve buttholes* at her as she walked home from school. Her childhood had been difficult, but it had prepared her for life. She was stronger now, tougher. "I didn't have a dad."

Her mom's eyes hardened. "And look where that's gotten you."

Mỹ looked down at her girl. "It also got me her." She regretted being with her daughter's heartless father, but she'd never regretted her baby. Not even for a second.

She brushed the damp baby hairs away from her girl's temple, and that enormous love expanded in her heart. Gazing at her daughter's face was like looking in a mirror that reflected a time twenty years past. Her girl looked exactly like Mỹ used to. They had the same eyebrows, cheekbones, nose, and skin tone. Even the shape of their lips was the same. But Ngọc Anh was far, far sweeter than Mỹ had ever been. She would do anything for this little one.

Except give her up.

Once Ngọc Anh's father had married, his wife had discovered she couldn't have babies, and they'd offered to raise Ngọc Anh as their own. Again, Mỹ had turned down an offer everyone expected her to accept. They'd called her selfish. His family could give Ngọc Anh all the *things* she needed.

But what about love? Love mattered, and no one could love her baby like Mỹ could. No one. She felt it in her heart.

Still, from time to time, she worried she'd done the wrong thing.

"If you don't like him," her mom said, "you can divorce him after you get your green card and marry someone else."

"I can't marry him just for a green card." He was a person, not a stack of paper, and if he decided to marry her, it would be because she'd succeeded in seducing him, because he cared about her. She couldn't use someone that way. That would make her just as bad as Ngọc Anh's dad.

Her mom nodded like she could hear the thoughts in Mỹ's head. "What happens if you go and you can't change his mind?"

"I come back at the end of the summer."

A disgusted sound came from the back of her mom's throat. "I can't believe you need to think about this. You have nothing to lose."

As Mỹ looked at the black screen on her phone, a thought occurred to her. "Cô Nga said he doesn't want a family. I have Ngọc Anh."

Her mom rolled her eyes. "What young man wants a family? If he loves you, he'll love Ngọc Anh."

"It doesn't work that way, and you know it. If a man knows you have a baby, most of the time he's not interested." And if he was interested, all he wanted was sex.

"Then don't tell him right away. Give him time to fall for you, and tell him later," her mom said.

Mỹ shook her head. "That feels wrong."

"If he tells you he loves you but backs out of marriage because you have a daughter, you don't want him anyway. But this woman knows her son, and she *chose* you. You have to try. At the very least, you get a whole summer in America. Do you know how lucky you are? Don't you want to see America? Where in America is it?"

"She said California, but I don't think I can stand being away that long." Mỹ brushed her fingers across her daughter's baby-soft cheek. She'd never been away from home longer than a day. What if Ngọc Anh thought she'd abandoned her?

Her mom's forehead creased with thought, and she got up to dig through a pile of boxes kept in the corner. They were her mom's personal things, and no one was allowed to open them. Growing up, Mỹ used to snoop through them when no one was looking, especially the bottom one. When her mom opened that box specifically and rustled through its contents, Mỹ's heart started sprinting.

"That's where your dad is from. Here, look." Her mom handed her a yellowed photo of a man with his arm thrown around her shoulders. Mỹ had spent countless hours peering at this photo, holding it close, looking at it upside down, squinting, anything to confirm the man's eyes were green and he was, in fact, her father, but nothing worked. The picture had been taken from too far away. His eyes could be any color. They appeared brown, if she was being honest with herself.

The lettering on his shirt, however, was easy to read. It clearly said *Cal Berkeley*.

"Is that what 'Cal' stands for?" she asked. "California?"

Her mom nodded. "I looked it up. It's a famous university. Maybe when you're there, you can go see it. Maybe . . . you can try to find him."

Mỹ's heart jumped so hard her fingers tingled. "Are you finally going to tell me his name?" she asked, her voice whisper thin. All she knew was "Phil." That was the name her grandma whispered with hate when she and Mỹ were alone. *That* Phil. *Mister* Phil. *Your mother's* Phil.

A bitter smile touched her mom's lips. "He said his full name was ugly. All anyone ever called him was Phil. I think his surname started with an *L*."

Mỹ's hopes shattered before they'd fully formed. "It's impossible, then."

Her mom's expression went determined. "You don't know until you try. Maybe if they use the expensive computers, they can make a list for you. If you work hard, there's a chance."

Mỹ gazed at the picture of her dad, feeling the yearning in her chest grow bigger with every second. Did he live in California? How would he react if he opened his door . . . and saw her? Would he accuse her of coming to ask for money?

Or would he be happy to find a daughter he'd never known he had?

She opened up the picture of Khải on her phone and held the two photos side by side on her lap. What had Cô Nga seen in her that she thought Mỹ was a good match for her son? Would her son see it, too? And would he accept her daughter? Would her own father accept his daughter?

Either way, her mom was right. She wouldn't know until she tried. On both accounts.

Mỹ typed out a text message to Cô Nga and hit send.

Yes, I want to try.

"I'm going to do it," she told her mom. She tried to sound confident, but she was quaking inside. What had she just agreed to?

"I knew you would, and I'm glad. We'll take good care of Ngọc Anh while you're gone. Now, go to sleep. You still have to work tomorrow." The light clicked off. But after the room went dark, her mom said, "You should know with just one summer, you don't have time to do things the traditional way. You have to play to win, even if you're not sure you want him. As long as he's not evil, love can grow. And remember, good girls don't get the man. You need to be bad, Mỹ."

Mỹ swallowed. She had a good idea what "bad" meant, and she was surprised her mom dared to suggest it with her grandma in the room.

CHAPTER TWO

Present day

As Khai's running shoes hit the cracked concrete of the driveway leading to his Sunnyvale fixer-upper, which he never got around to fixing up, the timer on his watch beeped. Exactly fifteen minutes.

Yes.

There was nothing as satisfying as perfect increments of time. Except for hitting whole dollar amounts when filling up at the gas station. Or when the restaurant bill was a prime number or a segment of the Fibonacci sequence or just all eights. Eight was such an elegant number. If he added a minute to his run, he could set a checkpoint in the middle. Wouldn't that be entertaining?

He was mentally rerouting his daily commute when he noticed the black Ducati parked next to his bird-shit-smattered Porsche on the curb. Quan was here, and he'd driven *that*, even though their mom hated it and Khai had provided him with all the death and brain damage statistics multiple times. Giving the motorcycle a wide berth, he jogged to his front door, avoided the thorny weed bush that thrived in the shade beneath the awning, and let himself in.

Inside, he removed his shoes and immediately peeled his socks off. Heaven was bare feet sinking into his house's 1970s shag carpet. Initially, he'd hated it—the pea-green color was offensive—but walking on it felt a lot like taking a stroll in the clouds Mary Poppins style. It used to smell funny, but time had fixed it. Either that, or he'd assimilated the scents of mothballs and old ladies into his identity. He was going to keep the carpet until the house became officially condemned by Santa Clara County.

There Quan was, sitting on Khai's couch with his feet up on Khai's coffee table, watching some finance program on CNBC as he drank Khai's only cold can of Coca-Cola—he could see the condensation dripping over the cursive lettering just like in a commercial. The rest of his soda was room temperature because you could only fit one can into his fridge at a time. The valuable real estate was taken by Tupperware containers filled with his mom's cooking. She thought he was going to starve to death if she didn't personally feed him, and in true Mom fashion, she never did anything halfway.

"Yo, you're home. How's it going?" Quan asked as he took a long slurp of Coke and then hissed as the burn worked down his throat.

"Fine." Khai narrowed his eyes at his brother. The hiss and burn from the cold Coke was one of Khai's favorite things, and now he had to wait four hours until a new can was ready. "Why are you here?"

"Dunno. Mom told me to come. Apparently, she's on her way."

Ah shit, he saw nonsensical errands in his near future. What would it be this time? Driving to the grocery store all the way in San Jose to buy discount oranges? Or importing commercial quantities of seaweed extract from Japan to cure his aunt's cancer? No, it had to be something worse, because she needed both her sons involved. He couldn't begin to imagine what it might be.

"I need to take a shower." His clothes were wet and sticky, and he wanted them off.

"You might wanna be fast. I just heard someone pull into the driveway." Quan took a good look at Khai then, and his eyebrows arched. "Did you just run home from work in a suit?"

"Yeah, I do every day. This kind is engineered for motion." He pointed to the elastic cuffs at his ankles. "And the fabric breathes really well. It's also machine washable."

Quan grinned and took another slurp from his pilfered Coke. "So my brother's been running the streets of Silicon Valley like an evil Asian Terminator. I like it."

The strange imagery made Khai hesitate, and just as he opened his mouth to respond, a familiar voice outside the house announced in Vietnamese, "Here, here, here, here, I have lots of food. Help me bring it in." His mom never spoke English unless she absolutely had to. Basically, she spoke English to the health inspector at her restaurant.

"What?" Khai asked in English. He honestly didn't know how to speak Vietnamese, though he understood it well enough. "I still *have* lots of food. I'm going to start feeding the homeless if you—"

His mom appeared in the doorway with a proud smile and three boxes of mangoes. "Hi, *con*."

Because he didn't want her to break her back, he stuffed his socks in his pocket and took the boxes from her. "I don't eat fruit, remember? They're going to go bad."

He was almost back out the door with them when she said, "No, no, they're not for you. They're for Mỹ. So she doesn't miss home too much."

He paused. Who the hell was Mỹ?

Quan got to his feet. "What's going on?"

"Help me bring in more fruit first." To Khai, she said, "Put those in the kitchen."

Khai walked the boxes into his kitchen in a state of utter confusion. Why was this fruit in *his* house when it was supposed to prevent *Mỹ*, whoever she was, from feeling homesick? He set the boxes on his Formica countertop and noted they were three different varieties of mango. There were big red-green ones, medium yellow ones, and small green ones in the box that bore Thai script. Had his mom purchased him some manner of fruit-eating jungle monkey? Why would she do that? She didn't even like dogs and cats.

Why was it taking Quan so long to bring the boxes inside? Khai went to investigate and found his brother and mom deep in discussion out by her beat-up Camry. Khai and his siblings had pitched in together to get her a Lexus SUV for Mother's Day last year, but she insisted upon driving this two-decades-old Toyota unless it was a special occasion. He noted there was no one sitting inside it. No *Mỹ*.

"Mom, it's wrong. This is the United States. People don't *do* that," Quan said, sounding more exasperated than usual with their mom.

"I had to do something, and you need to support me. He listens to you."

Quan looked heavenward. "He listens to me because I'm reasonable. This isn't."

"You're just like that stinky father of yours. You both let me down when I need you," their mom said. "Your brother is always reliable."

Quan made a huffing sound and scrubbed his hands over his face and buzzed head before he took three more fruit boxes from the trunk. When he saw Khai, he halted midstep. "Brace yourself." Then he carried the boxes inside.

Well, that was ominous. In Khai's head, the hypothetical jungle monkey morphed into a giant male gorilla. This fruit would probably feed such a creature for one day. On the positive side, he wouldn't need to pay to get his house bulldozed, and he might even be able to file a claim on his homeowner's insurance. *Reason for damage: rogue gorilla in a mango rage.*

"Grab the jackfruit and come inside. I need to talk to you," his mom said.

He hefted up the spiky jackfruit—holy fuck, it weighed like thirty pounds—and followed her into his kitchen, where Quan had set the new boxes next to the mangoes and seated himself at the kitchen table with his Coke. Worrying about the sturdiness of his counter, Khai carefully eased the jackfruit next to the other fruit. When the counter didn't immediately collapse to the floor, he sighed in relief.

His mom considered his seventies kitchen with a frown. That look on her face was textbook dissatisfaction. If he lined up his old facial expression flash cards with her face right now, they'd match perfectly.

"You need to get a new house," she said. "This one is too old. And you need to move all those exercise machines out of the living room. Only bachelors live like this."

Khai happened to *be* a bachelor, so he didn't see what the problem was. "This location is convenient for work, and I like exercising where I can watch TV."

She waved his comments away, muttering, "This boy."

A long silence ensued, broken only by the occasional slurping of Coke—Khai's Coke, goddammit. When he couldn't take it anymore, he looked from his brother to his mom and said, "So . . . who is Mỹ?" As far as he knew, *mỹ* meant *beautiful*, but it was also how you said *America* in Vietnamese. Whichever way he looked at it, it seemed an odd name for a gorilla, but what did he know?

His mom squared her shoulders. "She's the girl you need to pick up from the airport Saturday night."

"Oh, okay." That wasn't horrible. He didn't like the idea of ferrying around someone he didn't know and changing his schedule, but he was glad he didn't need a rabies shot or an FDA permit. "Just send me her flight schedule. Where do I drop her off?"

"She's staying here with you," she said.

"What? Why?" Khai's entire body stiffened at the idea. It was an invasion, clear and simple.

"Don't sound so upset," she said in a cajoling tone. "She's young and very pretty."

He looked to Quan. "Why can't she stay with you? You like women."

Quan choked in the middle of drinking Coke and pounded his chest with a fist as he coughed.

Their mom aimed her dissatisfied look at Quan before she focused on Khai and straightened to her full height of four feet ten inches. "She can't stay with Quan because she's *your* future wife."

"What?" He laughed a little. This had to be a joke, but he didn't understand the humor.

"I chose her for you when I went to Việt Nam. You'll like her. She's perfect for you," she said.

"I don't—You can't—I—" He shook his head. *"What?"*

"Yeah," Quan said. "That was my reaction, too. She got you a mail-order bride from Vietnam, Khai."

Their mom glowered at Quan. "Why do you say it so it sounds so bad? She's not a 'mail-order bride.' I met her in person. This is how they used to do it in the olden days. If I followed tradition, I would already have found you a wife the same way, but you don't need my help. Your brother does."

Khai didn't even try to talk then. His brain had shorted and refused to compute.

"I bought her all sorts of fruit." She moved the boxes on the counter around. "Lychees, rambutans . . ."

As she continued to list off tropical fruits, his mind finally caught up with him. "Mom, *no*." The words came out with unintentional strength and volume, but it was justified. He ignored the instinct that told him he was committing sacrilege by saying no to his mom. "I'm not *getting married*, and she's not staying here, and you can't *do* things like this." This was the twenty-first century, for fuck's sake. People didn't run around purchasing wives for their sons anymore.

She pursed her lips and propped her hands on her hips, looking like an aerobics instructor from the eighties in her hot-pink sweat suit and short hair with a flattening perm. "I already booked the banquet hall for the wedding. The deposit was a thousand dollars."

"*Mom.*"

"I picked August eighth. I know how much you like the number eight."

He raked his fingers through his hair and suppressed a growl. "I'll refund you the thousand dollars. Please give me the contact information for the banquet hall so I can cancel."

"Don't be this way, Khải. Keep an open mind," she said. "I don't want you to be lonely."

He released a disbelieving breath. "I'm not lonely. I *like* being alone."

Lonely was for people who had feelings, which he didn't.

It wasn't loneliness if it could be eradicated with work or a

Netflix marathon or a good book. Real loneliness would stick with you all the time. Real loneliness would hurt you nonstop.

Khai didn't hurt. He felt nothing most of the time.

That was exactly why he steered clear of romantic relationships. If someone liked him that way, he'd only end up disappointing them when he couldn't reciprocate. It wouldn't be right.

"Mom, I won't do it, and you can't force me."

She crossed her arms. "I know I can't force you. I don't *want* to force you. If you honestly don't like her, then you shouldn't marry her. But I'm asking you to give her a chance. Let her stay here for the summer. If you still don't like her at the end, send her home. It's that easy." She switched her attention to Quan. "Talk some sense into your brother."

Quan held his hands up as a constipated kind of smile stretched over his mouth. "I got nothing."

Their mom glared at him.

"This is all useless," Khai said. "I won't change my mind." And he really didn't want a strange woman living in his house. His house was his sanctuary, the one place where he could escape people and just be.

When his family wasn't breaking in, at least.

"You can't make up your mind before you've met her. That's not fair. Besides, I need her at the restaurant. The new waitress quit, and I need people for the daytime shift. Help me with this," she said.

Khai scowled at his mom. He keenly sensed she was manipulating him—he wasn't completely oblivious—but he didn't know how to get out of this. Also, when she was short on hands, she made Khai and his siblings take time off their day jobs and come in to help. If he had to choose between waiting tables while simultaneously dealing with his mom all day and having a strange woman in his house . . .

As if sensing weakness, she dove in for the kill. "Tolerate some difficulty and do it for me. It'll make me happy."

Shit, shit, shit. Frustration built into a giant ball inside of him, growing bigger and bigger and verging on explosion. There was nothing he could say to that, and she knew it.

She was his mom.

Clinging to his last shred of control, he said, "Only if you promise the matchmaking stops after this. You won't try to hook me up with Dr. Son's daughter or the dentist's daughter or Vy's friends or anyone. You won't ambush me with surprise guests when I come over for dinner."

"Of course," his mom said as she nodded eagerly. "I promise. Only this summer, only this one time. If you don't like her, I'll stop. I don't think I can find a better girl than Mỹ anyway, and . . ." She hesitated midsentence, and a thoughtful look crossed her face. "But you have to really *try*. If I don't see you trying to make it work, I'll *have* to do it again. Do you understand, Khải?"

He narrowed his eyes. "What does it mean 'to try'?"

"It means you'll do what a real fiancé does. You'll take her out, introduce her to your friends and family, do things together, things like that. You'll take her to all the weddings this summer."

That sounded *horrendous*.

He couldn't help grimacing, and Quan burst out laughing.

"You know, Mom, maybe this was a good idea after all," Quan said.

"See? You kids think I'm crazy, but Mom knows best."

That was questionable, but Khai had no choice but to say, "Fine. I'll do all that stuff this summer if you promise to stop with the wife planning after this."

"I promise, I promise, I promise. I'm so glad you're being reasonable on this. You'll like her. You'll see," she said, smiling ear to ear like she'd won the Powerball lottery.

Khai was one hundred percent certain *she'd* be the one seeing, but he kept that to himself. "I'm taking a shower." He spun around and marched toward his bedroom.

It was just like his mom to hatch a scheme like this. The entire thing was ridiculous. He wasn't going to change his mind. Mỹ could be the most perfect woman in the world, and it wouldn't change anything. His liking her was inconsequential. In fact, if he liked her, that was all the more reason why he shouldn't marry her.

CHAPTER THREE

Mỹ clawed the arms of her seat as the plane landed with a stomach-dipping jerk. Strange mechanical sounds reached her ears, and the lights flickered back on. She never wanted to fly again. Once in her life was enough. The loudspeakers dinged.

"Welcome to San Francisco, California. The local time is 4:20 P.M. Thank you for flying Air China..."

Thank sky and Buddha for English classes in high school, all the bootleg American movies she'd watched, and the audio English lessons she'd been listening to nonstop while she cleaned these past couple of months. She'd understood most of that.

California. She'd finally made it.

That meant she'd be meeting him soon.

Nausea hit her so hard the skin on her face prickled and her vision blurred. *Don't throw up. Don't throw up. Don't throw up.* That wasn't how she wanted to spend her first moments in the United States of America.

What if they dragged her somewhere for disrupting the peace

with her vomit? Or—she glanced at the nice old lady in a hand-knit sweater next to her—for spraying the people around her? Could she go to jail for that? Could she get *deported* for that? Maybe they'd send her back without letting her off the plane.

Everyone started lining up in the aisle, and Mỹ jumped to get her luggage from the overhead bin. A tall man in a brown leather jacket beat her to her suitcase and pulled it out. "Here, let me get it for you."

She opened her mouth to speak, but nothing came out. Embarrassment locked the English words in her throat. She'd learned the words in school long ago and could read and write a little—enough to fill out the disembarkation form and customs declaration, at least with help from the flight attendant—but actually talking had always been a challenge. She curled her fingers into ineffectual fists. How could she make him stop? All she had in her purse was Vietnamese *đồng*, and it amounted to basically nothing here. It wasn't enough to tip him.

He set the small navy-blue suitcase in the aisle and smiled, and she yanked it close to herself before he could take it hostage. His smile dimmed, and he turned to face the front of the plane. As they filed up the Jetway, she kept expecting him to "help" her more and request payment, but he never did.

When they reached the terminal, he disappeared into the massive crowd, and panic seized her. He'd known what he was doing. He could have told her where to go, but now she was all alone. What if she went to the wrong place and did the wrong thing? She was going to end up getting a full-body search and a lie detector test.

As she blindly followed the crowd, she tried to read the signs overhead, but her fear-scrambled mind couldn't make sense of the English words.

"Passport, please."

Somehow, she found herself at the front of a line. Heart pounding, she retrieved the little green booklet from her purse and handed it over along with all the forms the flight attendant had provided on the plane. This was it. This was the part she'd been dreading. The *paper* part. This was when everything could go wrong.

The airport employee scanned the forms, leafed through her passport, and stamped one of the pages before handing everything back to her. "Welcome to the United States, Esmeralda Tran. Enjoy your stay."

She stared at him blankly. Oh, right, *she* was Esmeralda Tran. It was going to take time to get used to her new name—which Ngọc Anh had given her because Esmeralda from Disney's *The Hunchback of Notre Dame* shared their coloring. Ngọc Anh had also chosen that moment to announce she wanted a new name, too. After a bit of research, they'd settled on Jade.

The airport employee motioned for her to move on. "Please proceed to baggage inspection. Next in line."

That was it? It took her longer to scrub a toilet. Hugging her passport to her chest with one hand, she rolled her suitcase toward the inspection line. She put everything she owned on the conveyor belt and walked through all the spaceship scanner devices.

Once she came out on the other side, she grabbed her suitcase and stood still for a moment, taking in the chaos of the airport terminal. Foreign languages all around. The smells of perfume and food and bodies. Expensive-looking shops. Colors, clothes, hands holding suitcases, hands holding other hands. Everyone calm, purposeful, on their way. She wished she knew her way.

All of this was too new. Even *she* felt new.

New place, new name, new person, new life. Maybe. For the summer, at least.

She should be excited. Hollywood and Disneyland were here. But all she felt was . . . scared. Home, however, wasn't an option right now. She had to do this for her girl.

Her mom's advice rang in her head: *Seduce first. Love will come.*
It was time to see a man.

She marched straight into the nearest bathroom, took an empty stall, and changed out of her comfortable travel clothes and into a tight pink dress. After exchanging her flat shoes for a pair of high heels that looked like weapons, she left the stall to brush her teeth until her gums hurt and apply the smallest amount of eyeliner, mascara, this shimmery stuff to hide the tired bags under her eyes, and bloodred lipstick. There. That was as good as it got.

When she checked herself in the floor-length mirror next to all the sinks, her reflection was completely unrecognizable to Mỹ. But that was a good thing. Mỹ was a naïve poor country girl who never quite fit in. She was leaving that girl behind. She was Esme now.

Lifting her chin, she exited the bathroom and joined the crowd. She sounded out the words on the overhead signs with determination and followed the foot traffic through the airport. After she passed security, she scanned the people and their faces, searching, searching, searching . . .

There he was.

W aiting on the other side of the security checkpoint was a surreal experience. Khai imagined it was a little like this when people took delivery of a special-order Schutzhund from the Netherlands. Only this wasn't a trained and certified protection dog. This was a *person*.

As minutes ticked by, he stood still, shoulders back and spine straight like years of martial arts practice had trained him to do. He didn't pace, tap his toes, or sway. He didn't do things like that anymore. But he wanted to.

If this girl actually showed up, he had to live with her for an entire summer. Even worse, he had to treat her like a fiancée. What the hell did he know about that?

He took his phone out of his pocket and pulled up the picture his mom had sent him. If she hadn't assured him she'd already met the girl, he would have thought this was a prime example of catfishing. The person in the photograph was almost too beautiful to be—

Someone stepped into his personal space. *"Chào Anh."*

He glanced up from his phone. And found himself staring into the same light-green eyes from the picture. Only in real life.

It was her.

"Hi," he said reflexively.

She smiled, and his thought processes hiccupped. Bright-red lips, straight white teeth, stunning eyes. People would call her pretty. No, she was more than that. Hot. Gorgeous. Breathtaking. Not that he cared about stuff like—

His gaze accidentally dropped below her chest, and his mouth went dry. *Holy fuck.* She was some kind of walking sex fantasy. Apparently, he was a boob man. And an hourglass-figure man. And a leg man. How did they look so long when she was so short? Maybe it was those three-inch heels she was wearing.

When he realized what he was doing, he forced his gaze back to her face. Back when his family still had hopes of him dating, his sister had made him memorize a set of rules since he was so good at following them.

THE RULES WHEN YOU'RE WITH A GIRL:

1. Open *and* shut doors.
2. Pull out chairs and push them back in.
3. Pay for everything.

4. Carry everything. (That included her purse if she wanted. Never mind the fact that he preferred keeping his hands free.)
5. Give her your coat if she seems cold. (No, it didn't matter if he was cold, too.)
6. No matter how she's dressed, don't check out inappropriate areas of her body.*
*Specifically, boobs, butt, and thighs. He could make an exception if she was grievously wounded.

Uncomfortable heat flushed his face and singed the tips of his ears. He'd just gone to town on Rule Number Six. In his defense, he had no practice being with a woman like this.

She positioned her suitcase in front of her legs and took and released a fast breath before smiling again. "You're Diệp Khải. I'm Esme," she said in Vietnamese.

That surreal sensation came back. This was really happening. His mail-order bride was introducing herself. But wasn't her name Mỹ?

Please don't let there be two of them. He didn't know what he was going to do with one woman. If his mom had acquired him an entire harem, he'd need therapy. After a heart-pounding second, logic returned to his brain, and he concluded she must have adopted a Western name to help her in the States. He did not have a harem.

Thank God.

"Just Khai," he said in English, dropping the surname and the tones. His mom was the only one who called him Diệp Khải, and usually when he was in trouble.

Her response was a puzzled tilt of her head, and he wondered if she'd understood what he'd said. As she looked him over, a crease formed between her eyebrows. "Why are you wearing all black? Black is for funerals in America. I've seen that in movies. Did someone die?" she asked in Vietnamese again.

"No, no one died. I just like it." Picking out clothes was so much easier when it was all one color. Besides, black didn't stain, and it was socially versatile, appropriate for every occasion from work functions to bar mitzvahs.

While she appeared to absorb that information, he grabbed her suitcase by the handle and started toward the parking garage.

"This way," he said.

With each step through the airport, words pounded in Khai's head.

What. Had. His. Mom. Been. Thinking.

His mail-order bride was nothing like he'd expected—which was a younger replica of his mom, complete with the matching sweat suits and the sriracha and hoisin sauce she always kept in her purse. That, he could have handled. But this girl, *Esme*, looked like a Playboy bunny. She lacked the trademark platinum hair, but the rest of her fit the description. What did you do with a Playboy bunny? Aside from sex. Not that he was thinking about sex.

Except, clearly, he *was* thinking of sex. *Fuck.* No, there wouldn't be any fucking. A sneaky part of his brain reminded him he'd promised to do all the things a fiancé would do. Fiancés had sex . . .

He shook his head to clear it of the porn thoughts. It was wrong to reduce a person to their sexual value. He was a rational being. He should be better than this. Besides, she could be the kind of person who regularly performed ritual animal sacrifices in her backyard. Was it safe to drop your pants around such a woman? That killed the sex thoughts quickly, and the rest of his trip through the airport went smoothly.

Once he passed through a set of sliding glass doors, the clacking of Esme's shoes on the parking structure's concrete floor followed him to his car. He stashed her suitcase in the trunk up front and prepared to walk around the car and follow Rule Number One, but

Esme opened her door and lowered herself into her seat. Then she shut the door, too.

For a moment, he stood still, staring at her side of the car. Did she know she'd just breached social etiquette? Should he tell her? And wasn't that ironic? That he knew the Rules better than she did? Or maybe they weren't international?

With a mental shrug, he got behind the wheel, started the engine, and shifted the gear into reverse.

"Wait a little," she said. "Can we talk?"

He sighed and put the car back in park. It looked like they were going to do more of this thing where they both spoke their own languages and neither entirely understood the other, just like when he and his mom talked.

"Thank you, Anh Khải." *Anh* meant *brother*, but when they weren't related it was more of an endearment. He didn't find it endearing. But when she flashed another of her disruptive smiles at him, he forgot to be annoyed. Right as his brain function started to stutter, she looked about the interior of his car. "This car is nice."

"Thanks." He didn't generally like flashy things, but he loved to drive. His car was by far the most self-indulgent thing he owned. Too bad about all the bird shit on the windshield.

She took a deep breath. "I know you don't want to marry me."

"That's right." He saw no reason why he should lie.

Silence hung in the air as she worried her bottom lip, and his muscles tightened unpleasantly.

"Are you going to cry?" he asked. "There are tissues in the center console." Should he get them out for her? He didn't know what else to do. Pat her on the arm maybe.

She shook her head before she lifted her chin and met his gaze. "Your mom wants me to change your mind."

"You can't change my mind."

"Do you have . . ." She glanced to the side as she searched for words. "A perfect woman in your mind? What is she like?"

"She leaves me alone." He already had a mom, a sister, and a bazillion aunts and girl cousins to send him on senseless errands, harass him about his clothing choices, and tell him to cut his hair. He didn't need any more women in his life.

"You don't want that," she said with a decisive shake of her head. "I'll help you be happy. You'll see."

He stiffened. "I don't need that kind of help." Her suggestion was galling in unprecedented ways. If she was going to spend the summer pushing him to dance and sing, he was probably going to have some manner of an epic mental breakdown. Happiness, like grief, was not in his personal emotional card deck. But minor emotions like irritation and frustration were. He was feeling those in healthy measure right this moment.

A skeptical look crossed her face. "Happy people don't wear all black."

His clothes again. He tightened his fingers on the steering wheel. "I disagree." Black was perfectly acceptable at weddings, and those were happy events. For other people, anyway. He'd rather have a prostate exam. Physicians only tortured you for a few seconds, whereas weddings went on for hours and hours.

Her lips thinned, and a tense moment stretched out before she asked, "What work do you do? Do you like it?"

"It's complicated to explain, but yes, I like it."

Her lips moved quietly for a moment, and he was fairly certain she was testing out the feel of the word *complicated*. But then she glanced about the car, took in his black suit and shirt again, and gave him a funny look. Her lips curved ever so slightly. "Are you a spy like James Bond?"

He blinked several times. "No."

"An assassin?"

"No, I'm not an assassin." What was wrong with her?

"Too bad." But she didn't *look* disappointed, not with that smile on her face. What weird things were going on in her brain?

Shaking his head, he said, "You're stranger than I am."

She confused him even more by hugging her arms to her chest and laughing down at her lap. It was a pretty sound, musical in a way. When she crossed her legs, his eyes were drawn helplessly to her thighs. Her skirt slid up, revealing another inch of flawless skin.

Rule Number Six, Rule Number Six, Rule Number Six.

He wrenched his eyes away and stared blindly at the dashboard. "I was an accounting major in school, but I'm more of a tax specialist now. My friend and I started an accounting software company. He's in charge of the programming, and I handle the accounting, which means I need to stay up-to-date on generally accepted accounting principles and tax law as set forth in the Internal Revenue Code. Lately, we've added transfer pricing analysis to our software package, so I've had to get particularly familiar with section 482 of the IRC. It's very interesting figuring out how to test if business transactions are at 'arm's length' when you have large multinational corporations. Sometimes, they'll create tax shelters in low-tax jurisdictions in, say, the Bahamas, so you have to—"

He forced himself to stop midsentence. People got bored when he talked about work. He even bored other accounting people from time to time. The intricacies and elegance of accounting principles and tax law weren't for everyone. He had no idea why.

"Accounting," she said slowly, this time in English.

"Not exactly, but I do have a CPA license. I'm certified to provide tax documentation for public companies in the United States."

"Me, too."

He took a surprised breath. She was an accountant? That was unexpectedly wonderful.

The hem of her dress became very interesting to her, and she fiddled with a loose thread as she said in Vietnamese, "In Việt Nam. Not here. It's probably really different."

"I bet it's different. I don't have any experience with Vietnamese tax regulation. It's probably fascinating. Do they expense bribery as a cost of doing business? Is it tax deductible?" It would be entertaining to see bribery as a line item on an income statement. This was why he liked accounting so much. It wasn't just numbers on paper. If you knew how to look at them, the numbers meant something and reflected culture and values.

She hugged herself like she was cold, saying nothing.

Had he accidentally insulted her? He replayed his comments in his head, trying to pinpoint the offensive thing, but it was no use. After an awkward pause, he asked, "Can we go now? I don't enjoy chitchat like this." And clearly, he was bad at it.

"Yes, let's go. Thank you, Anh." Sinking back against her seat, she stared out the side window.

He pulled out of the spot, paid for parking, and exited the garage. At first, his muscles tensed in anticipation of more probing questions, but as he left the airport and merged onto the freeway, she was blessedly quiet. Unlike his mom and sister, who could maintain one-sided conversations for hours.

Maybe she'd fallen asleep, but every time he glanced her way, he found her watching the landscape beside the freeway, which consisted of squat office buildings, scraggly grass, and the occasional bunch of eucalyptus or pine. Not very glamorous. Well, at least to him it wasn't. He couldn't imagine what it might look like from her eyes.

"Uni-vers-ity Av," she said out of the blue. She straightened in her seat and torqued her body so she could see the exit he'd just passed. "Is that where Cal Berkeley is?"

"No, that's where Stanford is."

"Oh." She turned back around and slumped in her seat.

"Berkeley is an hour north of here. That's where I went for undergrad and grad school."

"Really?" The enthusiasm in her voice caught him by surprise. A lot of people around here weren't impressed unless you'd gone to Stanford or an Ivy League school.

"Yeah, they have a good accounting program." He continued driving, keeping his eyes on the road, but he could almost feel the weight of her gaze on his skin. Sending her a sideways glance, he asked, "What?"

"Are the students close there? They know each other?"

"Not really," he said. "It's a huge school. Each year, they admit more than ten thousand undergrads. Why do you ask?"

She shrugged and shook her head as she peered out the window.

He returned his attention to the early evening traffic, exited at Mathilda Avenue, and drove down streets lined with tall, leafy oaks, townhome complexes, apartment buildings, and strip malls.

Ten minutes later, he turned onto the side street that led to his two-bedroom fixer-upper with demolition potential. Compared to the other remodeled and newly built homes in the area, his was a bit of an eyesore, but he bet no one else had the finely aged shag carpet. He pulled up next to his section of curb, cranked the parking brake, and turned the engine off.

"This is it," he said.

CHAPTER FOUR

Esme still couldn't forgive herself for lying like that. Did she want to get struck by the heavens? Why had she done it?

She knew why. Because she was a janitor/maid, and he was so much better. She'd wanted to impress him, to show him she *was* worth his time. But now she had to pretend she worked in accounting, when she didn't even know what it was, and continue to keep her baby a secret. She was a liar, and she was ashamed of herself.

If she were a good person, she'd confess right now, but this feeling of being his equal was too addicting. It didn't even matter that it was fake. She liked it anyway. She was already pretending to be something she wasn't—a worldly sexy woman (though not very successfully, judging by her failed attempt at flirting earlier in the car). Why not go all the way and add smart and sophisticated to the list while she was at it?

When she died, demons were going to torment her for eternity instead of letting her reincarnate. Or worse, they'd let her reincarnate, but she'd be a catfish who lived under a river outhouse. It was only fair. That was what she got for wishing food poisoning on people.

Khải got out of the car, and she followed suit. The crunch of her shoes on rocks was unnaturally loud to her ears, and her head spun as she looked down at her feet. When was the last time she'd eaten? She was too tired to remember.

Working her jaw to wake herself up, she forced herself to take in the surrounding area. The houses were so plain compared to the mansions she'd imagined. And short—one level only, for most of them. The air. She filled her lungs. What was this smell?

After a moment, she realized it was the *lack* of smell. She couldn't smell garbage and rotting fruit. A haze of exhaust didn't darken the sunset to tamarind-colored rust. She rubbed her jet-lagged eyes and admired a sky painted in bright hues of apricot and hyacinth.

What a difference an ocean made.

Homesickness hit her then, and she almost missed the pollution. Something familiar would have been nice as she stood there, on an unknown street, in an unknown city, in a world far away from everyone she loved. What time was it in Việt Nam? Was Ngọc Anh—no, it was *Jade* now—sleeping? Did she miss her momma? Her momma missed her.

If she were home, she'd lie down next to her, kiss her little hands, and press their foreheads together like she always did before she went to sleep.

She tripped and would have fallen if it weren't for the mailbox, and Khải aimed a disapproving look at her shoes after he pulled her suitcase out of the trunk. "You're better off walking barefoot than wearing those."

"But they're so useful. It's like having a shoe *and* a knife." She slipped both shoes off and made a stabbing motion with one of them.

He considered her for a serious moment, not laughing, not even smiling, and she pursed her lips and stared down at her bare toes. There she went, failing at flirting again. In her defense, it had been a long time since she'd dated a man, and she'd forgotten how.

As she gazed at her unattractive toes—she hated the unshapely hands and feet she'd inherited from her green-eyed dad; there was nothing elegant or appealing about them—she noticed the scary weeds choking Khải's yard. "What if I step on all the thorns?" She sent him a smile that she hoped looked sexy. "Will you carry me?"

He brought her suitcase to the front door without looking at her. "Stay on the concrete, and you'll be fine."

Skipping after him, she said, "I can clean the yard for you. I'm good at it."

He fished his keys out of his pocket and unlocked the door. "I like it the way it is."

She glanced over her shoulder at the yard again to make sure she hadn't imagined everything, and, nope, it was still a jungle of thorns, tangled vines, and dried-up bushes.

He'd been wrong earlier when he said Esme was the stranger of the two of them. He won that contest without even trying. He was easily the strangest person she'd ever met. She didn't know him well yet, but she'd picked up on his strangeness right away. He didn't look her in the eyes when he spoke, he wore all black, he liked this wasteland of a yard, and he said the oddest things. It gave her hope.

Odd was good. Odd was an opportunity.

Besides, she was odd, too. Just not as odd as he was.

"You're very . . . open-minded," she hedged.

He looked at her like he thought she was crazy, and she mentally kicked herself.

"Why do you park on the street when you have that?" She pointed to his garage. Judging from the size of the door, he could fit two cars in there. It didn't make sense that he parked his nice car on the street. Not unless he had three cars, which she doubted he could afford based on the state of his yard and house.

Instead of answering her question, he let them into the house. She wondered if he hadn't heard or if he'd purposely ignored her, but she let it slide. The inside of his house was stranger than the outside, with thick carpet that looked more like grass than his lawn, exercise equipment all over the main room, and fixtures and blinds from a different era. After setting her shoes on the floor, she followed Khải down a narrow hall, and the soft carpet fibers hugged her bare feet with every step.

He set her suitcase in a small room that contained a desk, sofa, and closet. When she noticed the old wallpaper, tears stung her eyes. Teddy bears, beach balls, dolls, ballet slippers, and building blocks. This used to be a child's room. She touched her fingertips to the ballet slippers. Jade would love this.

"This is your room," he said. "You'll have to make do with the couch."

"It's nice. Thank you, Anh Khải." She'd never slept on anything as nice as a couch in her life. She'd never *owned* a couch. But she didn't mention any of that. She was sophisticated Esme in Accounting now. Esme in Accounting probably had a nice apartment with two or three couches and had never slept on a straw mat over a packed-dirt floor.

The lonely country girl inside of her looked at the big empty couch and felt homesick all over again. She wanted the straw mat, the dirt floor, the single-room house, and the sleeping bodies of her little girl, grandma, and mom. She was exhausted, but she didn't know how she was going to sleep by herself.

"The phone on the desk is for you." He pointed at the desk before turning to leave.

"Wait a little, for *me*?" She hurried to the desk and lowered a hand toward the shiny silver phone but curled her fingers into a fist before she made contact. It would be a shame to smudge the fancy phone with her fingertips.

"My mom said you needed a new SIM card, but a new phone is easier. If you don't like it, I can probably exchange it for the larger model."

But that would cost even more. "It's *new*," she said.

He stuffed a hand in his pocket. "Yeah." He said it like it was the most normal thing in the world.

"Can you return it?"

He frowned as he tilted his head to the side. "I don't think so. You really don't like it?"

She wrung her hands together. "No, I *like* it, but—"

"Then it's not a problem. Just use it."

A wave of anxious heat washed over her face, but she made herself say, "I'll pay you back as soon as I'm working." She hoped she'd make enough to pay for it. Back home, she'd have to save for the better part of a year to pay for something this nice.

"You don't have to."

She lifted her chin. "I do." It was important he knew she wasn't marrying him for his money. This had never been about money to her. If anything, she liked that he *didn't* have as much money as his neighbors. They were a better match that way. She didn't need a rich man. She just needed someone who was hers. And Jade's.

He merely shrugged. "Suit yourself. I'm going to heat up dinner. Come out when you're hungry."

Her shoulders sagged. He didn't understand she wanted to earn things herself. "I'm going to call home first, okay?"

"Yeah, go ahead."

As soon as he left the room, she carefully shut the door, unplugged the white charging cable from the phone, and sat on the couch, staring at her unbelievably fancy *new* phone. She hadn't expected this at all. It was the best gift he could have gotten her, the absolute best. And he didn't even like her.

He was strange and tactless and very possibly an assassin, but when she looked at his actions, all she saw was kindness. Cô Nga had been right. Khải *was* good stuff. Very, very good stuff.

She'd memorized how to dial internationally from the United States before she left and dialed her mom's cell phone number. Her mom picked up on the first ring. "Hi, Má."

"Already, already, tell me everything."

"First, how is Ngọc Anh? Can I talk to her?"

"She's fine, excited to have a dad soon. Talk to me a little. How are things? Do you like him?" her mom asked.

"Yes, I like him."

A pleased *hmmmmm* sounded on the line. "That's good. What about his house? Is it nice?"

"I like it," Esme said. "The room I'm staying in has pretty paper on the wall. If Ngọc Anh saw it, she'd like it. There's a couch for me."

"You're not sleeping with him?"

She rolled her eyes. "No, Má, I'm not sleeping with him. Do you remember? He doesn't want a wife."

"That doesn't mean he wants to sleep alone."

"I just got off the plane," she reminded her mom. She needed time to work her seductive powers on him. If she even had such powers anymore. Working as much as she did, she didn't have the time to date. Or the desire. Just the memory of her mom's and grandma's faces when they'd found out about her pregnancy was enough to make any man look uninteresting.

"Oh, that's right, long flight," her mom said. After a quiet moment, her mom continued. "Can you unscrew one of the legs off the couch and say it broke?"

"Why would I do that?"

"So you can sleep with him, daughter of mine."

Esme pulled the phone away and stared at it. Who was this woman she was talking to? The voice sounded like her mom's, but not the words. "I can't do that. It's *wrong*."

"Fine, forget I said it," her mom grumbled. "Here, talk to your girl."

"*Má.*" The little voice made Esme's heart melt even as it broke her. She should be there, not here on the other side of the world chasing a man.

"Hi, my girl. I miss you too much. What have you been doing since I've been gone?"

"I caught a big fish in the pond yesterday. Great-Grandma killed it by slamming it against a tree, and after that, we ate it for dinner. My fish was *good*."

Esme covered her eyes with a hand. *Killed it by slamming it against a tree* . . . Esme in Accounting would be appalled by this conversation. Not only would she not have a five-year-old daughter out of wedlock, but her daughter wouldn't be catching her own dinner. There certainly wouldn't be any killing by slamming anything against a tree.

But at least her girl was happy. It was sinful to take a life, even a fish life, but Esme would gladly sacrifice an entire school of trout to distract Jade from missing her momma too much. She put her feet up and rested her heavy head against the couch's armrest as Jade rambled on about fish, worms, and crickets. When her eyelids drifted shut, she could almost sense the Việt Nam sun on her skin, almost feel her baby in her arms. She fell asleep with a smile on her lips.

CHAPTER FIVE

Something wet landed on Khai's face. And again. Like raindrops.
Except he was in bed. Was the ceiling leaking? Was his house
going to cave in on him?

He opened his eyes and almost shouted.

Esme stood next to his bed, dripping wet in nothing but a towel.
"I think I broke your shower. Water is all over." She bunched the
towel closer to her chest.

He sat upright, rubbed a hand over his face, and prepared to get
out of bed. "Lemme get it. It's probably just the setting—*Shit.*"

He yanked the covers back over his crotch. He was sporting some
mega-monster morning wood. She didn't need to see this. The way
he was pitching a tent in his boxers was grotesque, and she'd probably mistake it as a reaction to *her.* When it wasn't.

Most days, he woke up like this, and it wasn't like he was nursing
an out-of-control porn addiction or something. It was just a natural
biological response to morning levels of testosterone. One that he

could've done without. His mornings would be so much more efficient if he didn't have to jack off in the shower every day.

When he caught her looking at his naked chest and abs, however, he stopped thinking about efficiency and inconvenient hormone levels. She bit her bottom lip, and he swore he felt her teeth on his own lip. His stomach muscles tightened, and his senses sharpened. She was pretty even without makeup, wholesome, more *real*. The water drops on her smooth skin stood out in perfect clarity, calling to him. Something told him they would taste better than regular water. He hadn't thought it was possible, but he hardened even further.

Fuck.

Doing his best to shield his boner from hell, he got up from bed and limp-scuffled into the bathroom—the only renovated room in his house. Then he stood in front of the shower and watched in awe as the lights flashed rainbow colors and water spurted from the nozzles concealed in the ceiling and along the sides. How had she done that? He hadn't known there was a car-wash mode.

"Is the shower broken? I'll pay to fix it," Esme said.

"No, I think you just hit the wrong buttons." A lot of them. Maybe all of them at once. Or perhaps it was like in a video game where you had to hit the buttons in a certain order. She'd accidentally found the secret combination they didn't disclose in the manual.

There was nothing else for it. He had to go in.

He took a breath and marched in there in his boxers. Warm water soaked him from all directions, drenching his hair and massaging his muscles. It would have been nice if it weren't for the flashing lights, his now-wet underwear, and his audience. When he reached the control panel, he hit the power button. The lights stopped cycling color, and the deluge cut off. Residual water trickled from the nozzles and hit the floor with intimate drips.

He slicked his hair back and said, "Come here, and I'll show you how to turn it on."

Ducking her head and hugging her towel to her chest, she came to stand next to him.

"You hit the power button first, here. This turns it off, too. And I usually use rain mode, which is here. Just two buttons. Like this, see?" He pressed the buttons, and water washed down on them in a gentle downpour. "Got it?"

She nodded. "You fixed it?"

"It wasn't broken."

Her shoulders sagged as she released a relieved breath and smiled at him. When the water ran into her eyes, she swiped a hand over her face, but it was no use. They were standing in the shower with the water on. Each second, her towel got more soaked. She should remove it.

But then she'd be naked. With him. Surrounded by water and steam and misted stone walls.

That odd state of heightened awareness returned, stronger this time. The roar of the pouring water grew louder, and he felt each water drop dissolving against his skin like a tiny kiss. Images of him peeling the wet towel off her flashed in his mind, but her body remained fuzzy from her chest down to her thighs. He didn't know how to envision her there. But he wanted to. No, he didn't. Yes, he did. No, he really didn't. He didn't need that imagery rambling around his perverted head.

"We're smart, huh?" she said with a grin. "We're cleaning clothes, towels, and bodies at the same time. It saves water."

"I'm not sure we're getting any cleaner."

She ducked her head and wiped the water from her eyes. "I'm just joking around."

"Are you ever serious?" he asked.

She lifted an elegant shoulder and aimed a helpless sort of smile at him. "I only want you to be yourself with me."

"I am." Wasn't he? He certainly wasn't pretending to be someone else, but if he looked at things objectively, that was what the people around him usually wanted—for him to act differently, more appropriate, more intuitive, more considerate, less eccentric, less . . . himself. Did she really not mind him as he was?

Her smile widened, and all he could do was stare. Strange, incomprehensible, beautiful woman. She said the funniest things and smiled *all the time*. His fingers itched to touch that smile, and he stepped away out of self-preservation.

"I'll leave you to shower. Feel free to use the other towel over there."

He fled. The next thing he knew, he stood in his closet, dripping water onto the carpet as he stared blankly at the black clothes hanging on the racks. His heart crashed like he'd had five cans of Red Bull, and his cock did obscene things to the front of his wet boxers.

It took conscious effort to recall what day it was and the corresponding schedule, but then frustration pumped through his body. She'd thrown everything off with her shower fiasco. He couldn't even brush his teeth with her in there. Not without getting an eyeful, which, honestly speaking, he'd probably enjoy far too— He banged his forehead against the wall in his closet. Damn it all, he had to stop this.

Determined to get the rest of the day right, he pulled on his workout clothes, tied the laces of his indoor cross-training shoes, grabbed a spare toothbrush and toothpaste from the linen closet, and went to the kitchen to brush his teeth over the sink, inhale a protein bar, and drink a cup of water. It was Sunday morning, and that meant upper-body-workout time. If he strayed from his exercise routine, he started to lose weight really fast, and he disliked that. It reminded him too much of when he was younger and clumsy and extremely awkward. He might still be awkward on occasion, but not clumsy. He'd trained it out of his muscles with hours upon hours of practice.

Like always, he padded into his living room and took his spot at the proper machine. As he did overhead presses at 125 pounds, he was aware of Esme walking into the kitchen, helping herself to the fruit smorgasbord his mom had provided, and getting herself a glass of water, which she forgot on the counter, but he stayed focused and efficiently worked through five sets of five repetitions.

By the time he finished with his bicep curls, he'd lost track of Esme's whereabouts, but that was fine. She was an adult. She didn't need to be supervised. He started his pull-up repetitions, always five sets of ten.

One, two, three . . .

He used to hate pull-ups, but now that he'd gotten good at them, he liked them. He had the timing of his breathing and the pulling of his arms perfectly synchronized.

Four, five, six . . .

If he tried, he'd probably be able to do a ridiculous number of them before his body gave, especially if he didn't have the twenty-five-pound weight strapped to his waist.

Seven, eight, nine—

Movement outside the window caught his eye, and he froze with his feet dangling over the ground. Esme was in his backyard, hair in a ponytail, wearing baggy floral-print pants—were those *Hammer pants?*—and a white T-shirt with no goddamned bra underneath.

Her breasts swayed seductively as she hacked a tree down with . . .
one of his Japanese kitchen knives.

His feet hit the carpet with a hard thud, and he was vaguely conscious of how lucky he was that he hadn't injured himself with the
weight hanging between his legs. Still, he couldn't drag his eyes away
from the window.

Oh hell, it was the meat cleaver. She was cutting down a tree
with a meat cleaver. He doubted lumber work was one of the knife's
intended uses, but in the manner of most Japanese engineering, the
knife exceeded expectations. And he could see her dark nipples
through her sheer shirt.

He couldn't be the only person who would find this utterly baf-
fling. It was arousing and fascinating but scary, as she was weaponized,
and also a little frustrating because she'd so grievously repurposed his
fine cutlery.

He marched to the window, cranked it open, and asked, "Why
are you cutting that tree down?" With a meat cleaver.

She pulled the cleaver out of the tree's narrow trunk and smiled
at him like all of this was perfectly normal. "I'm cleaning up a little."

His lips worked without making a sound for a bit before he finally said, "You don't have to."

"I'm making the yard nicer. You'll see."

But he didn't care what it looked like. No, that wasn't right. He
cared a little. Just enough so he derived perverse pleasure from irri-
tating his neighbors with his dilapidated home exterior and lawn.
He'd been about to start fixing things up, but the pint-sized old lady
across the street, Ruthie, had sent him this letter, threatening to
take him to civil court if he didn't attempt to make his house fit in
better with the neighborhood.

He'd do almost anything if someone asked nicely—case in point
being his current predicament, in which a knife-wielding woman

was cohabitating with him—but if they threatened him . . . He and Ruthie were waging a silent battle, and he was going to demolish her. It didn't matter that she was a hundred years old.

Esme gave the sapling one more solid whack, and the trunk split in two. The leafy top of the tree crashed to the ground, and she held the cleaver up proudly, saying, "I'm good with knives."

He backed away from the window slowly.

What number had he been on? He had no idea, so he started back at the beginning.

One, two, three—

Esme set the knife down and bent over to haul the fallen tree away, and her pants stretched over her ass in the most beguiling manner. It shouldn't be sexy. He was absolutely certain those were Hammer pants now. But his cock didn't care. It stiffened and pressed against his workout shorts.

He shook his head and pushed himself to focus. Mind over penis. Mind over penis. He could do it. Rule Number Six, dammit.

Four, five, six—

The tree must have snagged on something because she began tugging on it, and her perfect Hammer-pants-clad ass shook like in a Beyoncé music video. Khai stared at her, caught helplessly in the most confusing arousal of his life.

When the tree came free, she stumbled backward a few steps and then dragged it to the far side of the yard. She found a shovel from somewhere—he didn't know where; he hadn't known he owned a shovel—and returned to drive it into the earth at the base of the newly severed trunk. Her tits bounced, and sweat glistened on her reddened face before she swiped it away with the back of her arm.

It occurred to him that maybe he should be helping instead of watching her like landscaper pornography. You weren't supposed to let women do any kind of manual labor. He might as well add that to the Rules. But he'd already told her she didn't have to do this. If her hands longed to till the Silicon Valley soil, what right did he have to steal her joy? Besides, he was philosophically opposed, what with his feud with Ruthie and all.

He tore his eyes away and got back to his pull-ups. Focus. Mind over penis.

One, two, three—

She leaned over, making her pants stretch across her ass again, and a groan rumbled from his chest. After digging out a rock from the dirt and tossing it aside, she got back to shoveling.

One, two, three . . .

With every stab of shovel into dry earth, Esme's determination grew. She'd woken up this morning with her new phone glued to her face and a blanket over her. He'd covered her in her sleep. It was a small thing to do, but the room had been cold. What if she'd gotten sick? It was a sign. He wasn't perfect by any means, but he was perfect *for her*. And Jade. She was going to do her best to marry him.

His name, Khải, meant *victory*, but the way he said it, flat like that without the accent, it meant *to open*. That was exactly what she needed to do. He was closed, and she had to open him. In her experience, when you wanted to open something, you cleaned it up first so you could see what you were dealing with, and then you worked on it really hard. Esme wasn't great at a lot of things, but she was good at cleaning and working hard. She could do this. Maybe she'd been made for this.

She'd start by straightening Khải's yard. Then she'd move on to his house. Last, his life. He'd said he wasn't unhappy with anything, but that was a lie if she'd ever heard one. For whatever reason, he'd built a thick wall around himself. She was going to knock it down, just like she'd taken down that tree, and work her way into his heart.

With that in mind, she cleared the yard until the sun was high in the sky. Then she went inside to have lunch with him and seduce him subtly, or not so subtly.

But he was gone.

He'd abandoned her alone in this house without a word.

CHAPTER SIX

When Khai's alarm rang the next morning, he smacked it off, sat up, and stared blearily at his room. He'd spent his Sunday in the office to escape her, but then she'd invaded his dreams. He was lucky if he'd gotten three hours of sleep. Fantasies had plagued him all night. Sexual ones. Featuring a certain pair of Hammer pants.

He was officially losing his mind, and look at that monster wood. His dick was so hard it was lifting his heavy down comforter all on its own. He needed to take care of this, but how did you do that with another person on the other side of the door? What if she barged in halfway through? None of the locks worked in this house. It hadn't mattered before now.

Walking with his dick pointing ahead like the needle on a compass, he went to the bathroom, turned on the light, and opened the drawer by the sink where he kept his toothbrush and toothpaste. They weren't there. He yanked the drawer out all the way, but they didn't roll out from the back. He knew he'd put them back last night. He always put them back.

Was he hallucinating? Was he in the middle of a nightmare? Or had some really weird person *stolen* his oral hygiene products? Why would anyone—

His toothbrush and toothpaste were laid out on the counter by the faucet next to a glass from the kitchen. What the hell?

Esme must have done this.

He picked up his toothbrush, squeezed toothpaste onto it, and crammed it in his mouth. As he brushed, he gazed at the bathroom. She must have gotten up at dawn, because there were new details everywhere. It hadn't been like this last night. His Kleenex box had been rotated so the sides were no longer parallel to the walls, and the tissue sticking out of the box was folded into a neat triangle. The towels hanging on the racks had been rearranged so they were folded in thirds with a hand towel and washcloth on top. It looked okay, but how was that practical? Barely refraining from growling, he turned the Kleenex box back to the way it'd been before, sides parallel to the walls.

In the shower, he accidentally conditioned his hair before shampooing it because she'd switched the locations of the bottles, and he had to condition his hair a second time, which was thoroughly obnoxious. On the way out, he grabbed his bath towel and sent the smaller ones scattering to the ground. He leaned down to grab them and banged his head on the towel rack on his way up.

By the time he'd dressed and left his bedroom, he was out of sorts, harried for time, and possibly nursing a concussion. He strode into the kitchen, and the smell immediately enveloped him. Pungent. Seafoody. So strong it startled a cough out of him. Esme stood at the stove, splashing fish sauce into a boiling pot of soup as she distractedly wiped at a spill by the flames with a wet towel.

For a stunned moment, he forgot all about the burnt-fish-sauce fumes. She was wearing a T-shirt—and nothing else. Wow, those legs of hers . . .

She beamed at him over her shoulder. "Hi, Anh Khải."

Her chipperness jolted him out of his dazed state, and the heavy fish-sauce scent descended upon him all over again. So potent. Yeah, it made things taste good, but who wanted to smell this all day? And his name, she kept saying it that way.

She sent him a puzzled look as he opened all the windows and the sliding glass door to the backyard and turned on the exhaust hood over the stove as well.

"Airing out the smell," he explained.

"What smell?"

He blinked once, twice. She didn't notice? It was everywhere. He imagined it was soaking into the paint on the walls at this very moment. "The fish sauce?" He pointed to the tall bottle in her hand with a squid on the label.

"Oh!" She set it down on the counter and awkwardly wiped her hands on the wet dish towel. After a tense moment, she whirled past him to open the cupboard next to him. "I made coffee already." She stretched onto her tiptoes to grab the mug from the middle shelf, and the hem of her shirt snuck upward, revealing the perfectly alluring cheeks of her ass and her white underwear.

His dick dug at his fly, reminding him he'd skipped an important part of his morning routine two days in a row now. After the land-scaping incident yesterday, it made a strange sort of sense that Esme could cause him to have a concussion, an overwhelmed sense of smell, and blue balls at the same time. The wide neckline of her shirt slipped to the side and revealed one of her graceful shoulders, and he drew in a slow, fish-sauce-laden breath. Blue and getting bluer.

She snatched a mug down, poured coffee in, and held it out,

smiling at him over the rim, green eyes sparkling. Sexy sleep-tousled dark brown hair with a widow's peak crowned a heart-shaped face. "For you."

He accepted the mug and took a sip.

"Good?" she asked.

He nodded, but he actually had no idea what it tasted like. His senses were overloaded. By the burning fish sauce. And her. Seafoam, he decided. Not the flavor of the coffee, but the shade of her eyes. Seafoam green.

Her smile widened, but after a moment she grew flustered and tucked the hair behind her ear. "Why are you looking at me like that?"

"Like what?"

"So long like that," she said.

"Oh." He made himself look away and took another drink of coffee to give himself something to do. He still didn't taste it. "I forget it makes people uncomfortable sometimes." He didn't have whatever sense it was most people possessed that told them when the eye contact was enough, so if he wasn't paying attention he easily looked too long—or not at all. He cleared his throat. "I'll try to do better."

She looked like she was going to say something, but she spun around and busied herself ladling soup into a bowl of thick rice noodles, which his mom had made by hand—*bánh canh*—with scallions, dry fried onions, shrimp, and thin strips of pork. Once she finished, she carried the bowl to the kitchen table and set it down next to a plate of sliced mango and other assorted fruits. Pulling out a chair, she said, "For you."

He approached the table and stared down at the food. "I don't eat fruit." And it was a workday. The routine was: inhale protein bar, drink a cup of water, run to work, shower in the work locker room, change, and be in his office in less than an hour. But today he had to drive Esme to the restaurant first, and now there was all this food someone had to eat. To top it all off, he really loathed being waited upon.

Dammit.

He had to deal with this for three more months. Three whole months of her in his life, folding his Kleenex and causing blue balls, confusion, concussions, and . . . fruit.

"Fruit is good for you," she insisted.

"I take a multivitamin."

"Fruit is better than a vitamin."

He shook his head and sat down when all he wanted to do was run out the door and get his day started. He should win an award for demonstrating this amount of self-control. A sainthood. Even better, a *knight*hood.

Sir Khai, CPA.

She took the chair across from him and put a cup of water on the table even though there was another one sitting on the counter, but instead of sitting in a regular fashion, she curled one leg underneath herself and hugged the other to her chest, waiting.

"Aren't you going to eat?" he asked.

"I already ate."

So . . . she was just going to watch him eat, then? And people called *him* strange.

He had a spoonful of chewy noodles and savory soup. It was saltier than normal since she'd added more fish sauce, but it was good. He wasn't in the habit of having soup for breakfast, though. When he glanced at her, she pursed her lips and pointedly eyed one of the slices of mango.

Fucking hell. He wasn't a two-year-old. Why was this happening to him? Heaving a beleaguered breath, he picked up the mango and took a large bite.

Extreme sourness exploded in his mouth, and he cringed as a hard shudder worked through his body. *Bla-uggity-bleh-gahhh.*

She burst out laughing, and he stared at her in horror.

How was this funny? He couldn't stop shuddering as he struggled to swallow the mouthful of pure citric acid. Shit, his eyes were watering.

She schooled her features and said, "Sorry. It's a little sour."

Fuck yeah, it was sour.

Without saying a word, he gulped from his coffee mug, shuddered again, and had another gulp of coffee. *Ugh.*

This was his life now. His life was hell.

"Sorry, I like sour," she said with an apologetic wince. "It's good with salt and chili pepper."

He held out his half-eaten mango slice. "You *like* this?"

She plucked it from his fingers and bit into it with complete disregard for germ transference. Didn't she care about bacteria or getting sick? She might as well have kissed him—a thoroughly disturbing thought. Smiling with the green mango caught between her white teeth, she said, "Too delicious."

He blinked and finished his noodles and soup. With that level of acid tolerance, her insides were probably corrosive enough to digest an entire seal pup. Nature was terrifying sometimes.

She helped him eat the rest of his fruit. No way he was touching any more of it. After they cleaned up, she raced to her room and came back thirty seconds later in a white T-shirt and black pants, hair up in a ponytail.

After he drove past the adult school and pulled into the parking space in front of his mom's restaurant, he refrained from drumming his fingers on the steering wheel as Esme gathered up her things, unbuckled her seat belt, and slowly climbed out of the car. As soon as she shut the door, he put the gear in reverse. Finally, he could *go.*

But she walked around to his side and motioned for him to open the window, which he did, even though he didn't want to. *What now, what now, what now?*

Meeting his eyes, she said, "Thank you for driving me. And about the looking . . ." Her lips curved into a smile that was almost shy. "You can look at me however long you like. I don't mind it. Good-bye, Anh Khải."

She turned around and strode toward the restaurant's front door, ponytail bobbing with each step. He was free, but he let the car idle there. He was still sleep deprived, still completely off routine and irritated as hell, his head still hurt, and his balls were still blue.

But something inside of him loosened, and he didn't mind so much the way she said his name now. He waited until the restaurant door shut behind her before driving away.

Here, here," Cô Nga said the second Esme walked in the door, waving her over to the booth where she was filling pepper shakers. "Come sit and tell me everything."

Esme slid into the red leather booth and cast a quick glance around the restaurant, taking in the orange walls, the red booths, the black tables, the large fish tank in back, and the familiar scents of cooking food. Surprisingly, aside from the booths, the restaurant wasn't that different from one you'd find back in Việt Nam. She felt like she'd come home.

Here, the smell of fish sauce was welcome. She brought a handful of her hair to her nose and inhaled, but she detected nothing. She'd washed last night. She was clean. But an uncomfortable embarrassment lingered as she remembered the way he'd opened all the windows and the door to air out a smell she didn't notice.

Cô Nga looked up from her pepper shaker. "How are things going?"

Esme shrugged and smiled. "It's too early to say."

"He's being difficult?" Cô Nga asked. "Do I need to talk to him? He promised he'd treat you like a fiancée."

Esme shook her head quickly. "No, he's been good. We ate together this morning and . . ." She considered telling Cô Nga her son had abandoned her at his house all day yesterday, but she didn't have the heart.

Cô Nga raised her eyebrows. "And . . . what else?"

"Nothing else." Esme took the large pepper container from Cô Nga and continued filling pepper shakers where Cô Nga had left off.

After a while, Cô Nga said, "There's a secret for dealing with my Khải."

"A secret?"

"He doesn't talk a lot and is really smart, so people think he's complicated, but in truth, he's simple. If you want something from him, all you have to do is tell him."

"Just tell him?" Esme couldn't keep the skepticism from her voice.

"Yes, just tell him. If he's being too quiet, tell him you want him to talk to you. If you're bored at home, tell him you want to go somewhere with him. Never assume he knows what you want. Because he doesn't. You *have* to tell him, but once you do, nine times out of ten, he'll listen. He doesn't look like it most of the time, but he cares about people. Even you."

Esme considered the serious expression on the lady's face. Cô Nga believed what she was saying. "I . . . Yes, Cô."

Cô Nga smiled and squeezed Esme's arm. "Now let me show you around, so you can get to work."

By the time the busy lunch hour was over, she was fighting tears. She didn't mind heavy lifting or staying on her feet—she was as strong as a water buffalo—but she'd forgotten that waitressing required talking. Oftentimes, in English. That was another thing she did about as well as a water buffalo. People had given her impatient looks as she forced herself to speak, a customer had yelled at her, another had openly mocked her, and she wanted to lock herself in the bathroom and hide for the rest of the week.

She stacked dirty dishes in the roller bin. Wiped, wiped, wiped the table. Moved on to the next. Tried to empty her mind and focus on the work.

Until she remembered she'd messed up this table's order. She'd run to the grocery store down the road to get them grapes, only to learn they'd said *crepes*, which was *bánh xèo*. What an embarrassing mistake. Who ordered grapes at a nice restaurant like this? She should have used her head. Her eyes watered, and she blinked furiously.

Don't cry.

Once the last customer left, she'd eat those grapes and laugh about all of this instead.

Dirty dishes in the bin. Wipe, wipe, wipe the table. Move on to—

Crash! She forgot to watch where she was going, and her hip knocked a chair over. With her stinky luck, the last customer's things had been on it, and now papers were spilled all over the floor.

"Sorry, so sorry," she said quickly and got down on her hands and knees. But once she was down there, the task seemed overwhelming. Papers were all over the place, under tables and chairs. It was too much. Her hip throbbed, and her head ached, and she wanted to scream, but she couldn't breathe—

"Enough, don't worry about them," a voice said in cultured Vietnamese.

Before she knew it, the papers were all gathered up, and she was sitting at a table, a vague memory in her mind of steady hands guiding her to the seat and a cup of tea in her hands.

"Drink it slowly," the lady customer said as she sat down across from her and watched her with kind eyes.

Esme took a sip, finding the jasmine tea lukewarm, grainy, and bitter, as it was the dregs of the pot. It still helped to calm her, though. She swiped at her face with the back of a hand, expecting to feel the wetness of tears, but there was nothing but her own over-warm skin. The lady had caught her before she could break.

"I eat here regularly, and I never saw you before today. It's probably your first day," the customer said. From the looks of her, she was twenty years or so older than Esme. With the lightweight scarf around her neck, sunglasses on her head, and fashionable sundress, the lady exuded sophistication, though maybe not wealth.

Esme nodded, feeling numb.

"You just crossed, didn't you?"

There was no need to clarify what she'd crossed or where she'd been before. Esme simply nodded again. With how the lunch hour had gone, it had to be painfully obvious that she was new to the country.

The lady reached across the table and squeezed Esme's hand. "It gets better over time. I was a lot like you when I first came."

Esme almost told her that she was only guaranteed to be here for one summer, but she thought better of it. She didn't want to explain things and change this woman's kindness to judgment. And what kind of impression was she making, sitting and drinking tea when she was on the job? She got to her feet, and as she continued wiping tables where she'd left off before, she said, "Thank you, Cô. I'm sorry about the papers."

"My name is Quyền, but call me Miss Q. That's what my students call me."

"You're a teacher?"

Miss Q held up the papers she'd gathered off the floor. "That's right. This is my students' homework." Then her face brightened, and she said, "You could join my class. I teach English in the evenings. The summer session just started."

Esme sucked in a surprised breath, and her towel froze in midswipe. Her first reaction was excitement. She would love to go to school again, and it would be so nice not to be embarrassed when she spoke to customers, and—

No, she told herself firmly. Evenings weren't for school. They were for seducing Khải. Besides, it was better to save the money for Jade. That was why she was here, after all. For Jade (and her dad). Not Esme. She couldn't justify it if it was just to make herself happy.

"I don't need it," she said finally. "I can manage like this."

A polite smile touched Miss Q's lips before she put a ten-dollar bill on the table, packed up her things, and got up. "Good-bye, then. If you change your mind, the adult school is just across the street there." She pointed out the window at the squat white building on the other side of the busy street and left.

Almost wistfully, Esme watched her dodge her way across the street without using the crosswalk. She didn't notice the stray sheet of paper on the far side of the room until the lady disappeared into the school.

Esme went to pick up the paper and found it covered with a handwritten essay by a person named Angelika K. She started reading, and kept reading, and stood there like a statue until she'd finished the whole thing. Then she stared out the window at the school.

Was Angelika K. going to school to benefit others? Or was she going just because she wanted to?

CHAPTER SEVEN

Over the following week, a new routine developed for Khai. In the mornings, they had breakfast. Khai ate whatever Esme forced on him, and she gleefully gorged herself on tropical fruit. They went to work, and he picked her up around six in the evening. That was the busiest time at the restaurant, but his mom insisted she had things covered. Khai suspected she just wanted him and Esme to have dinner together.

It wasn't candlelit romance or anything, so he didn't know why his mom bothered. Most of the time, they heated up containers from the fridge and ate like scavengers. Other times, Esme cooked, and he had to turn on the exhaust hood and open all the windows to vent the smell. While they ate, Esme made strange comments about work, current events, and whatever random things were going on in her head, and he tried to ignore her, mostly unsuccessfully. After dinner, he exercised and watched TV on low volume while he worked on his laptop. She used the time to torment him in new and creative ways.

On Tuesday, Khai found his socks rolled up the long way and stacked in his drawer like cigars. On Wednesday, she blasted Viet pop on her phone while she color coded the foodstuffs in his pantry, making it impossible for him to concentrate on the TV or anything, really. On Thursday, she wiped down the baseboards, wearing that oversized T-shirt, no bra, and a pair of his boxers. They were his underwear, for fuck's sake, not shorts, and they didn't even fit her. She rolled the waist down so many times she might as well have walked around in her panties.

By Friday, he was having fantasies of cramming her on the next plane back to Vietnam. He couldn't find anything in his house, he wasn't sleeping, and he was so sexually frustrated his molars hurt. He would seriously consider bribing her to leave if it weren't for his mom and her threats. No way was he doing this a second time.

Late Friday night, he was in bed, staring at the darkened ceiling and imagining Esme waving happily at him from the curb at the airport as he accelerated away, when the door to the bathroom, which connected their rooms, jerked open. The soft glow from the bathroom's night-light spread into his room, casting a dim light on Esme's tear-strewn face as she stumbled onto the foot of his bed.

He sat upright and swiped the hair from his face. "Are you okay? What—"

She crawled across the bed and straight onto his lap. Her arms wrapped around his neck, and she trembled as she held on to him tightly. Breaths quick and ragged, she pressed her wet face to his neck.

He held himself as stiff as a mannequin. What the hell did he do? He had a crying woman latched on to him like an octopus. He couldn't help recalling that the blue-ringed octopus was one of the most venomous animals in existence.

Don't upset the octopus.

After clearing his throat, he asked, "What's wrong? What happened?"

She hugged him harder, like she was trying to crawl straight inside of him. He was so used to keeping people away he hardly knew what to do with someone so close. Fortunately, this kind of firm touch was acceptable—he liked proprioception and deep pressure. But hot moisture drenched his bare skin, disturbing him. Tears, not deadly neurotoxin, he reminded himself.

"They took her from me," she said against his chest. He didn't know why he assumed it was a *her*. Pronouns weren't gendered in Vietnamese, so she could very well be talking about a *him*. There wasn't a good reason why he should dislike Esme crying about a man. Her trembling worsened as a sob tore from her throat.

"Who took who?"

"Her father and his wife."

Okay, that didn't make any sense. He was ninety-nine point nine percent positive she'd had a bad dream. It had been a long time since he'd had any nightmares—while inconvenient, sexual fantasies didn't qualify as nightmares—but back then, only one thing had made him feel better. He closed his arms around her and hugged her.

An uneven sigh warmed his chest, and she sagged against him with a murmur. Almost instantly, her trembling faded. An unusual kind of satisfaction spread through him, better than perfect increments of time or whole dollar amounts at the gas station.

He'd taken her sadness away. He usually did the exact opposite to people.

For long minutes, he continued hugging her, reasoning she needed time for the calm to stick. But maybe he liked holding her, too. There, in the near darkness of his room, it was okay to admit to himself she felt good and smelled good, like his soap but feminine, soft, no fish sauce. He enjoyed the weight of her body on his. She was better than three heavy blankets. He might have rested his cheek against her forehead.

Her breathing evened out, and her sniffles grew further and further apart until they stopped altogether. She shifted on his lap slightly, and he realized he was aroused, wildly and embarrassingly aroused. Shit. If she wiggled any more, she'd notice for sure.

"Are you done?" he asked.

She pulled away and scooted off his lap, thankfully missing his raging erection, and he rubbed his chest where her tears had dried.

A long silence followed. She started to talk several times but held back. Finally, she whispered, "Can I sleep here tonight? At home, I sleep with Má and Ngoại and . . . I won't touch you, I promise. Unless you want . . ." Her eyes glittered mysteriously as she gazed at him.

Unless he wanted what? Wait, did she mean *sex*? No, he didn't want sex. Actually, he did. His body was enthusiastic about the idea. But mind over penis and all that. Sex was tangled with romantic relationships in his mind, and because he wasn't suited for relationships, it only made sense to avoid the sex. Besides, touching was complicated for him. Hugs were mostly okay, but anything else was likely to be a problem. It was bad enough he had to give his haircutter instructions for how to manage. He didn't want to do that with a woman before the act.

He looked at the empty half of his large bed. The blankets were completely undisturbed, pristine. And he liked them that way. He always felt a certain accomplishment when he woke up in the morning and didn't have to make the other side of the bed.

Rubbing at her elbow, she edged away from him. In a small voice, she said, "Sorry, I'll go—"

He pulled the blankets down. "You can sleep here, I guess."

Dammit, what was he doing? He didn't want her sharing his

bed. But she looked like she was going to start crying again. She wasn't supposed to be sad. Esme was always happy, always smiling.

She covered her mouth. "Really?"

He swiped the hair away from his forehead. This was a horrible idea. He could already tell. "I might snore."

"My grandma snores like a motorcycle. It doesn't bother me," she said with a big grin.

There it was. Her smile. It was important somehow. Muscles relaxed that he hadn't been aware of tensing.

She crawled under the covers and plopped her head down on the pillow, lying on her side so she faced him. He stretched out on his back and stared up at the ceiling. They were a good arm's length apart, but his heart threatened to go into cardiac arrest anyway.

This was weird. He'd done sleepovers with girl cousins. This was nothing like that. He wasn't attracted to his girl cousins. His girl cousins didn't cut down trees with meat cleavers, wear his boxers, or want to marry him. His girl cousins didn't run to him when they had nightmares.

Only Esme.

"Thank you, Anh Khải," she said.

He pulled the blankets up to his neck. "You're welcome. Try to get some sleep. My cousin Sara's wedding is tomorrow." His brow creased when he realized he'd never mentioned it to her. "You don't have to go if you don't want to, but I do. *Do* you want to?"

"Your mom told me about it. I want to go." Her voice vibrated with excitement, and he almost sighed. At least one of them was going to have a good time.

"Okay, then. Good night, Esme."

"Sleep well, Anh Khải."

For several moments, he was aware of her watching him. He could almost feel the happiness rays beaming off her and bouncing against the side of his face, but it wasn't long before she fell asleep. She didn't snore, and she didn't take up much space. But her mere presence sent him into a state of alarm.

There was a woman in his bed, his life was completely out of order, and there was a wedding tomorrow.

That night, he didn't sleep at all.

CHAPTER EIGHT

The following evening, as Esme and Khải waited for the ceremony to start in the hotel's gold-encrusted ballroom, the last thing she expected him to say was, "This wedding is missing something."

She took in the tall floral arrangements, crystal chandeliers, and French palace ambience and shook her head. "Missing what?"

"I thought you'd know."

"Me?"

"I can't figure it out." He cleared his throat and pulled at his collar like his tie was too tight.

She scanned their surroundings again, but nothing obvious stuck out. Of course, she had no idea what to expect at an American wedding. She barely knew Vietnamese weddings, since she'd personally skipped that part of the baby-making process. It said a lot about them that he could think this wedding was missing something when it was as close to perfect as she could imagine.

A flutist started playing, and a little flower girl with pigtails tossed rose petals as she walked down the aisle between row after row of men in suits and women in *áo dài* and cocktail dresses. The bride wore a filmy gown that looked like it was made of clouds. She took her father's arm and walked to the wedding altar, where the groom waited, watching her like she was everything.

Esme's throat knotted, and though she tried to ignore it, her wanting grew so big her chest ached. She didn't need live music or a place this nice or a gown this beautiful, but the rest . . .

As the ceremony went on, she found herself watching Khải more often than the bride and groom. He concentrated on the couple's vows with his usual intensity, and she wanted to reach up and trace the strong lines of his profile, anything to feel closer to him. They were side by side, but they felt so far apart.

Was he going to be hers someday? He'd held her last night, and she'd enjoyed her first good night of sleep since she'd come here. No nightmares about her baby's playboy daddy and heiress wife taking Jade or the accompanying guilt that she'd been selfish in keeping her child. She told herself repeatedly that she hadn't done it just for herself. She'd mostly done it for Jade. Because her love for her child was strong enough to make a difference. That love had brought her here, hadn't it?

Maybe another kind of love could grow between her and Khải. If he opened up to her. She felt like she was on the verge of reaching him, so very close. Maybe it would happen tonight. Maybe when they danced.

The couple kissed, and the crowd broke into applause. Everyone stood up as Sara and her new husband strode past, huge grins on their faces. Cameras flashed, phone screens glowed, and bubbles floated in the air. An announcer said it was time to move to the banquet room for the reception, and Esme gathered her courage and hooked her hand around Khải's arm. His body tensed as he looked down at her fingers on his coat sleeve. She held her breath, horribly conscious of how unpretty her hand looked on him. Those short nails and inelegant fingers. Her mom had nice hands and often lamented that Esme hadn't inherited them. She said Esme had truckdriver hands.

Silly comments flitted through her mind, things she could say to possibly make him crack a smile, but she didn't say them. She was too anxious to be funny. In the end, he didn't relax, but he didn't brush her off, either. That was good. Right?

"Well, isn't this cute?" asked a feminine voice in a dry tone.

A pretty woman with straight bangs, natural-toned lipstick, and a severe black cocktail dress approached them, and Khải broke away to hug her.

"Hi, baby brother."

"Hi, Vy."

The woman brushed away invisible lint from the shoulders of his suit and inspected him like a momma cat did her kittens. "You need a haircut."

"It's fine." But Khải swiped the hair away from his face anyway.

It was on the tip of Esme's tongue to offer to cut his hair, but she swallowed her words. These weren't the kind of people who cut their own hair. Judging by this place and their designer clothes, they probably went to fancy salons where they gave you tea and a neck massage.

Vy's lips thinned. "It's getting messy. Unless you're growing it out. That could work for you."

"I'll take care of it," he said.

She fingered the lapel of his suit coat. "Is this the one I picked out for you?"

"Yeah."

"That's probably why I like it so much." Appeased, the woman finally looked away from Khải and focused on Esme. "So here she is."

Esme smiled tentatively, unsure of what to expect. "Hi, Chị Vy."

Vy shook her hand and returned her smile just as tentatively. "You're Mỹ." Her eyes swept over Esme's tiny green dress and mostly naked limbs, and her expression went carefully blank.

Esme tried to pull on the hem of her skirt without people noticing. She should have worn something else, something Grandma-approved that didn't have cheap sequins and glitter, but she hadn't known it wasn't acceptable until she'd seen all the conservative dresses here. "I changed it to Esme when I came here."

"Oh, that's nice," Vy said in slow, awkward Vietnamese, which suggested she didn't speak it often but had switched over for Esme's sake.

"It's from my dau—*my* favorite Disney movie," she said quickly, and then she bit her lip. Now that she'd explained that out loud, it didn't sound like a very classy way to pick a name. She needed to be classy, like Vy, like Khải, like all these people. "I am an accountant. Back in Việt Nam."

A genuine smile stretched over Vy's mouth as she looked at her brother. "I didn't know that. How perfect." She squeezed Khải's arm like he'd run into great luck.

Esme's lying heart twisted and beat faster. The heavens needed to strike her down right now because she was a horrible person. At least she had a rough idea of what accounting was now. She'd been sneak reading his textbooks since she was supposed to be an expert, but more often than not, she ended up lost inside dictionaries instead.

"Here, here, here, here. Precious Girl is here," a familiar voice said.

As Cô Nga wrapped her in a tight hug, Esme's stomach tied itself in a big knot. Had Khải's mom heard Esme lying? Was the woman ashamed of her now? Sky, earth, demons, and gods, why was she such a big liar? She wasn't this person.

"*Chào*, Cô Nga," Esme said.

Cô Nga took in Esme's green dress and smiled in approval, not caring that it was prostitutey. "You're too beautiful. Did you like the ceremony? Are you having fun, Precious Girl?"

"Yes, it was beautiful as a dream, and—"

"You're calling her that now?" Vy interrupted. "You know you have a daughter, right?"

Cô Nga pulled away from Esme and rubbed Vy's arm. She meant it to be comforting, but that was also how she shredded carrots at the restaurant. "You're my precious girl, too."

A tight grimace of a smile stretched over Vy's mouth.

"Eh? What's this?" Cô Nga waved both hands at the space in between Esme and Khải. "Why are you two so far apart? This doesn't look like an engaged couple."

Khải rolled his eyes and took a step toward Esme. "Better?"

Cô Nga pressed her hands closer together, and he took another step. "*Ơi*, put your arm around her."

He released a harassed breath and wrapped an arm around Esme's shoulders, pulling her close. Esme knew it was wrong—he'd been forced to do it—but she liked him holding her this way, here, among all these people. It made them look like a couple and helped her feel less like she was trespassing.

Someone in the middle of the room called for Cô Nga, and she patted Esme on the cheek. "You kids have fun tonight, ha? Let me know if you need anything."

As soon as his mom left, Khải dropped his arm from Esme's shoulders, and they followed the crowd to a second ballroom even more golden than the first. Huge bouquets with golden ornaments hovered over the tables on top of tall golden vases. Even the champagne glasses were rimmed with gold.

Esme, Khải, and his sister sat at a round table for ten next to several of his girl cousins. Introductions were made and hands shaken. Ang*ie*, Soph*ie*, Ev*ie*, Jan*ie*, Madd*ie*. They complained that their brother, Michael, would be absent tonight because his fiancée didn't like big parties, and he was "whipped." At first glance, Esme recognized they were mixed just like she was—something about them resonated with her as familiar—but instead of feeling like she belonged, she felt even more out of place. They possessed an American polish Esme lacked. They also had pretty hands. Esme sat on her hands to hide them. Wouldn't it be nice if Khải had ugly hands, too? If that was so, they were an ideal couple. When she snuck a peek at his hands, however, she found them wrapped around a book. He was reading. At a wedding.

And wearing black-rimmed reading glasses.

The glasses made him look smarter and more intense, absolutely irresistible. Had they been in his pocket? And where had that book come from? Was it about something sexy like accounting or math?

She angled her head to see the cover. She couldn't make out the title, but she was pretty sure she saw a spaceship and a green-skinned creature with horns. There was no way that was work related. He was ignoring everyone, including her, at this expensive wedding. So he could read a novel about alien demon things.

Her confusion must have been written all over her face, because Khải's sister sent Esme an apologetic glance.

"He always does something like this at weddings," Vy said. "He hates them, but my mom makes him come. He'd prefer to go to a tax seminar."

Like magic, he looked up from his book. "What about tax seminars?"

Vy laughed and rested her chin in her hands. "You two should talk about taxes. You're both accountants, after all. It's a match made in heaven."

Esme manipulated her lips into a smile. "Tell me about your work."

He shut his book with his finger inside to keep the page, looking breathtakingly smart-gorgeous with those glasses. "I'm still working on the transfer pricing project. Are you familiar with that kind of work?"

She nodded enthusiastically even though she had no idea what he was talking about. "Of course." No doubt about it, she was going to be an outhouse catfish in her next life. She'd have to look up *transfer pricing* tomorrow.

"I'm having trouble automating the process for making sure transactions between subsidiaries are at arm's length. It's challenging because no two subsidiaries are the same. There are always individual factors to consider," he said.

"The length of an arm? That's a strange saying. And so lonely."

He laughed—*she'd made him laugh*—and the sound was deep and rich and beautiful. She wanted to hear him laugh more. A lot more. "That's funny. They're companies, not people."

"Companies have people."

"Companies don't have feelings."

"If companies have people, and people have feelings, then companies have feelings."

"Pretty sure transfer pricing has nothing to do with feelings," Vy said as she sent her a skeptical look, and Esme's face heated with embarrassment.

But Khải surprised her by saying, "I like your reasoning, though. I can't argue with the transitive property." Then he grinned, and she realized it was the first real smile she'd seen on him. The corners of his eyes wrinkled, and dimples formed on either side of his face. Too man-beautiful. His gaze was direct and went on far too long, but she didn't mind. For this moment in time, he belonged to her. Well, he belonged to Esme in Accounting. Real Esme wasn't smart.

"There is no tax deduction for bribery in Việt Nam," she added, remembering he'd been interested in this their first day together. This was another thing she'd looked up, but once she'd understood, she'd gotten angry at the entire concept. "I hate bribery."

He tilted his head to the side. "That's surprising to me. In a lot of countries, that's just a part of business."

"And what about people who can't pay bribes? No business for them." That was how the rich stayed rich, and the poor stayed poor unless they cheated, stole, got amazingly lucky, or . . . married.

"You're right." Khải looked at her in a new way then, and it made her warm all over. That was respect. For Esme in Accounting or the person beneath the lies?

She searched her mind for more things she might say to make him keep looking at her this way, but he worked at his collar again like it was choking him, took a gulp of ice water, and cleared his throat, distracted now. "There is something missing at this wedding."

She pointed to the empty chair next to her. "This person is missing."

"That's Quan's seat. He told me he can't make it. That's not it." But he stared at the empty chair for a good minute, saying nothing. Something was wrong. She could tell by the way he repeatedly flipped through the pages of his book with his thumb on the corner. *Fliiip. Fliiip. Fliiip.* She'd never seen him fidget like this.

What could possibly be missing from this perfect wedding?

Waitstaff served salad followed by an entree consisting of a hunk of bloody meat and a lobster's tail. Where was the delicious lobster head and all the chewy legs? She was stabbing the lobster meat with her fork and prying the shell off with her spoon—people acted like they'd die if they touched the food with their fingers—when the bride, groom, and entire wedding party approached their table. Everyone stood up to toast the new couple, and Khải pressed a champagne flute into her hands.

Vy and all the cousins held their glasses up. "Congratulations, Derrick and Sara."

They drank champagne and *awww*ed when the couple kissed. As the sweet bubbles fizzed on Esme's tongue, she peered at Khải over the rim of her glass. He'd exchanged his champagne flute for his book and was flipping the pages again. *Fliiip. Fliiip. Fliiip.*

Did he still think something was missing?

Sara, the bride, separated from her husband and approached Khải. She'd changed into a red wedding *aó dài* with gold embroidered dragons and phoenixes, but Esme missed the white wedding gown with its billowing skirts. If she ever married, she'd wear her wedding gown the whole time, even for dancing. Forget tradition.

"Thanks for coming. I know you don't like weddings," Sara said.

Khải continued flipping the pages of his book. "No problem."

Sara smiled wryly. "I remember how when we went to weddings when we were little, you and Andy used to hide in the bathroom during the dancing and play video games."

His fingers froze on the book, and he went unnaturally still. "That's what it is. It's Andy."

Sara drew in a quick breath. "What do you mean?"

"I've been wondering all night what's wrong with this wedding," Khải said. "It's Andy. He should be here."

After a second of suspended belief, his cousin's face collapsed, and fat teardrops tracked down her face, ruining her carefully applied makeup. "Why would you—What can I—How can I—"

She covered her mouth and fled the room. The groom looked at Khải for the longest moment like there were things he wanted to say, but in the end, he raced after his wife without a word. All the people from their table stared at each other, stunned speechless.

"Find me when you're ready to leave." Khải tapped his book against his thigh once and turned to leave.

Esme stepped toward him. "I'll go with—"

"No, stay, dance, have fun. I'll be out there." He waved toward the exit, swiped the hair out of his eyes, and left.

Standing woodenly, she watched as he wove between the round tables and exited the ballroom. When the door swayed shut behind him, she sank into her seat, which was now between two empty chairs.

What had just happened? Why was he leaving? Who was Andy? Was he Sara's ex-boyfriend, someone Khải preferred over the groom? She wanted to ask the others at the table, but they spoke among themselves in quiet tones, avoiding her questioning looks.

How did he expect her to enjoy the wedding alone? Was she supposed to dance with some random man? Maybe that middle-aged guy at the next table with three beers, a red leather jacket, and shoulder-length curls? She pressed a hand to her forehead. She didn't want to dance with Asian Michael Jackson. She only wanted to dance with Khải.

She pushed away from the table. "I'm going to find him."

Vy shook her head. "He might not want—"

Esme didn't hear the rest of what his sister said. She rushed after Khải, but she searched and searched and couldn't find him anywhere. He wasn't in the hotel's opulent lobby, the sitting rooms, or even the valet area out front. Was he reading in a bathroom somewhere while she was searching for him until her feet throbbed? She was about to knock on the men's room door, but a sign on a nearby door caught her eye.

It read *Kieu-Ly Changing Suite*. Maybe he was in there? When she found the door unlocked, she let herself in.

The space inside looked like a disaster zone, complete with flats of Coca-Cola, giant bags of chips, and shoes all over the floor. Piles of clothes took up all the sitting space on the small sofa. No Khải in sight.

She spied an open door on the far wall and picked her way through the wreckage to check what was on the other side.

And lost her breath.

The bride's wedding gown hung from the curtain bar above a tall window. White gossamer fabric caught the soft light just right. Before Esme knew what she was doing, she was floating across the changing room and running her fingertips over the cool skirts. She doubted she would ever wear anything so nice, not even at her own wedding, if she ever got married. She'd heard people whispering that it was a Vera Wang gown and cost *ten thousand dollars*.

But as she stood in the empty room, it occurred to her maybe she *could* wear a dress like this. And she didn't need to get married to do it. She could wear this dress. Right now. She could do it quickly, just so she knew what it was like, and then continue searching the hotel for Khải. No one had to know.

She unzipped her green dress and let it fall to her feet before she stepped out of her shoes, sighing when her sore feet flattened against the carpet. She hadn't worn a bra under her dress, and goose bumps rippled over her naked breasts. Wearing nothing but panties, she reached for the dress's hanger. She arched onto her tiptoes and reached as high as she could. High, higher, but her fingertips couldn't quite grasp it.

Just as she was coiling up to make a jump for it, the door in the other room squeaked open.

No.

Was it the bride? Was she going to change her dress *again*?

She stood still and held her breath. Measured footsteps padded around. Who was it?

There was the pop and hiss of a can of soda being opened, and the footsteps came closer.

No, no, no, no.

She couldn't get caught in her underwear like this. Holding her arms to her breasts, she glanced about the room in a blind panic. No way out, only a closet. Without further thought, she sprinted into the closet and shut herself inside.

The door was the shuttered kind, and looking through the slats, she had a good view of the doorway. *Step, step, step, step.* The footsteps sounded heavy, male. Was it the groom? A hotel janitor? What was the most embarrassing thing that could happen? Knowing her stinky luck, she should expect that.

Khải strode into the room.

She pressed her forehead to the closet door in defeat. Of course it was him. He scanned the room and sat in an empty armchair across from the closet. After taking a sip of his Coca-Cola, he set it on the floor by his feet and continued reading the book with the spaceship and alien demon thing on the cover.

She almost groaned in frustration. She couldn't continue hiding in the closet waiting for him to finish reading when he was reading waiting for her. She had to walk out and explain herself. How could she word things so he didn't laugh as much?

He reached for his Coke can, but as he was lifting it to his mouth, his gaze caught on something. Following his line of sight, she saw her discarded dress and shoes. Did he recognize them?

Oh no, was he drawing certain conclusions?

There was nothing for it. She had to come out and explain herself. She pressed her palms to the closet door, preparing to push it open, but Khải jumped to his feet.

He angled his head to the side like he was listening to something. That was when she heard it.

Stumbling footsteps in the adjoining room. They came closer. And closer. A loud thump sounded, like someone had slammed themselves against the wall. A moan.

Khải backed away from the door. He contemplated the window before his gaze locked on the closet.

Another thump on the wall. The footsteps grew louder. Another moan.

In three long strides, he crossed the room and yanked the closet door open. His jaw fell when he saw her, but there wasn't time for surprise. He shut himself in the closet with her right as a couple stumbled through the door.

CHAPTER NINE

*N*aked.

That was the only thought Khai's brain was capable of.

Naked.

He'd looked at her for less than a second before he shut them both in the closet, but it had been enough to see almost everything. Bare shoulders, full breasts that threatened to overflow the cage of her arms, tucked-in waist, lush hips, and white cotton panties with a little bow in the middle.

Delete, delete, delete. He squeezed his eyes shut as he tried to erase the image from his mind. But that made the sounds from the other side of the closet door louder.

Heavy breathing. Wet kissing sounds. Hands on fabric. The *zzzzip* of pants coming undone. Oh fuck, were they doing what he thought they were doing?

He looked through the slats and saw the couple intertwined on the floor. He didn't recognize the woman, but her blond hair marked her as a friend of the family. With his Jheri curls and red leather jacket, the man couldn't be mistaken as anyone other than his cousin Van. Maybe he was pursuing his fourth marriage now. Khai had no clue how that look worked so well for his cousin.

The two moaned simultaneously before their bodies began writhing rhythmically.

Dammit.

Khai turned away from the slats, but then he was looking at Esme again. Light spilled in alluring stripes over her smooth skin, outlining the length of her neck, the ripe curve of her breast, and—

Rule Number Six.

He covered his eyes with a hand and wished he was anywhere else in the world. He'd had enough of thinking about Andy, making people cry, and wanting Esme.

Antarctica would be a good change of pace. Glacial mountain peaks, barren expanses of pristine snow, emptiness, calm, the smallness of man—

"Oh wow. Wow. *Wow,*" the woman cried out. *"Wowie!"*

Khai's focus shattered, and he dropped his hand away from his eyes. *Wowie?* Really? What the hell was Van doing out there?

A smothered choking sound drew his attention before he could spy on the couple again, and he found Esme's shoulders shaking as she laughed into her palm. He supposed it was kind of funny, but he never laughed along with her. She'd taken an arm away from her chest, and he swore he could almost see one of her nipples. He wasn't sure with all the shadows, but there was a dark—

Hell. He was in hell.

He stared at the wall, trying his best not to respond to the live porn both outside and inside the closet. It was impossible. The woman's cries kept getting louder. Did Esme make those sounds? He hoped she didn't say *wowie.* But something else. Like maybe . . . his name. His entire body hardened at the thought, and his skin went ultrasensitive. His pulse sped up. He attempted to put more space between them, but the side of the closet brought him up short. There was no escape.

How much longer could this go on? Were Van and his lady trying to set some sort of world record?

Eventually, the noises came to a horrible crescendo and then quieted. Van tottered drunkenly to his feet and helped his partner up. They straightened their clothes with awkward conversation and disappeared. Khai waited for a count of sixty before he pushed the closet door open and walked out. He took a breath, and the air smelled like—no, he wasn't going to think about what the air smelled like. An involuntary shudder coursed through him.

Esme followed him out of the closet, her cheeks reddened to a fantastic lobstery sheen, and went to get her green dress and shoes— he'd thought they looked familiar. Keeping her back to him, she stepped into her dress and pulled it up. A woman's back wasn't one of the restricted body parts mentioned in the footnotes of the Rules, so he let himself look. But it still felt like rule breaking. The curve at the base of her spine was one of the most elegant things he'd ever seen.

"Help me?" she asked, looking at him over her shoulder.

His feet took him to her on their own. As his heart pounded loudly in his ears, he fumbled with the zipper and pulled it along the graceful line of her back, covering her perfect skin. When he finished, she turned around, and their eyes met.

"I wanted to wear the wedding dress," she whispered. "But I couldn't reach it."

He glanced at the wedding gown hanging on the curtain rod. Yeah, she was definitely too short for that. "Do you want me to get it down for you?"

A smile worked over her face, one of those mind-scrambling, breathtaking smiles that made her eyes greener. He'd caused that smile. The knowledge sent warmth melting through him, better than a big sweater fresh from the dryer.

"Why are you smiling?" he asked.

Her smile widened. "You didn't laugh."

"Why would I?"

She lifted a shoulder. "Where did you go? I looked everywhere for you."

"I took a walk outside. To clear my head. I'm not . . . good with people." And the banquet hall and hotel had felt suffocating. Once he'd realized what was missing, he'd started to notice all the places where Andy should have been. Getting a drink at the wet bar, standing with the groomsmen, at Khai's side . . .

"I'm also not good with people," she said.

That was a revelation to Khai, and when he looked at her then, her imperfections stuck out for the first time. One of her eyebrows arched more than the other. Her nose wasn't as straight as he'd thought. There, on the left side of her neck, a tiny birthmark. She wasn't a photoshopped image on a magazine. She was a real person, flawed. Oddly, that made her more beautiful. She was also smart in her own strange way, with a sense of fairness that resonated with his own. She wasn't at all what he'd thought in the beginning.

She stepped toward him, and when she bit her bottom lip, his eyes tracked the movement, mesmerized by the way her white teeth scraped over the full red skin. What if he leaned down and kissed her?

Would she let him? What would it be like to bring their mouths together? To feel those red lips against his own? To delve inside and claim—

Something skated lightly against his hand.

Cold. Unexpected. Wrong.

"What the—" He jerked away on reflex, way too quickly and violently, and she startled and backed away from him with wide eyes.

"Sorry," she said as she hugged her hand to her chest. She'd touched him, maybe to hold hands, and he'd frightened her. He hated frightening people.

Explanations piled up on his tongue, but he didn't know where to start. He didn't even know if he should bother. What was the point? After this summer, they were never going to see each other again.

The impression of her touch remained on his skin, shimmery and unpleasant, and he knew from experience the sensation wouldn't fade for another day. Light touches did that, and it was worse when people caught him by surprise. Like she had. If she'd warned him, and if she'd touched him the right way, maybe . . . He shook his head at his thoughts. There was no maybe.

The incident today with Sara had confirmed he wasn't meant for relationships. Since that was the case, he couldn't encourage touching. What if—he didn't know—what if they explored this attraction between them, and she fell in love with him? That would be horribly irresponsible of him, wouldn't it? He could never love her back. He'd just hurt her. And he never wanted to do that. She was supposed to be happy.

When he rubbed his hand against his pant leg in an effort to blunt the feeling, she watched the motion with a tightening of her lips.

"If you want to eat cake and dance, I don't mind waiting for you here." But he wasn't going to join her. He was finished with that banquet room. And maybe it was cowardly, but he didn't want to see Sara crying anymore.

"No, no, let's go." She flashed a smile at him and walked efficiently from the room.

As they strode down the hotel's lavish hallways, Khai was very aware that she didn't rest her hand in the crook of his arm. She kept a healthy distance between them, and he couldn't decide if he was disappointed or relieved. He honestly hadn't liked it before, but he liked this even less.

The ground shook with a rhythmic bass when they passed the doors to the banquet hall where the reception was taking place. The dancing had started. That meant dinner was over, the fruit-filled wedding cake had been eaten, speeches spoken, and the wedding was basically done.

Andy had missed all of it.

He should have been here. He probably would have been a groomsman. If not, he definitely would have been an usher. He would have sat next to Khai during the ceremony and reception. He would have given a speech that embarrassed Sara and made everyone laugh. Right now, he'd be in there dancing because it was Sara's wedding and he was that kind of brother.

The fact that he *wasn't* in there dancing made Khai's shoulders, lungs, and feet heavy. He pulled at his collar again because it was strangling him. At least he knew what was wrong now. It was his sense of order. Things weren't in their proper place.

It was so important to him to have things in their proper place.

When they got back to Khải's house, he parked by the curb again. Esme wondered why he didn't like using his garage, but she didn't want to ask him. She couldn't forget the way he'd wiped her touch off his hand.

Why had he acted so disgusted?

He'd had that look in his eyes, the one men got when they wanted to kiss you. She *knew* that look. Or she thought she did. In that moment, all she'd wanted was for him to do it. She hadn't stopped to think about marriage, green cards, and finding a daddy for her baby. She'd been too mesmerized by the intensity of his gaze and the pull that always drew her to him. She'd wanted to feel his lips on hers, to be close to him, to know him.

But he'd pushed her away.

As she showered and got ready for bed, her eyes pricked with tears a few times, but she didn't cry. She'd been rejected before. This wasn't new. It meant she needed to try harder. She could do that. She certainly wasn't giving up.

Determined, she pulled on her favorite T-shirt, crossed the bathroom, and opened his door like she owned it. He propped himself up on an elbow and frowned at her as he swiped the overlong hair from his eyes. The blankets slid down, revealing his defined chest and part of his muscled stomach. Beautiful man.

Before he could come up with an excuse to send her away, she boldly helped herself to the empty half of his bed and stretched out on her side, facing him. Her shirt cooperated by exposing her shoulder and a good amount of cleavage. He looked. She saw him look. And since she had his attention, she reached up and gathered her hair above her head, away from her neck. The motion caused the neckline of her shirt to shift even lower, scandalously low. Cool air touched a fair amount of her chest, and she didn't cover herself, even though her heart pounded.

Khải's Adam's apple bobbed on a loud swallow before he lay down and turned his back to her, and she suppressed a pleased smile. He wasn't immune. He didn't want to, but he liked what he saw.

In the dim light provided by the bathroom night-light, she judged the distance between them to be almost exactly one arm's length. He worked all day keeping companies that far apart, and then at home, he kept the two of them that far apart. If she worked at it, she'd figure out how to close this distance.

CHAPTER TEN

Khai woke up on Sunday to bright sunlight spilling in through the windows and the insistent tweeting of chatty birds—they were probably the same ones who regularly shat on his car. He'd been certain he'd stay awake all night again, but as he'd lain there cursing Esme, her breasty Esmeness, and his body's response to her, he'd nodded off and slept clear until morning.

He must have been dead tired, because he hadn't noticed when she left. Her side of the bed was empty, but the blankets were thoroughly wrinkled. When he reached over, they were cool to the touch. She'd been gone for a while. He hoped she wasn't ironing his underwear or trimming his lawn with his desk scissors.

Instead of going to hunt for her and do damage control, however, he pulled her pillow close and buried his face in it. It smelled of clean laundry, shampoo . . . and her. The smell was faint, but he recognized it. Soft and sweet, gentle. She'd spent the night here, in his bed, in his space, with him, and left part of herself behind. He let himself drag in a lungful of her scent, one more, and a last one before he grew disgusted with himself and got out of bed. So what if she smelled good? She still drove him crazy.

Once he'd gone through his regular morning routine, he headed to the kitchen, expecting to find her covered in jackfruit, cooking, or flipping his refrigerator upside down. But she wasn't there.

He opened the sliding glass door connected to his kitchen and stepped into his backyard for the first time since he'd moved in. Nothing but dead grass and dirt where that tree used to be. Not even the roots remained, and all the weeds were gone. He had to admit she'd done a good job.

Where was she? She didn't work Sundays, so his mom couldn't have come and gotten her—not that she'd ever do that when she could just call and make him drive.

Had Esme . . . left him?

He'd been hoping for that all week, but now that it might have happened, he wasn't as glad as he'd thought he'd be. But why would she want to stay after last night? He'd made his cousin cry at her own wedding, and then he'd frightened Esme when she'd tried to hold his hand. He'd clearly demonstrated why he should be alone.

A heavy sigh gusted from his lungs, and he went back inside and checked her room. She wasn't there, but her suitcase was. His stomach relaxed, and he cursed himself every way he knew how. Why the fuck was he relieved she hadn't gone yet?

Shit, he must be getting used to her. He didn't *want* to get used to her.

He shoved his feet into his shoes and walked out onto the front porch to look for her. It was warm and sunny, but too early in the day to be humid. Those birds were tweeting, probably laughing because they'd left something new for him on his windshield. The lawn was only partially cleared, but it was already a great improvement. He grimaced. Ruthie had to be ecstatic.

Pink and peach begonias bloomed from neat bushes in the manicured lawn across the street. Ruthie gave those to the neighbors sometimes. He'd seen her do it. None for him, but that was fine. He didn't want her damned begonias.

No Esme in sight. He stepped down from the porch to see if she was hidden between his house and the neighbor's, and that was when he saw it.

The garage door was open.

A sick sensation surged through him, shortening his breath and making his palms sweat. *Why* was the garage door open?

He ran into the empty musty space, and reality hit him like a punch to the gut.

It was gone.

And Esme was gone.

When he did the math, a horrible certainty dawned upon him.

Esme was going to die.

E sme loved the Asian grocery store 99 Ranch. It was like they'd scooped up a bit of home and planted it on the other side of the ocean. The workers were all Chinese, but the food items were familiar. She knew this fishy smell. She was excited to eat the spicy tamarind candy she'd found in the checkout aisle. At the cash register, the process was quick and painless. She handed the cashier a twenty, and he gave her the change without saying a single thing. No translation needed. Everyone belonged here.

She carried her plastic grocery bags outside and admired the blue motorcycle parked close to the store's front doors. She'd squealed with joy when she'd found it earlier today. All last week, she'd passed by that door in Khải's kitchen without checking what was on the other side. She'd been too busy cleaning and plotting ways to get into Khải's heart and pants.

This morning, she'd turned the door handle by accident when she mistook it for the pantry door and come up short when it was locked. After unbolting it, she'd flipped the light on and discovered a spacious garage empty of anything save a tarp-covered *something* in the middle. From the size and shape of it, she'd suspected it was a motorcycle, and when she lifted the tarp, she hadn't been disappointed.

Transportation. Because she didn't like having to beg rides off people anytime she wanted to go somewhere, she'd stayed at home, but she didn't like being trapped and abandoned whenever Khải needed to go somewhere without her. There was a local bus system, but that was intimidating and likely to be slow with the different bus routes and connections. A motorcycle, on the other hand, could take her anywhere she wanted directly.

It didn't matter that it was a little scratched and banged up. When she'd turned the keys sitting conveniently in the ignition, it'd started right up. She'd hurried to grab her purse and shut the door, and then she'd headed out as possibilities raced in her mind, ways she could surprise Khải and make him addicted to her. The first thing to occur to her had been food. She could make him something fresh and nutritious like swim bladder soup.

Feeling hopeful and cautiously happy, she packed her purse and newly purchased groceries—including the swim bladders of twenty fish—onto the back of the motorcycle, pulled on the helmet, and headed out. There was something special in the air as she drove home. The houses and shops looked prettier, and the grass greener.

When she turned onto Central Expressway and headed west, soaring pines hugged either side of the street and occupied the center divide, which separated the traffic into coming and going lanes.

Funny how the trees were so tall but they made her feel bigger—inside, where it counted. She smiled as she passed exit after exit. She'd be home soon, and then she'd make Khải lunch. After that, she was going to finish clearing his front yard. Now that she had a motorcycle, she could go to the store and get things like grass seed and fresh flowers. She could make his yard really nice.

When Khải's exit approached, she turned on her right blinker, but before she could switch lanes, a silver car coming from the other direction skidded to a halt on the shoulder. Tires squealed and smoke rose off the blacktop. It looked alarmingly like Khải's car, and when the door opened, a man shot out who couldn't be anyone but Khải himself.

Over the roar of the motorcycle engine, she heard him shout, *"Stop. Get off. Get off right now."*

Her heart jumped into her throat, and her mouth went cotton dry. Was it the police? What kind of trouble could she be in? She slowed down and pulled over next to the center divide like he'd done.

He sprinted toward her. *"Get off the bike. Hurry."*

As soon as he came close enough for her to register the terror on his usually calm face, she started shaking. There had to be something wrong with the motorcycle. Was it going to explode?

She worked at the kickstand with a trembling foot, but before she'd managed to prop the bike up, Khải grabbed her by her upper arms and manually lifted her off the seat. The motorcycle crashed to its side, sending her things all over the rocks and scraggly grass.

His hair stood up in wild patches, and his face was a mask of fury. She'd never imagined he could be this angry. Without pausing to take breaths, he said, "Why did you take the bike why did you ride it I never said you could ride it."

Her shaking worsened to the point where she couldn't move. "S-sorry. I just went—"

He steered her across the grass toward his car. "Let's go."

"But I bought food. It fell all over. And the motorcycle. Someone will take it. I'll bring it back—"

"Stay. Away. From. It," he bit out.

Once she got into the car, he yanked the seat belt over her and buckled it, giving it a hard tug to make sure it was tight.

She flinched when he slammed the door shut, and after he marched around and threw himself into his seat, she cleared her throat and said, "My handbag. My money. It's over there, and I need—"

He leapt out of the car and crossed the divide to crouch beside the motorcycle, but instead of unfastening her purse from the rack, he pressed a fist to his forehead and stayed that way for several long moments. Cars sped by. One slowed down and then accelerated off. Another driver cranked his window down and asked if help was needed.

Khải shook his head and called out in a terse tone, "No, thank you." As the car drove away, he reached over, twisted the key out of the motorcycle's ignition, and pocketed it. Then he got her purse and returned to the car.

The drive back to his place took two minutes. Esme knew because she spent the entire time watching the clock and waiting for him to speak, but he never did. The garage was empty, but he parked along the curb as usual.

She followed him to the front door, unsure what to say or what to do. When he unlocked the door, she went inside and took her shoes off, expecting him to do the same, but he turned around without a word and started walking down the street. To get the motorcycle, she realized.

"Do you want me to come with you?" she asked.

No response. He simply continued walking, shoulders square and back straight, looking like an assassin out on his last mission.

She watched until he disappeared around the corner and then eased the door shut and sagged against it. Her heartbeat gradually slowed down, but her face remained hot with an intense mixture of embarrassment and confusion.

She shouldn't have taken the motorcycle without asking. But he was so easy with the rest of his things she hadn't thought it was a big deal.

Why was it a big deal? Why did he keep it in the garage without using it? There was enough room in there for both his motorcycle and his car. Why did he park outside?

Why had he been so angry?

No matter what it was, she had to make it up to him, and she could start doing that immediately. She slipped into the garage, grabbed the ladder she'd seen earlier, and carried it out to the front porch. There were so many leaves clogging the gutter she worried it might fall off and hit someone in the head. It also looked bad. After getting the ladder as stable as she could, she climbed up and tossed handfuls of leaves down to the ground. She'd cleared a good portion of the gutter when Khải walked the motorcycle up the driveway, returned it to the garage, and strode toward her.

Her plastic bags of groceries hung from his fingers by his side, but he let them plop to the ground as he stalked over and gripped the ladder, looking up at her with a deep frown on his face. "What are you doing?"

She tossed another handful of leaves down. "There are too many leaves in here."

"Come down," he said firmly. "It's not safe."

"But I'm not done. Wait a little—"

"*Now*, Esme." The words came out sharply, louder than she expected, and her foot slipped on the ladder.

She flailed about helplessly for a heart-stopping second but managed to get ahold of the gutter so she didn't fall. With her face pressed to the grimy metal, she whispered thanks to sky and Buddha. That fall would have broken her butt.

"Please. Come down now," he said in a hard monotone.

The instant her feet touched the ground, he turned the ladder on its side and carried it back into the garage.

She threw her hands up in the air and followed him. "Why are you doing this? I'm not done." She still had a lot of gutter left to clean, and she hated leaving a job unfinished. Without thinking, she grabbed his shoulder and said, "Anh Khải, put it back—"

He whipped around instantly and wrapped an arm across his chest so he could rub at the shoulder she'd touched. "You have to *stop* all of this."

"I'll finish later, then, but—"

"No, there won't be any finishing. You. Have. To. Stop. Do you understand? You. Have. To. Stop."

Her bottom lip trembled at his slow, exaggerated pronunciation. "You don't need to speak like that. I understand you."

He made a frustrated sound. "You don't. You've been reorganizing my stuff in ridiculous ways, cutting down trees with a *meat cleaver*, touching that motorcycle, touching *me*. It all has to stop. I can't live this way."

When his meaning sank in, Esmé's shoulders drooped. "Ridiculous?" she repeated in English. That didn't sound good.

He clawed both hands through his hair. "*Yes.*"

She looked at the half-cleared lawn and wiped her dirty hands on her pants as her heart shrank and her face flamed. *Ridiculous.* If she were classier, she'd know what that meant. Now that she thought about it, it probably wasn't very classy for her to do yard work or clean his house or any of this stuff. Esme in Accounting probably hired people to do this work. But the real Esme, the country girl Mỹ who always smelled like fish sauce, just wanted to be useful. She hadn't thought about how it looked.

Had she been embarrassing him and herself all this time?

"I'll stop," she made herself say.

"Really?" he asked, sounding so hopeful it made her pride smart even more.

She nodded. "I promise I'll stop now." She would have shaken hands on it, but he'd included touching him in the list of things that had to stop. She wiped her palms on her pants again, but something told her the thing that disgusted him wasn't something she could wash away.

CHAPTER ELEVEN

ENGLISH DICTIONARY
Ridiculous: inviting derision or mockery; absurd

VIETNAMESE DICTIONARY
Absurd: *đáng cười*

Ridiculous, a dry monkey's ass. She'd show him how ridiculous she wasn't.

On Monday, Esme began treating customer interactions at the restaurant like language practice. She *had* to improve, so she pushed herself to chat with the customers even though she felt like a water buffalo mooing from the fields. She asked about people's days; she played with their cute kids, who reminded her of Jade; she recommended new dishes. It felt unnatural and awkward at first, but aside from the one stinky woman who rolled her eyes at her and mocked her behind her back, the customers didn't seem to mind too much. After a while, it was kind of fun.

When she was cleaning tables after the lunch hour, she discovered that her "practice" had earned her bigger tips. Did that mean people *liked* it when she spoke to them? That made her laugh a little. Maybe she was a charming water buffalo.

"You've gotten better quickly," a familiar voice said in English.

Esme whipped around and saw Miss Q sitting at her regular table, absently munching on eggrolls wrapped in lettuce as she marked up more homework.

She almost responded in Vietnamese, but she didn't. Esme wasn't trying to marry Miss Q. She might as well practice on her.

"Thank you," she said.

Without looking up from her papers, Miss Q said, "I thought I'd see you in my class last week."

"I do not need class." Some people had to make do without.

Miss Q shook her head and continued marking the paper, her red pen scribbling quickly. "You would do better with class."

Esme bit her lip in frustration. She knew she'd do better with class. She loved school and loved teachers and loved to raise her hand all the time. School had always been something she excelled at. Until she'd quit early and disappointed everyone.

"I need to save money," she said. "For family."

Miss Q looked up, gave Esme an impatient look, and dug a flyer out of her bag. "It's not expensive. Here, look." As Esme pored over the prices, which *were* surprisingly affordable, Miss Q continued, "The difficult part for people is finding the time. Do you have the time?"

"No, I need . . ." Her voice dried up before she could say she needed to spend time with Khải. The truth was he didn't *want* to spend time with her. He'd made that very clear.

A section of the flyer listed the classes offered at the school, and one of them stuck right out: *Accounting*. A strange buzzing sensation spread through her veins. She tapped on the class listing. "Can I do this one?"

Miss Q put her red pen down and read the indicated words with a growing smile. "You want to be an accountant? I think you'd make a great accountant."

Esme frowned at that, not believing it for a second. In fact, the suggestion made her almost *angry*. Holding up the flyer, she asked, "I can keep this?"

"Sure, I brought it for you," Miss Q said.

"Thank you." Esme folded it neatly in half, tucked it into her apron's pocket, and got back to work.

The small table shook as she wiped it down, and she had to ease off before all the condiments fell to the ground. Miss Q made it sound like Esme could actually be an accountant one day, when she knew there was no way. It wasn't kind to put dreams like that in someone's head.

The best Esme could hope for was "almost an accountant." But luckily for her, that might be enough to win her Khải.

In the two weeks that followed, Esme put Khai's house back to rights and began taking the bus home. He assumed she'd taken on the night shift at his mom's. He should have been happy to have his evenings to himself again—his house didn't smell of fish-sauce fumes from her cooking and food doctoring anymore—but dinner wasn't the same without her odd chatter and cheeriness. If he was being honest, his evenings now sucked. The house felt empty, and even without her Viet pop blaring, he couldn't focus on his work or the TV. He checked the time a lot as he waited for her to walk through the door.

She still shared a bed with him, but she kept her back to him and balanced on the very edge, as far away from him as possible. Some-times, he worried she'd fall off. Other times, he *hoped* she'd fall off. So he'd have an excuse to tell her to come closer.

Tonight, it was nearly 10:30 P.M., and she still hadn't come home. She was usually back by this time, and his stomach churned. He considered calling or texting her, but those were cell phone func-tions he loathed.

Regardless, by the time 10:45 P.M. rolled around, he couldn't handle it anymore. He went into his contacts and scrolled down to the phone number for Esme T. His thumb was hovering over the call button when his phone vibrated with an incoming call.

From Esme T.

He accepted the call right away and brought the phone to his ear. "Hi."

"Oh hi, it's me. Esme. But you know that, ha? It says that on your phone," she said with a laugh.

He shook his head. Why was she talking so fast? "Yes, I know it's you."

"Sorry if I woke you up. I'm not on a date." She laughed and cleared her throat. "I just called to tell you I'll be late. Okay, bye-bye."

Then she hung up.

That was it? No explanation, no nothing? And why did she men-tion dating? He'd never imagined her with another man, but he sure as hell was now. The thought irritated the shit out of him.

Gritting his teeth, he called her back. The phone rang and rang and rang. Seriously? She'd just spoken to him. How come she'd—

"Hello?" she said over the background noise. Lots of people spoke at the same time, and was that a baby crying?

"Where are you?"

"I'll call you back. They just said my name."

"Wait, where *are* you?"

"The doctor. I'll talk later. I have to—"

His chest squeezed tight, knocking the breath out of him. "Which doctor? Where? Why?"

"The clinic by the Asian grocery store, but I'm okay. I just hurt—I have to go. Bye." For the second time that night, she hung up on him.

She'd hurt what? Herself? Someone else? He hurried out the door and jumped into his car.

Esme hugged her arms tight to her chest as a woman made soothing sounds for her wailing baby girl and walked back and forth across the waiting room. The baby's face was red and teary from several minutes of hard crying, and it made Esme's arms ache to hold her own girl. Jade had never gotten so sick, thankfully, but Esme had. She remembered when the fever and pain had been at their worst, she'd told Jade to keep her distance so she didn't get sick, too, and Jade had broken down into tears.

"Don't cry," Esme had said.

"I'm not crying because I'm scared I'll get sick," her girl had replied. "I'm crying because I love you."

Esme's longing for her girl grew unbearable, and she would have offered to bounce this stranger's baby if her ankle weren't swollen to two times its regular size and propped between a pillow and an ice pack.

When Khải marched through the waiting room door, her whole body went stiff. Seeing a ghost would have made more sense to her. What was he doing here? Why had he come? When he crossed the room and crouched in front of her, scowling at her ankle, she had no idea what to think. Was he going to yell at her?

"What happened?" he asked. "The doctor saw you already? What did they say?"

"I twisted it on the stairs. The doctor thinks it's sprained. He's waiting for the X-ray."

He lifted the ice pack away from her swollen ankle, and his frown deepened. "Can you move your foot?" When she wiggled it, he said, "Up and down? Side to side?"

A door cracked open, and a nurse called out, "Esmeralda Tran."

Esme stood and prepared to limp to the exam room just like she had earlier, but before her injured foot could touch the ground, the earth spun. She found herself cradled in Khải's arms like a heroine in a movie, and her muscles tensed.

"You don't need to carry me. I can walk. I'm heavy."

He rolled his eyes and followed the nurse through the halls. "You're not heavy. You're a tiny human."

"I'm not 'tiny.'" But she couldn't put much outrage into the words. His hold on her was secure, and he wasn't breathing heavily. He made her feel safe. And small. She loved it. Back home, her mom and grandma always asked her to get things down from the top shelf or carry the heavy packages because she was so much bigger than they were.

Khải didn't think she was too big.

"You can put her there." The nurse indicated the paper-covered exam bed. On his way out of the room, the nurse said, "Great boyfriend you've got. The doctor will be in shortly."

Boyfriend. The nurse was gone before either of them could correct him, and once Khải set her down, she fixed her attention on the picture of bones and muscles on the wall. "Thank you for . . ." She waved at her ankle, which he'd carefully positioned on the exam bed.

He shrugged and sat down in a chair against the wall. "You shouldn't walk on it for a while."

"It's not bad." Now. It had hurt something awful earlier, though.

She'd thought it was broken, and she'd panicked. She'd clearly failed with Khải. If she couldn't work, would Cô Nga send her back to Việt Nam early? She couldn't go home yet. She still needed to look for her dad. Rubbing her arm uncomfortably, she asked, "Why did you come?"

He gave her a funny look. "You're hurt."

Things collapsed inside her heart, and she turned her face away from him and stared down at her hands in her lap. He'd come . . . to be with her?

What a foreign concept.

Growing up, she'd been expected to take care of herself. Her mom and grandma were always busy working, and if she was hurt or sick, it was best to grit her teeth and deal with it on her own. That was even more the case now that she had Jade. When he fussed with the ice pack and repositioned it against her ankle, she felt more cared for than she ever had.

"I'm okay," she said.

"I hope so."

A knock sounded on the door, and the doctor strode in—the same one from before. He was extremely good-looking, with dark features, above-average height, and an Indian name she couldn't pronounce. Navneet Something. He held a black X-ray film in his hands.

"Good news, Esmeralda. No fracture. If you keep it compressed, elevated, and iced, it should be better in a couple weeks."

Esme's body loosened with relief. "Great. Thank you."

"My pleasure." The doctor flashed a white-toothed grin at her as he took a business card from his pocket and handed it to her. "It's not serious enough to need another checkup, but if you want to meet after hours sometime, I'd be happy to take another look."

Esme accepted the business card and flipped it around to see another phone number scrawled across the back. When her gaze jumped back to his face, he winked at her.

Khải stood up then, and the doctor's eyes widened as he took in Khải's height, dark clothes, and that intense air that made her think of assassins and bodyguards.

"I'm sorry. I didn't notice you here," the doctor said.

"What do you mean by 'after hours'?" Khải asked in his serious way.

The doctor swallowed. "It means . . . whatever she wants it to mean." He backed toward the door. "That's it for this visit. I'll send in the nurse to wrap the ankle." With one last tight smile, he left.

Khải scowled at the door as it swung shut and picked up a roll of cloth the doctor had left behind. "I can do it. I know how."

Then he shocked her by lifting her leg and winding the cloth around and around her ankle and the arch of her foot. His grip was firm, but he never hurt her. His warm fingers were gentle against the icy skin of her calf, her heel, and the ball of her foot, sending goose bumps up her leg.

When she caught her breath, he looked up at her. "Is it too tight?"

She was too distracted to speak. He was touching her ugly foot, and he wasn't jerking away or wiping his palms on his pants. Instead, he held her like she was precious. It was a heady sensation having his beautiful mind focused entirely on her, even if it was only her ankle.

Belatedly, she answered, "No, not too tight."

He returned his attention to her ankle, and the edges of the business card pressed into Esme's skin as she tightened her fingers. She wanted to touch his face, the brooding lines of his profile, his forehead, his jaw, the sharp bridge of his nose, his oh-so-kissable lips . . .

"That should do it," he said, and when he pulled his hands away, she saw he'd wrapped her ankle neatly and secured the end with a metal clasp. "If you start to lose feeling in your toes, let me know, and I'll loosen it."

"Okay, thank you, Anh."

"Ready to go?"

She nodded and dropped her legs over the edge of the bed, intending to stand, but again, he gathered her up in his arms and carried her out of the room.

"I can walk," she whispered.

"It's better if you don't. I don't mind carrying you."

After that, she didn't protest. She didn't mind him carrying her, either. No one had held her like this since she was a child. As they traveled through the clinic, however, she fisted her hands and kept her arms tense. She couldn't forget how he'd responded each time she'd touched him in the past. She didn't want to ruin this. Or surprise him into dropping her.

After setting her down briefly at the front desk to pay for her visit—she didn't know how much it cost because he handed his credit card to the receptionist before she could show Esme the bill—she was carried outside and buckled into his car. Sleepily, she watched the lights flicker by as he drove back to his house.

He broke the silence by asking, "What stairs were you on when you fell? There aren't any by my mom's restaurant."

At his question, adrenaline spiked, and cold sweat misted her skin. "The stairs across the street."

Please don't ask more.

"The ones at the adult school?"

She tried to sink into her seat and traced her fingertips along the handrail on her door. "I like your car. What kind is it?"

"It's a Porsche 911 Turbo S."

"Por-sha," she repeated. "That's a pretty-sounding name."

He shrugged and said, "I guess so."

Her muscles relaxed. She'd succeeded in distracting him.

But when he parked in front of his house, he didn't get out of the car right away. "What were you doing at the adult school?"

She squirmed in her seat and shifted her legs. Her clothes grew damp under her arms, and her hair stuck to her neck. All of her efforts were for nothing if he found out about them.

"Were you—"

Before he could complete the question, she opened the door and climbed out. She'd limped a quarter of the way up the driveway when the car beeped and he came up behind her.

"You really shouldn't be walking on it yet," he said. "Let me carry you in."

She didn't need it. Her ankle was already much better. But she nodded anyway.

He gave her his keys and picked her up like she was a "tiny human." After she unlocked the front door for him, he carried her inside, and she reveled in his closeness. If she leaned forward a bit, she could kiss him. That would probably startle him, though.

No kissing. No touching.

Nonetheless, the pads of her fingertips itched to stroke his lightly stubbled jaw and the strong cords of his neck. What would it feel like to run her fingers through his hair? The strands were thicker and darker than her own, and some of the uneven locks fell beneath his jaw. She stopped herself before she touched the ends.

"You need a haircut."

He sent her a wry look. "I know."

"I can do it. I know how. I used to cut hair for my cousins. I'm good at it," she said, but then she held her breath. Was getting his hair cut at home too unclassy for him? Maybe she shouldn't have offered.

He paused in the hallway and considered her. "You'd cut my hair for me?"

"Of course."

"You have to do it a certain way."

"Show me a picture. If I see it, I can do it."

He looked like he wanted to say more, but he carried her into her room instead. After setting her on the couch, he asked, "Will you cut my hair tomorrow morning? Please?"

She bit her lip, but that couldn't stop the wide smile from spreading across her face. "I'm happy to do it."

He nodded. "Okay. Thanks."

"How do you like it? Do you have a picture?"

He swiped a hand through his hair. "I'll leave the style up to you. I just want it shorter."

"I can pick?"

"Yeah, sure." He smiled lightly as he stuffed his hands in his pockets and strolled aimlessly through the room, stopping by the desk. A thoughtful look crossed his face, and he picked up something from the desk's surface. The photograph of her dad. "Who are these people?"

She focused on her injured ankle and wiggled her toes a few times. "My mom and dad."

His eyebrows arched as he glanced her way. "He went to Berkeley."

She took a breath and released it. "I think so, but I'm not sure. I've never met him before."

"Oh." Khải flipped the picture around to inspect the back, but she knew there wasn't anything written there.

"Do you think if we go there, they can help me find him?"

"To Berkeley?" he asked.

She nodded.

He shrugged. "It's possible."

Hope bloomed in her chest. "Can we go . . . tomorrow? After the haircut?"

He hesitated a second before he said, "Yeah, okay. We can go."

She got to her feet, so happy she wanted to hug him, but she squeezed her hands into fists instead and grinned. "Thank you, Anh Khải."

An awkward smile touched his mouth. "Yeah, sure." He walked toward the bathroom that connected their rooms but paused with his hand on the doorknob. "Remember to take the binding off when you shower. I'll wrap it again when you're ready to sleep."

"Okay."

When he left, she took a moment to admire her ankle binding. It had been perfectly done, not too tight, not too loose, with evenly spaced loops. So this was what it was like when Khải took care of someone.

A daydream of him taking care of Jade ran through her mind. If he wanted to, he could be so great with her little girl.

But Esme had no confidence that was in the cards. This didn't *mean* anything. She shouldn't let it go to her head. He was just a good person. She'd been working on it, but she was still . . . herself. Surprisingly, experience from her previous life as Mỹ was going to be useful tomorrow.

She got her phone out and searched through photographs of movie stars and musicians until images of beautiful men were stuck to the backs of her eyelids. Tomorrow, she was going to give Khải the best haircut of his life.

CHAPTER TWELVE

The next morning, Esme had everything ready. A chair was set up in the middle of the kitchen, sharp scissors lay on the counter, and the broom and dustpan were ready for cleanup afterward. The only thing missing was Khải. She clasped her hands together and took several breaths. There was no need to be nervous. She'd given lots of haircuts. She was going to do a good job.

But what if he didn't like it? What if he got mad because she'd "ruined" his hair?

The shower turned off, and shortly after that, Khải walked into the kitchen, wearing black shorts and a black T-shirt with *I love taxes* in white lettering. The sleeves were tight around the hard muscles of his upper arms, and she made herself look at his hair before she got completely distracted. Fresh from the shower, it was the ideal dampness for a haircut.

He considered her feet. "Does it hurt to stand? We can do this another time."

She smiled. He didn't seem to notice hurt feelings so much, but a hurt ankle got his attention. "No, it's much better. Here." She clasped the back of the chair. "Anh Khải, sit down."

He obeyed and clasped his knees, ready.

Acting like a professional, which she wasn't, she picked up the scissors, but Khải said, "I need you to do this a certain way."

"You want to see the hairstyle I picked for you? I can show you—"

He shook his head. "No, it's not that. I trust your taste. Maybe . . ." He ran his hands up and down his thighs a few times. Was he *nervous*? "Maybe put the scissors down for now."

She put the scissors down. Great, he was scared she was going to mess up. She didn't think she would. She'd picked out something classic and sophisticated. At least, *she* thought so.

Focusing on the wall, he said, "I'm autistic, and I have sensory issues. There's a certain way to touch me, especially my face and hair." He switched his attention to her face. "It's probably best if I show you. Can you give me one of your hands?"

He held his palm out, and Esme approached him. She didn't know what "autistic" was, or "sensory issues," either, but she understood he was trusting her with something important—himself. Holding her breath, she slowly lowered her hand. Closer. Closer. Until they touched.

She bit her lip, expecting him to jerk away or grimace. His warm fingers closed around her and squeezed, and heat melted outward as she exhaled.

They were holding hands.

He cleared his throat. "Light touches bother me, and it's worse when I don't know it's coming. So, when you cut my hair, I'd appreciate it if you kept your touch firm. Like this." He gathered her hand in both of his and pressed her palm to the middle of his chest, keeping his hands over hers.

He looked calm on the surface, steady, competent, like he always did, but his heart beat wildly beneath her palm. He *was* nervous. But not for the reason she'd thought.

"All those other times when I . . ." she whispered.

His chest lifted on a deep inhalation. "Too light, and you caught me by surprise."

"I didn't know . . ." She'd thought it was *her* touch. She'd never imagined it was *everyone's* touch. "What does it feel like when people touch you too lightly?"

His brow wrinkled. "It's just too much. It almost hurts, but actual pain is preferable. It's difficult to describe."

"If I need to touch you, I should tell you first?" she asked.

"Yeah, it's best to warn me if I'm not expecting it."

She tugged on her arm slightly. "Can I touch your face?"

He nodded and let his hands drop away from hers, but his throat bobbed on a loud swallow.

She lifted her fingers toward his jaw but stopped before making contact. "Can you help me?" She didn't want to get it wrong.

His lips curved with the beginning of a smile, and he brought her hand to his face as he pressed his cheek into her palm. "You don't need to be so worried. I know what's going on now. If we work together, I can control my reactions."

"Is this bad?" she asked, afraid to move a single finger.

"No, it's fine. For my hair, it's best if you can keep good tension on the strands while you cut them. I don't mind if you pull hard. It doesn't hurt. But no light touch. Please."

"No light touch." She reached her other hand toward him, curled the fingers as she hesitated, and then threaded them into his damp hair, pressing her fingertips firmly to his scalp. "Is that okay?"

When his eyelids drooped with pleasure and he nodded, she grew braver. She pushed her other hand from his jaw up to his temple and into his hairline.

"How is that?" she whispered.

"Good." The word rumbled out of him, deep, almost gravelly.

His hair was thick and cool between her fingers, smooth as silk, and before she realized what she was doing, she was massaging his scalp with slow, sweeping motions. And he was letting her. His eyes fell shut, and he leaned into her touch like he was soaking it up. His breaths came slow, easy. If she pressed her palm over his heart now, she would have bet everything his heartbeat had calmed down. She'd done that.

She pulled on the strands like she usually did while cutting. "How is this?"

He frowned, but his eyes didn't open. "Tighter."

"Like this?" She pulled harder.

"More."

She bit her lip and pulled harder yet, scared of hurting him. "This?"

A long breath sighed out of him. "That's better."

She shook her head as she smiled to herself. He was a puzzle she never would have been able to solve if he hadn't shown her how. Those were the best kinds of puzzles, though, weren't they? The ones no one else could figure out?

"I'm cutting now," she said.

He opened his eyes and focused on her. "All right."

She heard his words, recognized them as permission to go forward, but in that moment, she couldn't pull her hands back. She wanted to be closer to him, not farther away. Her massage had brought color to his cheeks and a drowsy cast to his dark, dark eyes. His lips had never looked so kissable. The need to kiss him grew into a wild craving, urging her to crawl right onto his lap, press her body against his, and take, take, take.

She wrenched herself away before she could do something she'd regret and took a moment to gather her thoughts. This was a haircut. That was it. His words echoed in her head, a reminder.

You. Have. To. Stop. Do you understand? You. Have. To. Stop.

If he wanted more, he would have to make the first move. She couldn't do it.

The coldness of the scissors grounded her, and her mind sharpened into focus like a surgeon's did when they picked up a scalpel. All things considered, Khải had been really tolerant of her, and he was taking her to hunt for her dad today. This was a good thing to do in return, and she wanted to do it well.

Moving to stand behind him, she said, "I'm starting."

"Okay."

But just like before, she had difficulty making the first move. He couldn't see her from here. What if she surprised him and ruined this whole thing before it began?

She held her left hand by his ear. "Can you put my hand in your hair?"

He glanced at her over his shoulder, gave her a puzzled smile, and pressed her hand to his hair before facing forward again.

Her motions were tentative at first, but she gained confidence with every snip of the scissors. She gathered his hair between her fingers, taking care to keep the tension tight, cut, and smoothed her fingers over his scalp before gathering more hair. Over and over, she did this, and before long, the rhythmic nature of it relaxed her as much as it did him.

She trimmed the back and sides and ended up in front of him. With a last snip of the scissors, dark hair floated to the kitchen floor. She took a step back to assess her work, widening her focus to take in more than just his hair, and the transformation made her gasp. He'd been good-looking before. *This* was too much.

The short haircut opened up his face, showing off his strong features to full advantage. Girls were going to throw themselves at him. Starting with her, if she wasn't careful.

"How is it?" he asked.

Making sure to keep her touches firm, she tugged on the strands to see if the lengths were even on both sides. "It's good." Tapping the handle of the scissors on her jaw, she let a smile sneak onto her lips. "*I'm* good."

He dug his cell phone out of his pocket, unlocked it, and handed it to her. "Take a picture for Vy, please. She's the hair police."

Esme took pictures from several different angles, but before returning the phone to him, she sent her favorite one to herself. "She's going to like it."

He scratched at his neck where small hairs stuck to his skin as he sent the same picture to his sister. "We'll see."

She got the broom and dustpan and had half of the hair on the floor swept up when his phone buzzed. Chuckling, he showed her the text messages on his screen.

Finally!

Who cut it? Tip 50%!

My baby brother is a hottie!!!

"I guess she approves," he said.

Esme grinned. "I told you she'd like it."

"Thank you." He returned her smile, and it was one of his rare *real* smiles that wrinkled his eyes, dimpled his cheeks, and revealed even white teeth.

Sky and earth, she wanted to taste that smile. And each of those dimples. Pure wanting speared through her body on electric currents, making the fine hairs on her skin stand up, and she almost swayed toward him. If she was better at being Esme in Accounting, would he want her back?

His smile dimmed. "What is it? Is something wrong?"

Without taking time to think, she answered, "I want to kiss you."

When she heard the words fall from her mouth, a furious blush heated her cheeks, and she spun around and busied herself emptying the dustpan into the garbage. Why had she said that? *Why?*

He approached her. "Esme . . ."

She stepped around him and swept up the rest of the hair on the floor. "Sorry. Forget I said that." She dumped everything in the garbage again and hurried to return the broom to the closet. "When do you want to go to Cal Berkeley?"

Rubbing at the back of his neck, he said, "We can go after I eat something and shower again, I guess."

"Okay, I'll get ready." She limped toward the hallway.

"Wait, aren't you hungry?"

Not for food. "No, thank you, Anh."

"I'll get you when it's time to go, then," he said as he ran his hands through his newly short hair.

"Take your time."

She'd just be in her room, trying not to think about him.

CHAPTER THIRTEEN

As Khai drove Esme to Berkeley, he couldn't get her confession out of his head.

She wanted to kiss him.

He wanted to kiss her back.

But he couldn't.

You kissed a woman if you wanted to date her and have a relationship, if you wanted to love and be loved in return, if you *could* love. If you kissed a woman when you couldn't deliver on the rest, you were an asshole. It was better to jack off in the shower.

He wished that was an option. Ever since Esme had come into his life, he was in a constant state of arousal, and there was no relief—except for what happened by accident in his sleep. To date, he'd had to get up four times in the middle of the night and change his boxers. It was embarrassing as fuck. Like being twelve again. And his dreams always involved her. Always. Half the time, they involved her Hammer pants, too.

It had been a while since he'd seen those particular pants.

Currently, she wore a pair of blue jeans that looked like they'd been painted onto her legs. He didn't care for denim himself, but he wouldn't have minded running his palms along her thighs. For someone who didn't like touching, he spent an awful lot of time fantasizing about it.

When they reached campus, he parked as close as was humanly possible to the registrar's office, and they walked down the road together. More accurately, he walked. She limped.

"The doctor should have given you crutches." Instead of his phone number. Opportunistic bastard. "How are you feeling? Do you need help?"

"It's not too bad." The smile she beamed at him was sunnier than the yellow long-sleeved shirt she wore. One of the sleeves had orange text down the side that read *Em yêu anh yêu em*. His written Vietnamese was god-awful, but he knew enough to roughly translate that as *Girl loves boy loves girl*. It was a nice concept. The circle of love and all that. Too bad he could never complete that circle.

"Let me know if you want to rest. I can just carry you there, too."

She tucked the hair behind her ear. "If you do that, people will think you're my boyfriend."

He looked at the students walking around campus and shrugged. "Why does it matter?"

"In that case, I hurt really bad. Carry me all the way," she said as she smirked and took an exaggerated limp.

He knew her well enough now to catch when she was joking with him, but he picked her up anyway. She laughed and wrapped her arms around him, grinning at him as her eyes sparkled in the sunlight. Right then and there, Khai decided green was his favorite color, but it had to be this specific shade of seafoam green.

She grew self-conscious all of a sudden, and her hands curled into fists. "I can walk."

"We're there." He nodded toward the large white building with its four massive pillars and *Sproul Hall* engraved over the middle set of double doors. "The registrar's office is in there. They should have a database of all the students who've gone here. I don't know if they'll give us the information you want, though."

Staring up at the building, she nodded. "He walked up these same stairs."

She wiggled her legs, and he let her down. She aimed a distracted smile at him before she hobbled up the stairs to the building. When they made it inside, she looked around with roaming eyes and parted lips.

He shoved his hands in his pockets and gave her space to explore. He didn't really understand her fascination. It was just a building, and it wasn't like her dad had left part of himself here. Well, if he had, that was nasty.

There wasn't a line at the registrar's, so they walked directly to the counter.

"Hi, how can I help you?" the guy asked through his enormous orange beard.

Esme hugged her purse to her chest, wet her lips, and glanced at Khai quickly before she said in rehearsed-sounding English, "My dad went to school here a long time ago. His name is Phil. Can you find him for me, please?"

So she *could* speak English. She just chose not to. With him. The guy looked at both of them over the tops of his purple plastic-rimmed glasses. "Are you serious?"

Esme nodded.

"You don't know his last name?" the guy asked.

She swallowed, shook her head, and replied in English again, "No. All I know is Phil."

Khai slowly turned his head so he could analyze her. She only knew her dad's first name. That was surprising and . . . sad. This decreased her chances of finding him dramatically.

"There are probably thousands of Phils here. *I'm* a Phil." The guy tapped his name badge where it said *Philip Philipson*.

Khai arched his eyebrows. The guy was about two hundred percent Phil, but his age and coloring were all off. "She has a picture."

She hurried to pull it out of her purse and handed it over. "Twenty-four years ago." She tried to smile, but her lips barely curved before she cleared her throat.

Philip Philipson offered Esme an apologetic smile. "I totally want to help you, but I'm not allowed to give you this information. I'm so sorry."

"But he was here," she insisted.

"I'm really so sorry. Maybe you should hire a private investigator," Philip said.

She hugged the picture to her chest as her eyes went glossy, and Khai wanted to reach across the counter and shake an apology out of Phil. Before he could act, Esme pushed away from the counter and limped from the room.

He followed behind as she rushed out of the building, hobbled down the steps, and limped across the plaza to sit by the round water fountain. She dragged in deep breath after deep breath, but as far as he could tell, she wasn't crying. She might as well have been, though. He didn't see how it was that different from what she was doing.

A familiar sense of ineffectualness seized him. He never knew what to do when people were emotional like this, but he wanted to do *something*.

For lack of any better ideas, he sat down next to her and said, "My parents divorced when I was little. I know my dad, but we never see him."

She turned to look at him. "Why not?" Back to Vietnamese again. What did it mean?

"He's busy with his new family and lives in Santa Ana. He's an accountant. Like me. Or maybe I'm like him. I don't know." He rubbed his neck. "Maybe . . . it's better that you don't know your dad. You can imagine he's better than mine."

"That's true." A small smile touched her lips, but it faded quickly. "But I just—I just wanted to know, and if I go without seeing him, I'll have wasted the trip here, and . . ." She swiped a sleeve over her eyes and tried to take more deep breaths, but then her face collapsed and her shoulders shook.

Fuck, she was crying for real now. Something much like panic gripped him. She couldn't cry. She was supposed to be happy for the both of them because he didn't know how.

He grabbed one of her hands. Hand-holding was good, right? But then she leaned toward him, and soon he was hugging her as she buried her face against his neck. The air rushed out of his lungs. She was in his arms, turning to him, trusting him, just like that time she'd had the nightmare.

It was terrifying. It was wonderful.

He didn't know what to do other than hold her tighter. Students crossed the plaza. Birds chirped in the trees, and a soft breeze blew. Sunlight was warm against his face. She nuzzled closer, and the weight of her body pressed on him. He felt the impression of lips on his neck.

Did that count as a kiss?

She turned her face to the side and peered up at him through damp eyelashes, and he brushed the residual moisture on her cheek away with his thumb. So soft, so pretty. He stroked wet tendrils of hair back from her temples, and her lips parted.

In an instant, everything changed. The wind became velvet, and sound was the loudness of his heart and the rush of his blood. Colors brightened and danced. The green of her eyes, the yellow of her shirt, the blue of the summer sky, it all centered around the pink of her mouth.

He didn't realize what he was doing until he saw his fingertips smooth over her bottom lip. What a sight to see his tanned skin against her pale face. Her eyes went luminous and dreamy, and when he ran his fingertip over her lip again, her mouth opened wider. He found himself leaning toward her, wanting, wanting, wanting, but he managed to stop before he broke all his rules.

"You can kiss me," she said, her voice half whisper, half husky rasp. "Anytime you want, you can kiss me."

Girl loves boy loves girl repeated in his head. He couldn't love her, couldn't make her any promises. He should stay away from her.

Eyes steady on his, she continued, "You can kiss me . . . and touch me . . . and not marry me. I just . . . want to be with you. Before I go."

Her words sent clashing reactions through him. His stomach bottomed out at the idea of her leaving, but concurrently, tension drained from his muscles. She'd given permission and made it clear she had no expectations. Kissing her wasn't connected to dating or a relationship or marriage or love. He could just kiss her because he wanted to.

He could kiss her.

His skin went hot, and he knew it was going to happen. He was going to kiss Esme. It was inevitable now.

He brushed the backs of his fingers across her cheek, and a shaky breath sighed between her lips. He had to taste them, had to know them.

Now.

Cradling her jaw in his hand, he leaned toward her.

"Esmeralda, it *is* you," a loud voice interrupted in a thick Russian accent.

O h no, that voice was familiar.

Esme jerked away from Khải with a start, and her heart dropped when her fears were confirmed. It was her. "Hi, Angelika."

Khải looked from her to the tall blond Russian woman, and Esme broke out in a cold sweat. He was going to find out she was a big liar, and then he was going to look down on her more.

"I did not know you have a boyfriend," Angelika said.

Khải didn't correct Angelika. Maybe that meant something, but Esme didn't have time to think about it. They needed to leave right away. Maybe if they were fast, Khải wouldn't figure it out.

She jumped to her feet. "We need to go. Later, Angelika." She wanted to grab Khải by the arm and drag him after her, but she was afraid of touching him the wrong way. After a moment's hesitation, she limped off on her own, hoping he'd follow. Luckily, he did.

But instead of letting them leave in peace, Angelika tagged after them. "I am thinking of applying here if I pass the GED. But I do not know if I will pass. If you take the test, you will pass." To Khải, she said, "Esmeralda is very smart. She gets As on all of her tests in class."

Esme's heart jumped and started beating so fast her vision blurred. Too late.

"You're taking classes?" he asked. "At the adult school across from my mom's restaurant?"

She nodded as she stared down at the ground, wishing she could melt into the cracks between the bricks. Now he knew she wasn't Esme in Accounting. She was Esme who hadn't even graduated high school.

Angelika took an uncomfortable step back. "I, um, I will see you later. Have a nice weekend. Nice meeting you."

Esme waved, and Khải flashed his usual barely there smile at Angelika before focusing on Esme again.

When he opened his mouth to speak, Esme hurried to say, "We're done now. We should go."

As she limped back the way they'd come, she distracted herself by taking in as much of the campus as she could. Her dad had walked on these same bricks, breathed this same air, seen these same trees. This was probably the closest she'd ever get to him.

Khải caught up to her with easy strides of his long, uninjured legs. "We should go the other way."

"The car is this way." She pointed toward the parking lot.

"There's another place we should try."

She paused. "Another place?"

"The alumni building. They might be more helpful. I probably should have taken you there first. Do you need help getting there? It's not far. It's just over there." He motioned in the other direction, toward a cluster of more modern buildings surrounded by old trees.

"I'll walk. Let's go."

Esme hobbled as fast as she could through the student traffic, hoping if they moved quickly, they couldn't talk. But that didn't stop Khải from asking, "What classes are you taking?"

She hugged her arms over her chest even though she wasn't cold. "English, social studies, and accounting."

"Isn't that a lot? Three classes?"

"Is it?" She didn't have anything to compare it to. All she knew was she spent a lot of time sneak studying when she thought people couldn't see her.

"I think so." He swiped at his hair, but when his hand encountered the shorter locks, he rubbed at his neck instead. "I was never very good at those classes—other than accounting, of course. I do better with numbers."

She had to smile at that. "Me, too." They were the same no matter what language you were speaking.

He smiled back at her before he focused on the tops of the passing trees. "If you ever need help, I can try. I don't mind."

She watched her feet pad unevenly over the ground, so she had something to look at other than him. Step-draaag, step-draaag, step-draaag. When she'd finally built up the courage, she made herself say, "I'm sorry. For lying. I'm not an accountant. I . . ." She inhaled. ". . . clean places." She exhaled, and her insides shriveled. "Back home. I didn't finish school. We needed money because Ngoại was too weak to work, so I started to clean, and then I—" She bit her lip before she mentioned having a baby.

When she glanced at him, she found him watching the way ahead with a small frown. "You didn't need to lie to me."

She winced and looked back down at her feet. Step-draaag, step-draaag, step-draaag. "I wanted you to like me." It wasn't a question, but she held her breath as she waited for him to respond.

That was when he stopped in front of a modest one-story building composed of glass and red brick. "This is it."

In the front reception area, a woman with short gray hair and a pantsuit greeted them. "Welcome to Alumni House. How can I help you?"

Esme wet her lips and took the photograph out of her purse as she struggled to put her thoughts into English. "I am looking for a man. This man. Twenty-four years ago—"

"I'm sorry. We specialize in alumni *events* here. You'll need to speak to someone else if you're looking for a specific alumnus. Did you try the registrar's office?" the lady asked.

"We were just there," Khải said.

"I see." The lady frowned, and after a moment she hurried to her desk, found a business card in one of the drawers, and handed it to

Esme. "This woman is in charge of the Alumni Association. Try giving her a call. I don't know if she'll be able to help you, but if anyone can, it would be her."

Esme tried to smile, but her lips refused to cooperate. "Thank you."

They were both quiet as they made the short walk back to the car. Someone had stuck a yellow slip of paper under one of the windshield wipers, and Khải pulled it out and read it. She caught the words *Parking Ticket* on the paper before he stuffed it in his pocket, and clear as daytime, right in front of the car, there was a big sign that said, *No parking without permit.*

He'd intentionally gotten a ticket, and she knew he'd done it for her. Because of her ankle. It was a small thing, but she didn't know anyone else who would have done something like that for her. Just Khải.

He left the parking lot, drove through campus, and merged onto the big road, and she watched as he wove in and out of the afternoon traffic like a getaway driver after a bank heist, fast but in perfect control. His hands looked strong and capable on the wheel and the gear shift, and she remembered he'd touched her with them earlier. Her face, her lips, her jaw.

Would he want to touch her again now that he knew she was a fake accountant? Would he want to touch her if he found out she had a baby?

"Give me that business card when we get home, okay?" he said unexpectedly. "I want to call that woman at the Alumni Association."

His words were so out of line with her thoughts, it took her a moment to understand what he meant. "You'll call her for me?"

Eyes on the road, he replied, "Yeah. I'll let you know if she gives me any useful information."

A weight she hadn't been aware of lifted off her shoulders, and gratitude swelled inside of her. For someone who was often tactless, he could be incredibly considerate when it mattered. She got the card from her purse and placed it in the center console. "Thank you, Anh."

He nodded and concentrated on driving.

When they arrived at his house, he put the car in park but didn't turn the ignition off. Her fingers hesitated over her seat belt buckle.

"Your classes are at night, right?" he asked.

She squirmed in the seat. "That's right."

"Do you want me to pick you up from now on, so you don't have to take the bus?"

"You don't mind?"

"I don't mind," he replied.

"Then, thank you, Anh."

He nodded once and left the car, and she followed behind as he went up the driveway and unlocked the front door of his house. She thought he might kiss her then, but he merely held the door open for her. Instead of passing straight through, she paused in front of him, inviting him to continue what had been interrupted earlier. Expectation built, and her lungs waited to draw breath. Even her heart waited to beat.

Kiss me. Kiss me.

His gaze dropped to her mouth, and her lips tingled like he'd touched them. Yes, he was going to—

He took a step back, looked away from her, and said, "I'm going to get some stuff done at the office. I'll see you later tonight."

Her chest sank, and she watched him grab his computer bag and return to his car. He *had* wanted to kiss her. Before he knew. But not anymore.

He'd done all those things—showing up at the doctor's office, carrying her, the haircut—with Esme in Accounting. He wasn't interested in the real Esme.

CHAPTER FOURTEEN

The following week, Khai pretended the almost kiss never happened. Esme's Russian friend had saved him from committing a grievous mistake in a moment of poor judgment.

Esme might be able to handle a physical relationship without any adverse effects, but he didn't think *he* could. She was already a song that played on endless repeat in his head. If he started having sex with her, this *thing* would escalate into pure addiction, and what the fuck would happen when she left near the end of the summer? If he didn't want to find out, he had to keep his distance.

He did a stellar job of it until Friday evening rolled around and it was time to attend the second wedding of the summer. He knocked on her door, and she opened it with a tentative smile.

For a long moment, he simply gazed at her. She didn't look like herself. Her dress was *black*. Didn't she think that was an unhappy color? It hung loosely over her body, hiding every area of interest, and holy shit, look at all that bling. Her ears, throat, and hands were blinding. There had to be a hundred dollars' worth of cubic zirconia there—no way those were real diamonds.

Even so, she was beautiful. Her makeup was subtle but for black liner that brought attention to her green eyes and her bloodred lipstick.

God, those lips. Painted like that they were enough to make him light-headed. Ever since he'd almost kissed her, he'd been seeing her mouth every time he shut his eyes. His imagination had done unspeakable things to that mouth this past week.

He cleared his throat. "Ready to go?"

She squared her shoulders and lifted her chin. "I'm ready."

They left the house and piled into his car. As soon as he merged onto 101S toward San Jose, he broke the silence by saying, "I called the Berkeley Alumni Association. They gave me a list of all Phils who attended Berkeley during the ten years before you were born."

She squealed and covered her mouth as she danced in her seat. Her movements made the loose hem of her skirt slide up, and *holy shit*. Rule Number Six might as well not exist anymore. There was no way he could follow it when it came to Esme. He wanted to touch her so badly his hands curled around the steering wheel in a death grip. He could almost see his fingers smoothing over those bare thighs and slipping under that sack of a dress.

The fly of his pants grew uncomfortably tight, distracting him from his X-rated thoughts. Fuck, he was sporting an erection in his damned car. If he hit a speed bump, he'd probably break his dick in half. He needed to think about the desert, the arctic, Statement Number 157 from the Financial Accounting Standards Board, anything else.

"How many names are on the list?" she asked.

Right. The list. "Nearly a thousand."

"Oh." She frowned in thought, unconsciously running her hands up and down her thighs in a manner that did nothing to help his current condition.

"One of Quan's friends is helping me sort through the list. He says it's easy to do with the proper software," he said. "I'm going to need a copy of that picture you have."

"Does it cost a lot?" she asked hesitantly.

"No. He's doing Quan a favor."

"That's too great." She beamed one of her signature grins at him. "I'll give it to you when we get home tonight. Can you tell your brother thank you for me?"

"You can tell him yourself. He's going to be at the wedding."

"Oh, okay, I'll tell him." She ran a hand over her hair and smoothed her skirt back over her thighs. "I'm nervous now," she said with a small laugh.

"Nervous about meeting Quan?"

She ducked her head. "He's your older brother. I want him to like me."

Khai shrugged. "He will. He likes everybody." And everybody liked Quan back. He had a unique kind of charisma. Unlike Khai, who blundered his way through life, making people cry left and right.

"I hope so." She didn't look entirely convinced, but Khai knew she didn't need to worry.

After making the half-hour drive to San Jose, he parked in front of a large two-story restaurant called Seafood Plaza. A giant neon crab and Chinese characters blinked above the roof. It was his mom's favorite restaurant, and he'd been here countless times over the years.

"This is it," he said. "The ceremony and reception are both here." For some people, nothing said *happily ever after* like lobster in ginger scallion sauce.

Esme stared at the building for several moments before asking, "Is the food good?"

Khai shrugged. "If you like Chinese food and jellyfish."

"Jellyfish?" she asked with interest.

He arched his eyebrows. "Jellyfish are those ocean creatures that sting you. Lots of tentacles." He wiggled his fingers to imitate them. "Weird texture. They taste like nothing."

She crossed her arms over her chest. "I know what jellyfish are, and they don't taste like nothing."

Understanding slowly dawned on him. "You're excited. About jellyfish."

"It's good."

"You weren't this excited about the San Francisco Fairmont." If you went by the price tag and venue exclusiveness, most people would be much more impressed by the Fairmont. Khai couldn't help finding Esme's enthusiasm for Seafood Plaza both entertaining and endearing.

She lifted a shoulder, but she smiled. "I like good food."

"Let's go in, then. I think you'll be happy."

As they crossed the parking lot, the gray smells of grease and age welcomed them. Yep, he knew this place, but it was different with Esme by his side. *Everything* was different with Esme. She didn't need him to open and shut doors for her, didn't want him to pay for everything or carry her stuff, didn't mind if he stared at her body all day . . .

She reached for his arm but stopped before touching him. "You don't like that." Her head tilted as she thought, and then a smile stretched over her lips. She skipped a few steps ahead of him and rested a hand on her lower back. "Men put their hand here sometimes. When they're walking or standing. If you do that, girls won't grab your arm."

It was on the tip of his tongue to tell her he didn't mind her grabbing his arm—not anymore—but he held the words back. They needed more distance, not less.

"Try it. Maybe you'll like it better." Watching him over her shoulder, she stood still and waited.

This was ridiculous, but he did what she asked anyway. Then he wished he hadn't. Seeing his large hand in the small of her back did things to him. Her spine had the most elegant curvature, this spot specifically, and some elemental part of him thrilled as he staked a claim on it.

His.

She smiled at him for a quick second before she continued toward the restaurant. With his hand there, he was achingly conscious of the way her hips swayed when she walked. Why was that so sexy?

They passed by huge aquariums in the front entryway that housed lobster, crab, and glum-looking fish and entered a seating area on the ground floor of the restaurant. All the chairs were vacant, and a hostess with a blue ballpoint pen in her hair directed them to take one of two spiral staircases up to the second level.

As they climbed the stairs, found their table assignment, and walked through the maze of round tables, keeping his hand in the small of her back became second nature to Khai. The heat of her skin soaked through the fabric of her dress and warmed his palm.

When they reached their table, Khai spotted a familiar buzzed head and set of shoulders. Quan turned around, grinned, and shot to his feet so he could give Khai a monster hug.

"Look at you." Quan scrubbed a hand through Khai's newly short hair. "Good haircut."

"Thanks." Khai pushed his brother's hand away and stepped back.

"So here she is," Quan said.

Khai suppressed the strange urge to wrap his arm around Esme's waist. Instead of pulling her close like he wanted, he took a step away from her. "Esme, this is my brother, Quan. Quan, Esme."

Quan took in the distance between Khai and Esme with a pensive expression on his face.

Esme rubbed at her elbow before smiling at him. "Hi, Anh Quân."

When his brother's face broke into a wide smile, Khai wasn't able to relax like he should have. Instead, his muscles tensed up, and he watched Esme's reaction, trying to interpret it. He didn't know what he was looking for, what he wanted, but something important hinged on this moment.

Esme held her hand out for Quan to shake, but he gave her a funny look. "Really? A handshake?" He pulled her in for a hug, and she laughed as she hugged him back.

Khai had known these two would like each other, but the sight made acid churn in his stomach. With Quan's designer suit and tattoos peeking above his collar, he had this reformed drug lord image, and Esme provided the perfect soft counterpoint to all that badassness. They looked good together.

Esme sat in the seat between Quan and Khai, but she turned toward Quan. In careful English, she said, "Thank you for helping with my dad."

"No problem. Happy to do it," Quan said, being his genuinely kind self. "So tell me about things so far here. How's work and stuff? Do you like it?"

The acidic feeling in Khai's stomach worsened as Esme grinned and told Quan all about her stay so far, speaking English like she wouldn't with Khai and sharing things Khai hadn't known. He never asked her about her day. That wasn't how their dynamic worked. He tried to ignore her, and she inflicted conversation on him. But now he wished he'd thought to ask her about herself. Esme facts went in a special place in his mind, never to be forgotten, and it bothered him how little he actually knew.

The waiter came to their table and set a giant platter in the middle. It contained three types of cold meats and seaweed salad, and there was the jellyfish. It looked like rice noodles or sautéed onions but crunched against your teeth in the most disconcerting way.

Esme could barely contain herself as she waited for her turn to fill her plate, and then she ate with an enthusiasm that had Quan grinning. When she blushed, Quan grinned even harder.

"Hungry?" Quan asked.

"This is good," she said as she wiped her mouth with a napkin self-consciously.

Quan chuckled. "I bet you're fun to take out." Switching his attention to Khai, he asked, "Did you take her to that cold noodles place in San Mateo?"

A bitter taste filled Khai's mouth as he shook his head. He hadn't thought to take her out. Between his mom's cooking and Esme's, there was way too much to eat. He'd never seen a reason to go out. Until now.

"Ah, well, you should go there next," Quan said. "Everything is good there. It'd be fun to see how much she can eat."

"A lot," Esme said with a laugh, and her green eyes sparkled brighter than all her cubic zirconia put together. She looked happy. Quan was making her happy.

The DJ started playing "Here Comes the Bride." The groom—a distant cousin he didn't know well—and his bride strode arm in arm between the tables and across the dance floor to the stage, where they exchanged vows entirely in Vietnamese. After that, their dads gave speeches, and Khai's attention wandered. He'd heard countless variations of these kinds of speeches. *So happy for the union of these*

two families, looking forward to a bright future, so proud of my daugh-
ter, etc. Esme, however, hung on every word.

She smiled, but Khai picked up on her sadness, an unusual feat
for him. Her eyes lost their shine, and when the bride's dad hugged
his daughter, she wiped a tear from her cheek. He was reaching for
her hand when she pulled away to cover her mouth, smothering a
laugh. Quan whispered something in her ear, and she laughed harder
and shook her head at him, like they were old friends.

Khai exhaled quietly and stared down at his hand. It hadn't occurred to him to make her laugh. He didn't even know how. Good
thing there were people like Quan in this world.

When the speeches finished, entrees arrived at the table in quick
succession: Peking duck, steamed fish, the usual wedding dishes.
The lobster with ginger scallion sauce came, and Esme tied her hair
back and dove in, cracking a claw open and eating the soft meat
inside. Funny how she was pretty even when she was being carni-
vorous.

When she caught him watching her, she glanced at the un-
touched lobster on his plate and asked, "Want me to crack it for you?
I'm good at it."

"No, thanks, I can do it." He wanted her focused on her own
dinner. He liked watching her enjoy the food.

"What? How can you turn that down?" Quan asked. To Esme,
he said, "You can do mine."

Suppressing a smile, she put a morsel of lobster meat on Quan's
plate, and Khai had the horrible urge to snatch the food off his
brother's plate and gobble it down. It made no sense, and he grabbed
his water glass and took a large gulp. A floral flavor had him frowning. What was that?

When he pulled the glass away from his lips, he found red lipstick on the rim. He'd accidentally used Esme's glass. *Germ transfer-*

ence. He wasn't excessively germophobic, but with all the new bacteria no doubt swarming in his mouth, he might as well have kissed her.

Except he'd never kissed her. Not even once.

He didn't know the softness of her lips or the taste of her mouth. By drinking from her cup, he'd gotten all the cost without any of the benefit. That hardly seemed fair. The scope of his vision narrowed to her lips. Full, red, and wet, they called to him.

When she sucked on her fingertips, Khai felt the draw deep inside of himself. The breath punched out of his lungs as his body hardened in a dizzying rush.

He drank the rest of her water and pushed away from the table. "I'm going to get a drink." Maybe alcohol would kill her bacteria and clear his mind.

Esme waved saucy fingers at him as he escaped to the bar to order something strong.

It wasn't much of an escape, though. Quan followed him there and rested a big arm on the bar's counter, looking relaxed and dangerous at the same time.

"How you doing?" Quan asked.

Khai had no idea how to articulate his current state, so he gave his usual answer, "Okay."

"You missed kendo practice last weekend."

That was kind of a big deal. Khai never missed practice—not even when he was sick—but Esme had asked him to take her to Berkeley. And if she asked, he knew he would give her anything. If he could.

"Sorry, I was busy," he said.

Quan laughed as he rubbed at his buzzed head. "Tell me about it. I'm so busy with this CEO shit I hardly have time for anything. That's why I haven't checked up on you before now. She's not who I expected Mom to pick for you, but she's great. I'm surprised you don't like her."

Khai started to correct his brother and say he *did* like her, but he frowned at his drink instead. If he said he liked her, Quan would probably start matchmaking. He didn't want that. It was hard enough to stay away from her as it was.

"What don't you like about her?" Quan asked. "She's fun and hot as fuck."

He couldn't answer that question. There wasn't anything about Esme he'd change. Not a single thing. "I'm just not interested."

As he said the words, however, they felt uncomfortably like a lie. Their relationship wasn't even physical, and he was already half addicted to her. He needed to keep them apart. For both their sakes.

He dug the paperback out of his inner coat pocket and flipped through the pages with his thumb once before he caught himself.

"You're kidding me," Quan said, pinning a disgusted look on the book. "You're going to read with her sitting there?"

"Yeah." That had been the plan. Weddings were bad enough on their own, but watching Esme and Quan interacting like best friends was even worse. He didn't bother analyzing why.

"Can't you try to be nice to her? It's obvious weddings are hard for her. She grew up without a father, and it has to suck seeing the bride with her dad."

Khai frowned. He hadn't made that connection earlier. Because of his stone heart. But now that he understood the reason for Esme's sadness, he swore he'd go through the list of Phils one by one if he had to, and then he'd send her dad to her wrapped in a red bow like a Lexus on Mother's Day. As for being nice to her, he recalled his brother's weakness for orphaned anything—dogs, cats, tiny gangsters from school, you name it. "She'll be fine with you there."

"Are you . . . handing your girl to me? You'd be okay with me and her being together?"

It took Khai a moment to comprehend what his brother was saying, but then his muscles flexed involuntarily. No, he wasn't okay with that. He didn't want Esme for himself, but he didn't want her with anyone else, either. He always pictured them apart but single.

"Because I'm interested," Quan continued. "Those eyes alone would do it, but the rest of her . . ." Quan made hourglass movements with his hands. "Jesus."

Listening to his brother talk about Esme that way was worse than hearing someone chew with their mouth open, and the unfamiliar desire rose to punch Quan in the nose. When Khai noticed he'd fisted his hands, he uncurled his fingers, appalled. He pushed away his violent thoughts and forced himself to be rational. When he thought about Esme's needs instead of his own, one thing became very clear.

Quan was perfect for her.

His brother could give Esme the things Khai couldn't. Quan could make her happy and understand her, and most important, Quan could love her. Khai wanted that for her. She deserved that.

"I'm okay with it," he heard himself say. After clearing his throat, he made himself clarify, "I'm okay with you two being together." Cold sweat beaded on Khai's forehead as sickness swam in his stomach, and he swallowed a mouthful of his drink. He couldn't remember what it was, but it tasted strong. He wished it was stronger. "I'm going to go read downstairs. Let her know, all right?"

Quan considered him for a moment, his gaze level and weighted. "Yeah, I'll let her know."

Khai tipped his glass in Quan's direction and fled the banquet room, feeling like he was leaving something priceless behind.

CHAPTER FIFTEEN

When Khải left the banquet room with a drink and a book in his hands, the lobster in Esme's mouth turned to chalk. It was the best lobster she'd ever eaten, the ideal blend of salty and sweet balanced with the freshness of ginger, but she was no longer hungry. He was abandoning her. Again. She swallowed with effort before wiping her hands clean and sitting back in her chair.

Quân took the seat next to her as servers cleared the table of dinner plates and placed fluffy slices of cake in front of everyone. She picked up her fork and considered her slice from different angles, trying to muster the enthusiasm to eat.

"What are you looking for?" Quân asked.

"It is too pretty to eat." The frosting flowers looked like they'd been painted with an airbrush. Roses, hibiscus, a lotus blossom, seeds, all colors. Normally, she'd be excited to stuff them in her mouth, but not now.

Quân laughed and pushed his plate toward her. "I already made mine ugly. You can share with me."

His offer brought a smile to her face despite her mood. He was one of the nicest people she'd ever met, and she was unspeakably glad he was sitting next to her. "Wasting food is bad. I will eat it." She pierced her cake's perfect surface with the tines of her fork.

As she took her first bite of airy vanilla cake, lightly sweet frosting, and strawberries, Quân leaned toward her and asked, "How are things with you and my brother?"

The cake went bland on her tongue. When she tried to wash it back with water, she found her glass empty and had to steal Khải's. "Fine."

"Really."

She poked at her cake with the tip of her fork and lifted a shoulder, saying nothing.

"The dancing starts soon," he said. "Want to dance with me?"

Her eyes jumped to his face. "You want to dance? With me?"

"Yeah, I want to dance with you." His lips curved into a smile, transforming his face from severe and dangerous to wildly handsome. Oh, this man.

"I, um . . ." She put her fork down, sensing this was important. "It looks bad if— *Why*?"

"I don't care what people think. It's just a dance, Esme," he said with a careless grin.

But it wasn't just a dance. It was more than that. She was in this for marriage, and people would be vicious if they saw her flitting between brothers. Cô Nga would be disappointed. Quân had to know that. Unless . . .

Was *he* interested in marrying her? No, he'd just met her. He couldn't possibly want to marry her already.

Right?

She began to rub her face, but the scent of lobster gave her pause. "I need to wash my hands. I will be right back," she said before rushing away from the table.

In the bathroom, she took the far back stall. It was funny, but bathrooms soothed her. Probably because they felt familiar—she'd cleaned so many. But she couldn't stay in here all night. She had a decision to make.

"You know she's after him for his money and a green card," a woman in one of the other stalls said.

"Of course she is," a second woman replied.

Esme released a measured breath. They had to be talking about her and Khải. She'd known these kinds of conversations would take place. It was surprising she hadn't heard talk like this until now.

"To be honest, if he wasn't family, *I'd* be after him for his money," the first woman said with a laugh.

"Well, me, too, actually." Both women laughed at the same time.

Were they talking about Khải? They made it sound like he was a billionaire, when Esme was certain he wasn't rich. She supposed it was perfectly possible these two women were worse off than he was. An old beat-up house was better than no house.

"Did you see her all over Quân?" the first woman asked.

"Yeah, if it doesn't work with one brother, try the next."

Esme scowled. Without a doubt, they were talking about her, but she hadn't been flirting with Quân. Had she? Definitely not on purpose. He *was* attractive, though, and funny, considerate, and kind. If she'd never met Khải, she'd jump at the chance to dance with him.

But she had met Khải.

Toilets flushed, heels clacked against the tile floor, and water ran as the women washed their hands.

"He *is* good-looking, though," the second woman said.

"He's also an asshole."

"Okay, I agree. I know he's . . . you know, but I heard he complained to Sara about her wedding. Right there at the table on her wedding day—"

Esme's tolerance for their secret bad-talking ended as a fire lit inside of her. She clawed the door of her stall open and marched out. "He is not an asshole. He is sweet."

It was fine if they thought the worst of her—she didn't care about them—but Khải was their family. Instead of spreading rumors and condemning him, they should have tried harder to understand him.

One of the women flushed and hurried to the door, but the other sent Esme a cutting glance. "*You* don't get to look down on anyone."

Esme lifted her chin, but she said nothing as the women left the bathroom. What *could* she say? They had judged both Esme and Khải without knowing their entire stories. Khải wasn't bad. He was misunderstood. As for Esme, she wasn't a gold digger. Her reasons for pursuing Khải had nothing to do with money. Too bad she couldn't tell anyone about them without ruining everything.

She finished washing her hands and looked in the mirror, and her shoulders sagged. No matter how hard she tried, something about her was always off. She searched through her purse until she found her lipstick and applied a fresh red coat to her lips, but that didn't fix the problem. She still wasn't Esme in Accounting, the one Khải wanted.

But Quân wanted her—maybe—and he seemed to like her as she was, without an accounting certification and GED. Unlike Khải, he wanted to dance with her. It might not be a big deal for Quân, but it was for her. The man radiated sex appeal. Their bodies would touch. He'd have his arms around her. They'd move together. And she'd respond to him. How could she not? She was human and starved for affection.

If she was smart, she'd switch to the brother who was a better bet. From where she was now, that brother appeared to be Quân, but when it came to matters of the heart, she'd never been good at listening to reason. The real question was: Who did her heart want?

Khai could not focus on his book. There was no sense in trying anymore. He slapped his book shut and paced about the bottom floor of the restaurant, running his thumb over the corner of the book and flipping through the pages. *Fliiip. Fliiip. Fliiip.*

He didn't pace anymore. He didn't do this fidgety stuff anymore. Except, clearly, he did.

The hostess and all the staff were busy upstairs with the wedding, and his footsteps were loud on the red carpet. The dancing was going to start soon.

Khai didn't dance. But Quan did. He suspected Esme did.

Quan's words from earlier repeated through Khai's head: *I'm interested. Those eyes alone would do it, but the rest of her . . .*

The building rumbled with a slow bass, and Khai's skin went cold and numb. It had started. First, it was the bride's dance with her dad. But after that . . .

Esme. With Quan. Bodies together. Moving slowly.

He was going to be sick. His skin hurt. Each breath hurt. His insides were splitting open. Why the hell did he want to smash everything to pieces?

Quan was going to put his hands in the small of Esme's back, that place Khai had claimed earlier today, touch her hips, her arms, her hands. And she was going to let him. She was going to touch him back.

As she should. Quan was the better man.

Khai realized he could leave. Quan would take care of her and drive her home. Maybe after spending time with Quan, she'd want to pack up her things and switch brothers and houses. That worked out nicely for Khai. He couldn't form a full-scale addiction to her if she was gone.

Setting his jaw, he marched to the front doors of the restaurant and pressed his hands to the metal handle. But his arms refused to push.

What if she didn't want to dance? What if she wanted to go home right now? It didn't make sense for Quan to take her when Khai was going there. That would be inefficient.

He turned around, planning to head up there and brave the music long enough to assure himself she was happy and tell her he was going home.

But there she was, at the bottom of the stairs, her hand resting on the railing.

So beautiful. And here. She'd come to find him again. No one ever looked for him. They all knew he wanted to be alone. Except it wasn't always that way. Sometimes he was alone out of habit. Sometimes it took effort to distract himself from the growing emptiness inside.

"Are you leaving?" she asked in a small voice.

"I was going to tell you." He heard the words as if from a distance, like someone else had spoken them. "If you want to dance, you should stay."

"Do you want me to dance?" She didn't say the words, but they hung in the air between them: *without you.*

He swallowed past a lump in his throat. "If it makes you happy."

She took a step toward him. "What if I want to dance with you?"

"I don't dance."

"Can you try?" She took another step toward him. "For me?"

His chest constricted. "I can't." He'd never danced in his life. He'd be terrible at it and injure her and humiliate himself. Not to mention the loud music. He couldn't function with those earsplitting decibels. Another reason why Quan was the better man. "If you want to stay, I know Quan will be glad to take you home."

"You want me . . . and him . . . to dance?" Her eyebrows drew together. "Is that right?"

"If you want to." And it was true. If that was what she wanted, he wanted her to have it, even if it made his chest feel like it was getting trampled on.

Several moments passed before she said, "I understand." Then she smiled, but tears trickled down her face. She swiped them away, took a deep breath, and smiled wider before turning around.

He'd made her cry.

"Esme . . ."

She ignored him and walked back to the stairs. She was going to find Quan. She was going to be perfectly happy.

Without him.

Something inside of him snapped, and the rational part of his mind blinked off. A foreign part of him took control. His skin went fever hot. Blood roared in his ears. He was aware of his feet taking him across the room, saw his hand wrapping around her arm, pulling so she faced him.

Those tears.

They shattered him. He brushed the saline away with his thumbs.

"I'm okay," she whispered. "Don't worry. I—"

He took her mouth, pressing his lips to hers as the feel of her shocked through his system. Soft. Silk. Sweet. Esme. When he realized she'd gone stiff, he started to pull back in horror. What had he been think—

She softened against him, kissing him back, and that was it. His thoughts burned away. Something else rose from the ashes, something he'd kept chained up so long it was all fierceness and animal hunger. He stroked his tongue over her lips, and when she sighed and parted her lips, savage victory swept through him. He claimed her lips, claimed her mouth, claimed the liquid heat inside that tasted of vanilla and strawberries and woman.

———

Esme melted beneath the intensity of Khải's kiss. She'd never been kissed like this, like he'd die if he stopped. His motions were tentative at first, as if he was learning her, but he gained confidence quickly. Each aching press of his lips, each dominating sweep of his tongue, weakened her more.

Her knees threatened to buckle, but she was afraid to anchor herself against him. If he stopped, she'd cry. She needed more, much more. She couldn't breathe for needing.

She kissed him back harder, and he groaned against her mouth and swept his hands down her back, across her shoulder blades, along her spine. Lower. He squeezed her behind, and her inner muscles tightened.

He pulled her close and rolled his hips so his hardness pressed against her. She gasped as an electric thrill shot straight to her core, and she arched against him, clinging to the lapels of his coat. It was either that or fall.

Closer, she needed closer. She tried to melt into him, rubbed her body against his, but it wasn't enough. Her palms ached to touch and explore, to know him. She resisted the urge and gripped his lapels tighter as he kissed her jaw, nipped her earlobe, and sucked on her neck. Goose bumps rippled over her skin.

The room spun in a dizzying swirl, leaving the two of them in a world of their own. All she knew was the safety of his embrace, the heat of his mouth, and his scent—soap, aftershave, man. They needed a bed, a wall, a table, anything. She wanted him now, and he was so ready—

"They put too much oil in the soup," a familiar loud voice said. "But the fish was—oh father of mine."

His mom and several of his aunts stared at them from midway down the stairs.

Esme and Khải tore apart at once. Blushing furiously, she smoothed shaky hands over her dress as the ladies finished descending the stairs.

"*Chào*, Cô Nga," she said before inclining her head toward the aunts. She pressed her thighs together, not used to being this aroused in a room full of people.

Khải ran a hand through his hair. "Hi, Mom, Dì Anh, Dì Mai, Dì Tuyết." Averting his eyes, he sucked his swollen bottom lip into his mouth. Oh sky, her lipstick was all over him.

"Anh Khải, let me—I . . ." She lifted a hand toward his face. When she hesitated to touch him, he brought her hand to his jaw.

"What is it?" he asked.

"My lipstick." She brushed her thumb over a smear at the corner of his reddened mouth, but it wouldn't come off. "Oh no, Khải."

Instead of getting upset like she thought he would, he smiled, flashing those dimples at her, and warmth flooded her heart.

He didn't mind getting caught kissing her.

"Young ones, ha?" one of his aunts commented, and the others tittered into their hands like schoolgirls.

"These two kids." Cô Nga tried to sound stern, but she couldn't keep a smile off her face. "Go home already. People will see you." She dug through her granddaddy-sized purse until she came up with a tissue and handed it to Esme. Then she dragged the aunts off.

As soon as the front doors swayed shut, Esme lifted the tissue toward Khải's mouth, but he dodged it and kissed her again, a slow, thorough press of lips to lips. The tissue bunched up in her hand, forgotten, as he threaded his fingers into her hair and tipped her head back so he could kiss her deeper.

A throat cleared.

But this time, when Esme tried to wrench herself away, Khải's arms wrapped around her and held her close. She looked over her shoulder and found Quân watching them with his arms crossed and a big grin on his face.

"The older folks are starting to leave," Quân said. "You guys might wanna . . . take this somewhere else. You know, so you don't give them heart attacks."

Khải looked from his brother to Esme and loosened his hold on her somewhat. "Do you want to go with me . . . or stay?"

"I want to be with you," she whispered.

That beautiful smile spread over his face again. "Let's go, then."

They separated, and Esme tucked the hair behind her ear, not sure how to act around Quân now. But he didn't seem angry or insulted. If anything, he seemed pleased. Had he orchestrated this somehow?

Quân gave Khải one of those American handshake/one-armed-hug/back-slap things. "Call me if you need anything. Have a good night, you two."

He winked at Esme and climbed back up the stairs, and she waved at him awkwardly. Khải opened the hand his brother had gripped earlier, and a shiny foil lay in his palm.

Heat exploded in Esme's cheeks, but she couldn't help grinning. Quân was the best brother ever.

Khải shifted the foil so he held it between his index and middle fingers and considered her with a steady gaze. "Will I have the chance to use this tonight?"

She bit her lip as breathless anticipation bubbled through her veins. After picking up the book he'd dropped on the ground earlier, she glanced at him over her shoulder and said, "I hope so."

CHAPTER SIXTEEN

K hai drove home in a state of madness. His heartbeat was so out of control it was a wonder he didn't get into ten car accidents. The condom in his pocket burned against his thigh.

He was going to have sex with Esme.

Sex.

With Esme.

Even in the midst of this fever, he recognized the fact that he shouldn't do it. He should stay away from her. *Girl loves boy loves girl.* What if she fell in love with him? He couldn't—

No, he told himself firmly. He could. She'd clearly stated she didn't expect anything, and he trusted her to know her own mind. As for himself and his fear of addiction, he'd manage. He'd gone too far to stop now. He wanted this too much. Besides, grown people did this all the time. *His brother* did this all the time, as evidenced by his reliable supply of prophylactics.

After Khai parked outside his place, they walked to the front door together. They'd done this countless times, but everything felt different tonight, surreal somehow. The air smelled sweeter even though the night-blooming jasmine had always grown here. How come he'd never heard the chirping of the crickets like this or noticed the stars as they blinked through the tree canopy?

As he unlocked the door, Esme hugged his paperback book to her chest, watching him from under her lashes. She wet her lips, and the desire to kiss her hit so hard his stomach muscles flexed. He tried to regulate his breathing, tried to calm the rush of his blood, tried to restore his usual functional state, but then he remembered he was *allowed* to kiss her.

Anytime. He. Wanted.

He pinned her to the door and claimed her lips, groaning as she softened and returned his kiss. He always expected her to turn him away, but she never did. It was a heady thing, her acceptance. What else would she let him do?

With one last parting kiss on her mouth, he trailed his lips down her neck. He hadn't meant to, but he'd left a mark there. Deep caveman satisfaction unfurled inside of him, and he didn't question it. He kissed the spot in greeting. When she tipped her head to the side, offering herself to him silently, he gave in to instincts he didn't understand and scraped his teeth across her sensitive skin. Her breath broke, and he saw the goose bumps stand up on her arm. He'd done that.

So soft, so responsive to him, just for him. For now.

Holding his breath, he did what he'd been yearning to do forever. He cupped her full breasts in his palms. And she let him. His thumbs registered the hard points of her nipples through her dress, and he stroked her, exhaling shakily when her eyes went hazy and she bit her bottom lip. He was ninety percent sure she liked that.

What else did she like? Could he make her feel as good as he felt right now? He was determined to try. He needed to please her. He needed that more than anything.

His mouth found hers again, and his mind went fuzzy. She overwhelmed his senses, made it impossible to think. There was only her strawberry taste, the silk of her skin, the curves filling his palms, and the softness that pressed against him every time his hips rocked into her.

Between kisses, she whispered, "Bed. Khải. Now."

Bed.

Sex.

Esme.

His body hardened to the point of pain, and he released her lips and pressed his forehead to hers, taking a moment to cool down and relearn how to use his brain. People told him he was smart. He should be able to figure out how to get them to a bed. It was a regular mundane task. It shouldn't seem so impossible. Break it into steps.

He opened the door, giving himself an extra point when he remembered to put his keys in his pocket, and then picked her up.

She laughed as he carried her into the house. "I can walk. I'm better."

"I like holding you."

Her eyes met his. Her lips didn't curve, but he felt like she was smiling. She was silent the rest of the way to his room. After he placed her in the center of his bed, she sat up, put his book on his nightstand, and slipped the high-heeled shoes off her feet, letting them drop to the shag carpet. Her necklace and other jewelry came off next. Then she curled her legs beneath her and watched him with heated eyes.

After a moment, he realized she was waiting. For him.

He took his shoes off—something he'd never done in his bed-

room because he did it at the front door. He'd probably left a trail of
street grime through his house. Before that could disturb him too
much, he shook his head, shrugged out of his suit coat, and sat on
the bed. Without meaning to, he'd put an arm's length between
them, a safe distance.

She considered that empty space for a second before she looked
him in the eyes, grabbed hold of her dress, and pulled it over her
head, completely obliterating him.

In a split second, she redefined perfection for him. His standards
aligned to her exact proportions and measurements. No one else
would ever live up to her.

Beautiful woman, beautiful sculpted breasts and dusky nipples,
beautiful thighs. She wore the same white cotton panties from the
night of the first wedding. He could tell by the little bow at the
waistband. Either that, or she had several just like it. Did women
buy underwear in packs of six like men did? The image of six white
panties with six little white bows flashed in his mind.

That little bow fascinated him. He wanted to touch it. And her
legs, her skin, all of her. Her breasts, definitely her breasts.

"Your turn." The husky edge to her voice had an almost tactile
quality, and the hairs on his body stood on end.

His mouth was too dry to form words, so he nodded. He felt like
he was shaking, but his hands were steady as he undid his tie and
unfastened the buttons of his shirt. It was the look on her face, the
way she watched every movement. To him, his body was just . . . his
body, this thing he lived inside of. Seeing himself from her eyes was
a new experience.

When he took his shirt off, her lips parted on a quick draw of
breath. When he removed his pants, leaving him in nothing but his
boxers, her gaze roamed over him. His skin heated everywhere she
looked, his chest, his arms, his belly, his legs.

She swept a hand through her long hair and bit a fingertip, and the air gusted from his lungs. Unable to resist any longer, he got to his knees and edged closer, closer. Half an arm's length. A quarter. Their bodies pressed together, skin to skin for the first time.

He'd grappled with men. That was a deliberate, non-light kind of touching, and acceptable. He knew what it was like to have someone against him—two matched planes bruising and punishing, one slip and he ended up in a choke hold.

This was nothing like that. Esme didn't smell like gym socks and man sweat, and her curves fit into his hollows, soft to hard, smooth to rough, the perfect debit to his credit. It hardly made sense when she was so much smaller than he was. He could overpower her in two seconds. But he never wanted to do that.

Her hot breath heated his neck, and he tipped her head back so he could see her face. Slumberous green eyes gazed at him, and her parted red lips seared away whatever remnants of resistance he might have had. He took her mouth, stroked his tongue deep, and she kissed him back just as fiercely.

He couldn't get close enough, couldn't breathe, couldn't think. He touched her everywhere as he mapped out her body in his mind. The ripe curves of her ass, the smooth glide of her back, her breasts. He groaned as her stiff nipples grazed against the centers of his palms. They seemed to be crying for his mouth, and before he knew it, he was sucking a hardened tip, rolling it against his tongue, crushing her to the bed, lost in her. Her legs parted to make room for his hips, and he shuddered as he rocked against her. Friction, her smell, the murmuring sounds she made, pure heaven.

"Now, Khải."

He didn't understand the words. He couldn't stop rubbing himself against her.

"Khải," she said on a gasp. *"Now."*

He pulled away, and her nipple popped from his mouth, wet, glistening. The sight was so erotic he had to look away before he could collect his thoughts. "What now?" he asked in an unrecognizable sandpaper voice.

Her lips opened, but words didn't come. Her chest heaved on quick breaths, making her breasts move in the most alluring way, and down by her sides, her hands opened and closed, opened and closed, like she was grasping for something that wasn't there.

Finally, she said, "Condom."

Everything clicked into place.

He climbed off the bed and retrieved the lone condom from his pants pocket. Watching her, he eased his boxers down so his cock sprang out. When her eyes darkened and the tip of her tongue licked over her upper lip, a surge of raw lust almost knocked him to his knees. He yanked his boxers all the way down and stepped out of them before easing onto the bed beside her.

The foil crinkled as he opened it, and he rolled the lubricated latex over his hypersensitive length. Finished, he let his hands drop to his sides.

It was time, but he hardly knew where to take things next. He'd always thought there'd be an inner voice telling him what to do. Humans had been mating for thousands of years. It came to them naturally, instinctively. But all Khai heard was his own breathing. He was going to fuck this up.

Eyes steady on his, she bit her bottom lip and removed her panties with a subtle lift of her hips. She kept her legs pressed together, but the cloud of curls between her thighs caught his attention. He swallowed hard. She was naked, gloriously naked.

"Come here," she said.

His body obeyed on its own, edging between her knees and covering her, lining them up just right. The lure of her lips was too much, and he kissed her with a touch of desperation. When he rolled his hips, his cock slid over her, and the tip lodged inside of her. Just the tip. He went flame hot everywhere, his back, the base of his skull, his scalp.

This was happening. Him and Esme. Together.

He kissed her deeper as he pushed in slowly. Each inch changed him, broke him down and put him back together again, until he finally seated himself inside her completely, and she threw her head back and moaned.

For a moment, he was too overwhelmed to move. *He'd pleased her.* He'd never dreamed it would be so easy to satisfy a woman. He smoothed the hair away from her face, kissed her lips, awash in tenderness and new sensation. There was nothing like being inside Esme. She was tight, fitting him like they were custom-made for each other, hot, soft.

When her hips lifted, pushing him in farther, pleasure sizzled through him, and those instincts he'd thought he didn't have fired to life. He pulled out and thrust back into her with a harsh groan, out, in, faster. Holy fuck, sex was good. Sex was *fantastic*, ten thousand times better than jacking off in the shower, a million times, a billion.

And he knew it was because he was with Esme. She made everything different. He was so glad she was his first.

E sme bunched the blankets in her hands as she fought against the need to touch Khải. His face was drawn like he was in pain. She wanted to soothe him, and then she wanted to stroke him all over. He was magnificent, all powerful muscle and hard lines.

It was good, so good, and even though he hadn't once touched her where she needed, she was achingly close. She arched her back and writhed against him, trying to find the perfect angle, but her motions only enflamed him.

His thrusts picked up speed and grew shallower, and his mouth fell open as he pushed in sharply and locked their hips together for the span of several heartbeats. Lungs heaving, he kissed her on the temple. Then he pulled out, climbed off the bed, and disappeared into the bathroom.

She sagged against the bed in disbelief. That was it? Surely, he had to be coming back soon. Her sex ached for him to return and finish what he'd begun.

The shower started.

She sat upright and stared at the door to the bathroom as her skin went cold. He was really done. He'd enjoyed himself, and now he was showering her off. It hadn't even been a minute since he'd finished. Her lips were still wet from his kisses.

Tears threatened, but she choked them back. She didn't know how long she sat there staring at the bathroom door. It could have been hours or seconds, but she eventually jumped off his bed, gathered her things, and plopped them on the floor in her room. After she perched on the couch, she wrapped her arms around herself tight. She'd wanted to be with him, and now she had. Her curiosity was satisfied. She'd told him she didn't expect anything, and that was what he'd given her. Nothing.

Hurt and anger spiraled through her. She focused on the anger.

When the shower turned off, she marched into the bathroom. He looked up in the middle of toweling himself. After an awkward second, he lifted the towel from his thigh and dried his hair, exposing his beautiful naked body. Defined muscle in his arms that bunched as he rubbed at his head, broad shoulders, firm belly, *that* part of him, strong legs. Everything perfect to her eyes, but not meant for her. He grinned at her, the kind with dimples, but the smile faded when she stared at him stonily.

She plodded into the shower stall and stabbed at the buttons. What was wrong with her that his smile still melted her? She had no self-respect at all. When she scrubbed between her legs, her sensitive flesh throbbed with need. He'd kissed and touched her until she was wild for him and then abandoned her. Again.

He would always be leaving her. Because she wasn't what he wanted. She'd known this, but she'd thrown herself at him anyway.

Foolish, foolish girl.

As the water washed over her and heat sank into her skin, she swore everything stopped here. No more. No more secret hoping, no more seducing, no more caring about him. She was done. She wasn't rich, classy, or smart, but she wasn't something you could use once and toss away. She had value. You couldn't see it in the clothes she wore or the abbreviations after her name or hear it in the way she spoke, but she *felt* it, even if she didn't entirely understand where it came from. It pounded inside her chest, big and strong and bright. She deserved better than this.

Strengthened by the force of her conviction, she turned the water off, yanked a fresh towel to her chest, and stepped out of the shower.

Khải paused in the middle of brushing his teeth and turned around to look at her, letting his gaze sweep over her bare skin. It was impossible not to notice he was hard again, and her treacherous body warmed in response. Foolish, foolish body.

She stalked past him and shut herself in her room without a word. If she tried speaking, she'd either cry or yell at him. After stepping into another pair of white panties and putting on her sleeping clothes, she shook out her blankets and made her bed on the couch. No more bed sharing.

As she pushed her legs under the covers, a knock sounded on

her door, and Khải stepped into the room, wearing a fresh pair of boxers.

He rubbed at his neck as he took in the blankets on the couch. "You're not sleeping . . . in my room? Like usual?"

"The couch is fine."

His brow wrinkled, but after a while, he nodded. "All right, then. Good night." Flashing a shadow of a smile at her, he shut the door, and his footsteps receded as he returned to his room.

She punched her pillow before she pulled it out from under her cheek and hugged it next to her body like it was a person. She didn't need to sleep with him. Her anger would keep her company.

CHAPTER SEVENTEEN

The first thing Khai saw the next morning was the empty other half of his bed. No Esme, not even a wrinkle on the blankets. Was it normal to want space from someone after you had sex with them? He didn't understand it, especially when she had nightmares when she slept alone, but he didn't know what to do other than leave her be.

He sat up, put his feet to the floor, and speared his fingers through his short hair. He'd slept like the dead—great sex probably did that—but everything felt off today. The walls were too gray, the room too dingy, his bed too big. Even his carpet looked extra ugly around his bare feet, and its softness wasn't enough to make up for its offensiveness.

Hoping routine would set things straight, he went about his regular Sunday morning tasks. He got ready, choked down a protein bar, and lifted weights, but Esme never left her room. He knew because he watched for her the entire time.

After he showered, he found her sitting on the couch reading a textbook as a cartoon movie played on the TV. He got his laptop and joined her on the couch, thinking to work while she studied, but as soon as he sat down, she got up and disappeared into her room.

What the hell was going on? Was she sick of him now that they'd had sex? He wasn't sick of *her*. If anything, he wanted her more, not less. Frowning, he left his computer on the couch and went after her. Outside her door, he took a bracing breath, opened his hands wide to stretch them out, and knocked.

The door swung open shortly after that, and Esme faced him. She wore her yellow *Em yêu anh yêu em* shirt over knee-length shorts and had her hair in a sloppy ponytail with a pencil over her ear. She was so beautiful she made his chest hurt.

"Are you mad at me?" he asked.

Her lips thinned as she stared at him.

"Why are you acting this way?" He wanted her back to the way she used to be.

She tipped her chin up, looking mutinously stubborn, and the perverse desire to kiss her rose. He almost acted on it, but she looked likely to bite him. Except then her eyes went glassy and her breaths quickened. "I do what I want."

"Are you hungry? I can—"

"No, thanks." She shut the door in his face.

He stared at the door for a good minute. What in the world was going on? Had he . . . done something wrong? He couldn't think of anything. There'd been the sex, which was amazing, and afterward, he'd showered right away so he didn't smear his sweat all over her. That had taken monumental effort since he'd felt like someone had shot him with a hippopotamus tranquilizer. What was it? He wished he understood people.

But he knew someone who did. Because he was an ideal human.

He grabbed his keys and let himself out of the house. It took forty-five minutes to get to Quan's neighborhood in San Francisco, and then fifteen more minutes to find street parking. When he finally hit the buzzer outside the condominium building, there was no answer.

He tried it again.

Still nothing.

One more time with feeling.

More nothing.

Grumbling to himself, he got his phone out of his pocket and dialed his brother.

Quan picked up on the first ring. "Yo, wassup?" he asked, his voice thick with sleep.

"I'm outside your building."

"Whoa, what? Is something wrong? Wait, I'm coming. Hold on a second." A softer female voice murmured something in the background, and he said, "It's my brother. Be right back." The call disconnected.

Khai kicked at a spot of dirt on the concrete as he waited. It sounded like he wasn't the only one who'd had an eventful night. He didn't think Quan's date would be ignoring and avoiding him all day, though.

The front door swung open, revealing Quan in nothing but tattoos and an old pair of jeans. "Hey."

For a moment, Khai was so distracted by Quan's tattoos he forgot why he'd come. "When did you get those new ones? Do you have plans for that bare patch?"

Quan scratched at the swirling calligraphy on his right side that melded with the Japanese-style art on his left. "Gonna leave it blank. Too much of a good thing and all."

"You don't think you already crossed the 'too much' line?" Khai asked.

"Shut up, you. My ass is still bare. Come on in."

Khai entered the building, and they rode up the elevator together.

"So what is it?" Quan asked as the numbers on the digital display climbed. "You never visit me."

Khai stretched his fingers out again before relaxing them. "I had sex last night. With Esme."

A giant smirk stretched over his brother's mouth. "Your first time, right?"

Khai nodded curtly. He'd never told anyone he was a virgin, but of course Quan, with all his excellent people intuition, had known.

"Good job, little brother." Quan held a fist out, and Khai bumped it with his own out of pure habit. Then he felt ridiculous.

"You don't mind? I know you said you were interested, and I—"

"No, I don't mind," Quan said with a small laugh. "You're my brother. I'll always pick you first. Plus, I like her for you. I'm glad you went for it."

Khai filled his chest with a big breath, relieved he hadn't ruined anything with his brother through his indecisiveness but also strangely proud Esme had chosen him over Quan. If Khai were a woman, he'd pick Quan, no competition. "She's acting weird now, and I don't know what to do."

"You mean like she's getting clingy and you want her to stop? That happens sometimes. You gotta let them down gently. What I do is—"

"No, it's not that." He wouldn't mind clinging. That would be better than what was going on right now. "I think she's mad at me, but I can't figure out what's wrong. She won't tell me."

Quan's eyebrows rose. "When did she start acting weird?"

"I think . . ." He looked to the side as he searched his memories. "I think right after we, uh, after the sex."

Quan's eyebrows rose even farther before his expression went blank. "Maybe that's it, then. Did she, you know, did she like it?"

"Yeah, that part was easy."

"Really," Quan said in a dry tone. "Your first time out the gate."

"Yeah."

Quan gave Khai a skeptical look. "What are you, the King Midas of Orgasms? I've been perfecting my craft since eighth grade, and sometimes I still don't know what I'm doing down there. Women are complicated."

"What craft? It's sex. You put bodies together, and shit happens. It's like the nature channel." He did bad on the emotional front, but he'd gotten this part right, dammit.

"I'm pretty sure we've figured out the problem," Quan said.

Khai shoved his hands into his pockets. "Tell me, then." He was ninety-nine percent certain Quan was wrong.

"How do you know she came?"

The elevator dinged, and as they walked down a narrow hallway toward Quan's place, Khai cleared his throat. "She made sounds. *Those* kinds of sounds." Really good sounds.

"Anything else?" Quan stopped at his door and turned the key in the lock.

"What else is there?"

"Oh, for fuck's sake, come in and sit down." Quan opened the door to his bachelor pad.

Khai stepped inside carefully, half convinced he'd find sperm on the walls, but it was mostly neat. There was definitely no sperm. That he could see. If you analyzed the black leather couches closely, who knew what you'd find. He didn't take his shoes off before he followed Quan to his kitchen.

"Have a seat. I need to fix my hangover." Quan puttered around his modern kitchen, breaking eggs into a blender and adding orange juice. Once he'd blended the mixture to a froth, he poured it into an old giant Slurpee cup and joined Khai at the kitchen table. "Want some?" He held it out toward Khai.

Khai grimaced. "No, thanks. Don't you have Advil?"

"Nah, ran out." Quan chugged half of his concoction, set the cup down, and wiped at his mouth with the back of his hand. "Okay, back to the sex. My guess is she didn't orgasm."

"What are the symptoms for orgasm?"

Quan burst out laughing and drank more of his orange hangover cure. "Only you would talk about orgasming like it was a sickness."

Khai drummed his fingers on the table. "Can you just get on with it?"

"Okay, okay, okay." Quan took a deep breath before he chuckled, shook his head, and scratched at the morning scruff on his jaw. "First, she—wait, wouldn't it be awesome if Michael were here? He's a pro at this shit. I know, let's *call him*."

"What? No. Can't you just tell me?"

Quan waved his fingers toward Khai's pockets. "Get your phone out and call him. He can verify what I say, so you can stop looking at me like I'm cheating off someone's test answers."

"*You* call him."

"He won't pick up if I call him. It's Saturday and not even eight yet. If you call him, he'll think it's an emergency. You never call anyone."

Rolling his eyes, Khai fished his phone out, dialed his cousin, and hit the speaker button. There was no way in hell he was doing all the talking alone.

Michael picked up on the fourth ring. "Hey, Khai, how's it going?"

Khai held the phone toward his brother, and Quan said, "Michael, we need your expertise. It's about orgasms."

"What the hell? Are you kidding me?" A frustrated sound crackled through the speaker. "I'm going back to sleep."

"We're not kidding," Khai said quickly.

There was a long pause before Michael said, "What did you want to know?"

Khai took and released a tight breath before asking, "How do you know when a woman is orgasming? What are the sym—signs?"

"Wow, okay. Orgasms. Um . . ." He cleared his throat. "There are lots of signs, but not every woman is the same. Generally, she'll . . ." He cleared his throat again. "Why is this so hard?" He laughed a little.

"Fine, since you're mature as a nine-year-old, I'll start," Quan said. "Sounds are really misleading. Half the time when you have a noisy woman, she's a faker, and she wants the sex to be over because she's not digging it. It's better to watch her body. When a woman is about to come, she tenses up, and her hips rise. Her skin flushes. And when the orgasm hits, she convulses hard and fast. Her whole body might shake. If you're paying attention, you'll feel it on your cock or your fingers or your tongue, whatever you've got going on. It's fucking awesome."

After another long pause, Michael said, "What he said."

An uncomfortable feeling crawled over Khai's skin as he stared at the phone and then his brother's face. "I don't know if she did all that. I was distracted by how good it felt."

"Were you inside her?" Quan asked.

"Well, yeah. That's how you have sex," Khai said. They taught that in fifth-grade health class.

Quan gave him an impatient look. "Did you touch her clit at all?"

"What's that?"

"Oh hell," Michael said.

Quan smacked his palm to his forehead. "Her clitoris. It's where you stimulate her to make her come."

"Where is it?"

Quan rubbed both hands over his face as Michael repeated, "Oh hell."

"What?" Khai asked. "They don't talk about the 'clitoris' in health class at school." It didn't even sound real. For all he knew, it was an urban myth, like the Chupacabra or Roswell aliens.

"They really should," Michael said, sounding pained.

"Why don't they?"

Michael and Quan both fell silent.

"So maybe she didn't orgasm. Is that enough reason for her to be mad at me?" he asked.

"Who is this we're talking about?" Michael asked.

"Esme," Khai said.

"Oh," Michael said.

"Who else would it be?" Quan said. "At the end, did you hold her? They need a couple minutes of that."

"Why?"

"The fuck, Quan?" Michael said. "You should have prepared him better."

"Prepared me for what?" Khai asked.

Quan scrubbed a hand over his buzzed head. "Shit."

"I was all sweaty, and I was afraid the condom would leak and get her pregnant. I took a shower. That seemed appropriate." Wasn't it?

Quan continued scrubbing his head. "Well, shit."

"Why do you keep saying that?" Khai asked.

Quan dropped his hands from his head and focused a steady gaze on Khai. "Imagine you're a girl, and—I'm serious, don't laugh—you let a guy touch you, but when things start to feel really good, he stops. And then you're telling yourself it's okay, you're glad he had a good time, but he leaves you right away and washes you off, leaving you alone in his bed. How would you feel?"

"Sexually frustrated?"

Quan looked up at the ceiling. "Yeah, and used and sad and shitty. They get extra sensitive after sex, and you gotta make sure they feel cared for."

"I second that," Michael said.

Khai released a heavy, defeated breath. When it came to women, what Michael said was as good as gold. Khai had fucked this up royally. Because of deficiencies in his fifth-grade health curriculum and his stone heart.

"What do I do now?" he asked, completely at a loss.

Michael and Quan spoke up at the same time.

"Apologize."

"Say sorry."

"Can you give an example of what I should say?" he asked. A script would be best. He could memorize it and repeat it to her.

"Don't tell him, Michael." To Khai, Quan said, "It's best if you come up with something on your own. It'll be genuine that way. But first, I have some books for you."

"What books?" Michael asked.

"Sex ed books. What? Yeah, I read. Surprising, I know." Quan shook his head at the phone. "I think you can go back to sleeping or banging your woman now. I got some stuff to talk to Khai about."

"Which books? I have—" There was a barely audible female whisper, followed by something that was distinctly a kiss. "I'll catch you guys later. Call me if you need anything."

The screen of Khai's phone went black, and Quan got up. "I'll be right back. They're in my bedroom."

Khai watched as his brother strode down the hall. It wasn't long before Quan returned with a stack of books under his arm.

"Really? *Sex for Dummies?*" Khai asked. "*You* read this?"

"It gives a good overview. I like this one best, though." Quan set the books on the table and moved *She Comes First* to the top. "Don't take everything in there as hard rules. They're just suggestions. I don't agree with all of it, but it's a good place to start."

Khai reached for the book but hesitated with his hand inches away. "Are these books safe for touching?"

"Yes, you dork, they're safe for touching. I prefer jerking off to porn, not how-to books. Keep them. I'm done with them."

"Okay, thanks." Khai picked up *She Comes First* and leafed through it, lifting his eyebrows at the diagrams. He hadn't done *that*.

But he wanted to.

"There are videos where they demonstrate stuff with fruit on YouTube. You should check them out. But I'd save those for later. You need to speed-read that book and then apologize ASAP."

Khai gathered up all the books. "Right, got it. Thanks again."

The corner of Quan's mouth kicked up. "Anytime, Khai. I shoulda prepped you earlier, but—"

"I wouldn't have listened. I wasn't ready." He probably never would have been ready if it weren't for Esme. "I am now."

Quan looked at him for a good long moment before he said, "Be careful, okay? You guys are both grown-ups, and you can make your own decisions and shit, but just . . . be careful. With yourself and with her. I really do like her for you, and—"

"Quan," someone called from the other side of the condo. "I'm getting cold."

Quan clapped his hands and rubbed them together like everything was settled. "I think we're done here. Feel free to call me if you have questions. But not until ten at the earliest. Good luck. Oh, and maybe you wanna buy a box of condoms on the way home. I'd give you some of mine, but I only have two left."

Khai headed for the door. "Got it." That seemed really optimistic, considering where things were with him and Esme right now, but it was best to be prepared.

As he headed out, he heard Quan say, "Don't forget to apologize. First with words. Then with your tongue."

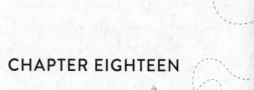

CHAPTER EIGHTEEN

Esme tried her best to focus on studying, but thoughts of Khải kept intruding on her United States history. Why had he looked so confused? Did he treat all his women that way? Was she supposed to be grateful he'd slept with her and beg for more?

She sneered. Not in this life. Not even in her next life when she was a catfish.

After reading the same page three times, she shut her textbook. She wasn't trying to impress him anymore. She wasn't sure why she continued studying. It wasn't like any of this information would help her clean bathrooms any better.

A wave of homesickness hit her. She checked the time, but it was too early to call home. When she couldn't talk to her family, the next best thing was fruit. Fruit and home were connected in her mind. Everything Cô Nga had bought was long gone, so she raided the pantry. Fresh was best, but canned was better than none. She opened a big can of lychees, poured them into a bowl with ice, and brought them to the living room, where she queued up *The Hunch-back of Notre Dame* on Netflix.

She was sitting cross-legged on the carpet in front of the TV, shoving lychees into her mouth with a soup spoon, when Khải walked through the front door. He glanced her way for a quick second before he focused on removing his shoes with a furrowed brow. He was wearing his reading glasses and looked especially accountant/assassin-like in his black T-shirt and pants. Beautiful mind, beautiful body.

This man had kissed her like he was drowning last night.

And then he'd discarded her as soon as he'd finished with her.

A lychee lodged in her throat, and she forced it down with an uncomfortable swallow. She picked up her half-finished bowl of lychees and prepared to run.

"No, don't go." Khải took a step toward her, and plastic bags swayed at his side. "Please. I wanted to talk to you."

She considered running anyway, but the pleading in his eyes kept her still. She prodded at a floating lychee with her spoon as she waited for him to say whatever it was he needed to. She had no idea what to expect. He'd never been predictable.

Instead of speaking right away, he crossed the room and sat on his heels in front of her. The plastic bags rustled as he set them down. "I got these for you."

The distinct red spiny shells of rambutan fruits were visible from the top of one of the bags, and she gasped and snatched them close. "For me? Where did you get them?" They didn't have these at the regular grocery store that was within walking distance of his house.

He smiled slightly. "I had to drive around a little, but I found them in San Jose."

"All day?" she asked.

"No, not all day." He ducked his head and laughed a little. Was it her, or did his cheeks redden? "I did some reading." He removed his glasses and stuck them on the coffee table.

"Thank you," she said, more touched than she cared to admit, but then she noticed the box inside the second plastic bag. She knew what kind of box that was.

Her eyes went round. If he thought she was having sex with him again after last night, he had a few things to learn. These fruits were coming with her to her room, and she hoped he got ants all over his house. She'd secretly feed them and lure them to his bedroom, so they bit him in his sleep.

Just as she lifted the bowl and bag and unfolded her legs so she could get up, he looked at her directly and said, "I'm sorry."

The words were so unexpected she didn't know what to do. She stared at him without blinking.

"I screwed up last night. I didn't realize—I didn't know—" He made a frustrated sound and looked down at his knees. "I swear I practiced this, but it's not coming out right." His eyes met hers again, determined now. "Last night was my first time."

She shook her head, not understanding.

"My first time. Ever. With a woman. With anyone."

"You never . . . ?" she said before her throat dried up.

"I know it's not a great excuse. I should have prepared ahead of time to make sure I did right by you, but . . ." His expression softened. "I'm glad it was you."

She didn't know how to respond. She'd never dreamed she'd be anyone's first, and being this guarded man's first meant something.

"I suppose that's a selfish thing to say, considering you didn't like it," he said, grimacing slightly. "Will you give me another chance? Let me make it up to you?"

She parted her lips to speak, but nothing came out.

"Or have I screwed things up too badly?" When she still couldn't bring herself to reply, his chest deflated. His lips curved with an almost-there smile, no dimples, and he averted his eyes and came up onto his knees. "I'm going to go to the office. I'll see—"

"If I give you another chance, what will you do?" she asked.

His eyes searched hers before they dropped to her lips and darkened. "More kissing. A lot more kissing."

"And then?"

"More touching."

She shivered as his gaze tracked over her body. "Who gets to touch? Only you?"

His brow creased. "You can touch me if you want."

"Anywhere?"

He was halfway through a nod when he said, "Except for one place."

"Your face."

"Ha, no. You can touch me there. You already have."

"Then, where?" she asked.

A thinking expression crossed his face. "It's not important unless you decide to give me another chance. Are you?"

She worried the inside of her lip before she said, "Maybe."

"How can I help you decide?"

She set her fruit aside and rose to her knees so they were nearly at eye level. "Kiss me like the first time."

For a suspended moment, he went completely motionless. Then his arms were wrapping around her, drawing her close, his hands tipping her head back. Their lips crushed together, and she gasped as heat arrowed through her. He gentled immediately, like he was afraid to hurt her, and the kisses turned slow, drugging.

She grabbed handfuls of his shirt as she struggled not to touch him, and he pulled back, saying, "Sorry, did I—"

"More."

He kissed her like she was his whole world, and if she weren't already kneeling, she would have collapsed to the floor. Grasping at his shirt, she returned each aching press of lips, each stroke of tongue.

They kissed until they were straining against each other on the floor, lips swollen and breathless, and then they kissed more, each lost in the other. When his hand slipped beneath the waistband of her pants, however, she snapped out of her daze, and her entire body tensed. She broke the kiss as a wave of inexplicable panic turned her skin cold.

"What is it?" he asked. His cheeks were flushed, but his eyes watched her with confusion and concern. "Have you changed your mind?"

She shook her head quickly. She wanted this, him. But that was the problem. She'd wanted him from the start, had opened herself up to him over and over, and what had that gotten her?

"I'm scared," she whispered.

His face creased with something that looked like pain. "Of me?"

She shook her head again. "No, I'm scared you'll push me away again when I touch you wrong, scared you'll leave me again." Against her will, her eyes watered, and tears spilled over. She turned her face away from him and swiped at her eyes with the back of a sleeve, embarrassed now. Even to her own ears, she sounded pathetic.

He cupped her cheek and gently urged her to look at him. "I won't," he said in a rough voice. "At least, I'll try not to."

She nodded and attempted to smile in response, but it felt off. "I'll try not to" didn't sound very convincing.

He surprised her by gathering her tightly fisted hands together and kissing her knuckles. "You did this yesterday, too." He eased her stiff fingers open, and when he saw the deep grooves her nails had left in her palms, his eyebrows drew together. "No more of this."

After a brief hesitation, he sat back on his heels and pulled his shirt off, revealing broad expanses of smooth skin stretched over sculpted muscle.

"The place I'm asking you not to touch is . . ." He took a breath, squared his shoulders, and said, "My bellybutton."

She couldn't help it, a smile spread over her mouth and a laugh threatened to escape. "Your bellybutton?"

"Yes, my bellybutton. I know it sounds funny."

"A little." She tried to wipe her smile away, but that only made her grin bigger.

"I mean it," he said with a level gaze. "I can't stand being touched there. If you try, I might accidentally hurt you. I can't control my reactions when it comes to that place. I don't even like *thinking* about it."

"I won't touch you there. I promise. But . . ." She edged closer to him. "I can touch everywhere else?"

He nodded once. "Yes, as long as—"

"No light touch, I know."

She lowered a hand toward his chest, and he held still, not making any move to stop her. Before making contact, she withdrew, paused for the span of a heart's beat, and took her shirt off just like he'd done. As usual, she wasn't wearing a bra—she hated them—and he consumed her with his gaze, making her feel like the most desired woman in the world. She brought their bodies together from chest to knees, rested her cheek against his shoulder, and gingerly wrapped her arms around him. Holding her breath, she pressed her palms firmly against the hard planes of his back, even though she knew he couldn't see.

Her heart pounded so hard she could feel her sternum shaking with each beat. This was the first time she'd dared to hug him since she'd crawled into his bed with that nightmare. If he was going to push her away, now was the time.

He didn't. He kissed the top of her head and hugged her in return, and moment by moment, Esme relaxed into him as the hurt slowly drained out of her.

Eventually, she dared to let her hands roam. She explored his strong shoulders, the swells of his biceps, and everything from the pads of muscle between his shoulder blades down to the twin grooves in the small of his back, and he let her; he trusted her.

Maybe she kissed his neck. And his jaw. His chin. When he turned toward her, their lips met, and sensation sang through her. The kiss started tenderly but quickly escalated into something intense as they tried to get closer to each other. She could hardly breathe, and she didn't care.

She boldly stroked him through his pants, loving the way he groaned and kissed her harder. And then it was happening. Hungry hands undid buttons, lowered zippers, pushed cloth down. She touched him there for the first time, loving how deliciously different he was from herself, and he touched her in return. His fingertips searched through damp curls and wet folds and settled there, there, *there*. She tore open the box he'd bought with trembling fingers and extracted a foil packet.

"No oral sex?" he asked. "The books I read highly recommended it . . . and I wanted to try."

It took her a few seconds to figure out what that was, and then her blush grew so hot she could feel heat coming off her body in waves. That was not something she'd ever known, and her grandma certainly wouldn't approve. The thought of him kissing her between her thighs was outrageous.

And intriguing.

"Later," she said and urged him to hurry. Once he'd rolled the condom onto his length, she pulled him down onto the floor with her. Their bodies lined up next to each other in that perfect way, and he pressed his cheek to hers like he was savoring being close to her.

"Please, don't let me make you cry," he whispered in her ear. "If something is wrong, tell me so I can fix it. Please."

Her heart squeezed, and she hugged him tight. "I'll tell you."

He swallowed once before he shifted his hips, and they came together with broken breaths and a long sigh. Filled with him, she couldn't help arching up, trying to get closer, until he reached between them and touched her. She clenched tightly around him as heat shimmered outward from the place where his fingertips stroked.

"Show me how to make it good for you, too," he said as he looked at her directly, no trace of shame on his face. "Because I need you to feel the way I do right now."

At first, she froze with a mixture of embarrassment and inhibition, but then she settled her hand over Khải's and showed him how to pleasure her. She'd always thought it was bad for a woman to participate like this in bed, but perceptions didn't matter when it was the two of them. She would be whatever he needed.

When he started to move his hips as he caressed her with his fingers, she couldn't stop the sounds escaping her throat. Stroked inside and out, treasured, loved. She wrapped her arms around him, holding him in every way she could as their bodies found a rhythm.

He was here. He was hers. He wasn't going anywhere.

Kisses everywhere, on her lips, on her throat, her shoulder. Temple to temple, heavy intimate breaths, whispers in her ear, answers.

Like this?

Like this and this and this.

Her hips rose sharply off the floor, pressing as close to him as possible, high, higher, higher. Head thrown back. Too much, too good, so good. A trembling moan. Strong convulsions, over and over and over.

And you?

All I need is you.

Her name, her name, her name, her name.

Pure stillness.

In her mind and in her heart.

Warm. Content. Safe in his arms. Him safe in hers. She hugged him tighter. He was bigger and stronger, but she would protect him with everything she had.

CHAPTER NINETEEN

Khai woke up from the deepest sleep of his life and blinked his bedroom into focus. When he saw how bright it was, he glanced at the clock: 10:23 A.M. Really? He never slept in this late. He tried to sit upright, but a warm weight kept him down. He lifted hands to the mass and encountered long silky hair and soft skin.

Esme.

Memories flooded his mind. Kissing her. Touching her. Being touched by her. Being inside her. Watching her come apart.

As he lay there staring at the popcorn ceiling, he recognized he should be losing his shit—his Sunday schedule was destroyed, and there was a woman in his bed, sleeping on him like a sloth in a tree. But her weight was calming, he'd gotten a full eight hours of sleep, and for the first time in a long time, he didn't have blue balls. He felt . . . good.

He analyzed the odd sense of well-being, not trusting it. Was it due to the oxytocin and endorphins released during intercourse? Was he addicted to sex now . . . or was it worse than that? Was he addicted to Esme? Should he get rid of her before it was too late?

The thought of losing her made his stomach drop and his body stiffen in rejection, and he brushed the hair away from her cheek and kissed the top of her head, needing to reassure himself she was still here.

Well, that explained everything.

Khai Diep, CPA, Esme addict.

He was surprisingly okay with it. It was hard to be upset when he had her in his arms. But the day would come when she had to go, and he didn't know what it would take to readjust to life without her. For now, however, he didn't have to think about it. The summer was only half over.

His phone buzzed, and he picked it up instantly, grateful for the distraction. An email from Quan's friend about the list of Phils. Before he could open it, Esme stirred.

"Oh, I'm on top of you," she said. "Did I sleep here all night?"

"I think so."

"Sorry." She eased off him. He was about to voice a protest but got preoccupied with her hair. It looked like she'd brushed it backward, applied hairspray while upside down, or both. She swiped at the extra-volumized strands and self-consciously tucked the only tame tendril behind her ear. "Do you hurt anywhere? From me sleeping on you?"

She patted her hands over his chest like she was searching for something—he didn't know what, signs of internal bleeding or broken bones maybe—and he covered her hands with his. If she touched him much more, they'd be having morning breath sex, and he wasn't sure how that worked.

"I'm fine. You're the perfect size for me," he said.

She grinned. "You think I'm pretty *and* the perfect size."

That was obvious, so he changed the subject. "I just got a narrowed-down list from Quan's friend." He sat up and accessed the email. "Looks like he narrowed it down to . . . nine. There are full names, attendance information, phone numbers, and the pictures from their old student IDs. Want to see?"

"*Yes, I want to.*" She grabbed the phone and immediately snuggled up next to him, pulling the blankets over her breasts—a crying shame. Oblivious to his disappointment, she flashed him an excited look before scanning the photographs. When she got to number eight, she grabbed Khai's far arm and wrapped it around her middle so he was hugging her, and he smiled.

He liked this, the snuggling, her smiles, the fact that she helped him be there for her. He hadn't known she needed to be hugged, and it was immensely freeing that instead of getting angry with him or sad, she communicated and showed him what to do.

"That's him," she whispered. "Number eight."

Khai considered the photograph skeptically. The man had green eyes, but everyone looked more or less the same to him. How had she settled on this one? "Judging by his 650 area code, he's local."

She covered her mouth. "Is it too early to call now?"

"It's not early. It's after ten."

Her eyes widened, and she glanced out the window like she was just noticing the time of day. "We were up late, huh?"

"We were." As memories of last night flitted through his head, he let his eyes trail over her profile, her fine jaw, and the graceful line of her neck. He cleared his throat and touched his fingertips to the little purple blemishes on her skin. "I, um, may have left marks on you."

Shit, were they permanent? He hadn't made them on purpose, though he had to admit he found the sight highly satisfying. Apparently, he was like a dog and felt the need to mark his territory—not with pee, though.

She pressed a hand to her neck and grinned as her cheeks bloomed with color. "They go away."

He nodded, relieved and disappointed at the same time.

After scrutinizing the other photographs again, she returned to number eight. Her finger hovered over the phone number as she took a deep breath, and then she pressed it and hit the speaker button. She chewed on her bottom lip as the phone rang once, twice, three times.

Four times, five, six . . .

Seven, eight, nine . . .

"Hi, you've reached Phil Jackson. I'm probably busy in the operating room. Leave a message, and I'll get back to you when I can."

When voice mail started recording, she hit the end button, and Khai looked at her in confusion.

"You don't want to leave a message?" he asked.

She shook her head quickly. For a long while, she continued worrying her lip as she stared at the photograph on the screen. "Do you think . . . he is a doctor?"

"Maybe. We can check." He got the phone from her and Googled "Phil Jackson MD." Sure enough, there was a Phil Jackson in Palo Alto who specialized in cardiovascular and thoracic surgery.

Esme snatched the phone from him and zoomed in on the man's picture. He looked nice enough with his distinguished white hair, glasses, and easy smile, kind of like if Santa Claus worked out and got a shave.

"He is a doctor," Esme whispered, but she didn't look happy about it. Her brow wrinkled, and she kept torturing her bottom lip.

"Is that a problem?"

She ran a hand through her headbanger hair and lifted a shoulder. "A man like that . . . for his daughter . . . I'm not . . ." She gave up and looked out the window.

"You don't think he'll like you?"

Her eyes searched his. "You think he will?"

"Of course he will." How could someone not like her?

She surprised him by tackling him with a hug and burying her face against his neck. After a shocked moment, he tightened his arms around her and rested his cheek against hers. Was she sad? Was she happy? Was she crying? He had no clue whatsoever, so he held her and waited.

But as he waited, he couldn't help noticing he had a very naked Esme straddling his very naked hips. Her breasts were plumped against his chest, and her sex was *right there*. It took a tenth of a second for his body to respond in the expected manner, and he winced. This didn't strike him as the right way to react when you had an emotional woman in your arms. He was wishing his erection away, when she brushed up against it, stiffened in realization, and deliberately rubbed herself over his length as she bit his ear.

"Again?" she whispered.

There was only one possible way to answer that question. It looked like they were having morning breath sex after all.

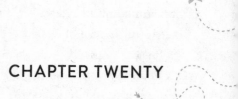

CHAPTER TWENTY

The month that followed was the best month of Esme's life. Now that she'd gotten the hang of things, waitressing suited her just fine, and she saved up enough to either fix her grandma's house or buy something better. Her grades in school stayed high. She couldn't become Esme in Accounting, but she was getting *close*.

Best of all, her time with Khải was like a dream. Things had become easy between them. She knew to turn the exhaust hood on when she cooked with fish sauce, and he'd learned to kiss her every morning when she left for work and hug her every evening when he picked her up from class. He still didn't speak much unless she asked him specific questions, but that was fine. She talked enough for both of them, and he was a good listener. She'd made an offhand comment about wanting to ride on a sailboat someday, and he'd surprised her today by taking her to Sunday brunch on the water in the San Francisco Bay. It had been lovely. Their first date.

Now they were settling onto the couch at his place. She had studying to do, and his work was seemingly endless. She'd highlighted a few textbook pages before she made the poor choice of glancing up at him. He was wearing his reading glasses again, dressed in formfitting black as usual, and brooding over his computer screen like he was masterminding an elite sniper attack. A peek at his computer, however, revealed spreadsheets instead of battle blueprints.

It was sexy anyway. And she couldn't prevent herself from setting her homework aside and cozying up next to him. He didn't seem to notice at first, and she kissed the strong cords in his neck and his jaw.

"Khải," she whispered. "How about—"

His lips met hers, and the rest of the words didn't matter. Like always, he kissed her with his entire attention and intensity, and it wasn't long before she displaced his computer and took up the space on his lap—her plan from the beginning.

They bumped his glasses askew, and he grabbed them like he was going to remove them.

"No," she said quickly and repositioned them for him. "I like them."

He sent her a puzzled look. "My reading glasses? You want me to wear them . . . now?"

She bit her lip as she grinned. "They're sexy."

"Reading glasses?" He shook his head as he chuckled, but he kept them on. "What else is sexy?"

"You. Naked." She grabbed the hem of his shirt and pulled upward, but then her phone rang and buzzed.

It was the cute little song that played every time she got a call from her mom's cell phone. She'd chosen it because she'd thought Jade would like it.

Khải reached for her purse, which she'd left on his side of the couch, and thoughts fired through her mind faster than lightning: He knew where she kept her phone. He was going to get it for her. He was going to see the picture of Esme and Jade on the screen. He was going to *know*.

She dove for her bag, but instead of intercepting him, she toppled off the couch and almost cracked her head on the coffee table.

"Are you okay?" Strong hands pulled her upright and smoothed over her head just to make sure.

Her phone continued ringing. "I'm fine. I just—the caller—maybe it's Phil Jackson." She winced. It wasn't Phil Jackson.

Khải picked up her bag, and when he started to unzip the outer pocket where she kept her phone, she snatched it out of his hands.

"I'll get it," she said in an overly bright voice, but when she finally retrieved the phone, it had stopped ringing.

Guilt niggled at her belly. Judging by the number of rings, it had probably been Jade.

"Are you going to call back?" Khải asked, looking at her phone curiously.

She bit her lip. "Um, maybe later. I—"

The phone starting ringing again. Same ringtone. Her mouth went dry, and sweat beaded upon her brow. She clutched the phone to her chest.

She should tell him. Right now. Things were going well. Maybe he'd take the news in stride.

"It's my mom," she heard herself say through the pounding of her heart.

"You should answer. I don't mind."

But did he?

What if it was too soon? What if she ruined everything?

"I'll talk in the other room, so you can work," she said, losing all courage at the last second. She ran to her room, shut the door, and hurried to answer the phone. "Hello?"

"*Má.*" Jade's unmistakable child's voice came across the line, and Esme's guilt worsened. What kind of mother kept her child a secret? She wasn't ashamed of her girl, but having a child when she was so young didn't look good. She already had so many drawbacks. How could she add another?

"Hi, my girl."

"I called you because I miss you," Jade said.

Esme's throat ached, and her eyes pricked. "I miss you, too."

"That's all I wanted to say. Ngoại said not to waste the phone minutes. Oh, and if they have horse toys there, you can get me one if you want. I love you too much. Bye."

After the call disconnected, a sound that was half laugh and half sob coughed from her lips, and she buried her face in her hands. She had to tell Khải.

Soon.

But not yet.

On Monday, Esme was sitting in a booth after the lunch rush deliberating between two toy stores on her phone—one was a forty-five-minute walk away and the other was a half-hour walk away followed by a half-hour bus ride—when Cô Nga marched in from the kitchens.

"Here, what are you doing all by yourself?" Cô Nga asked.

Esme scrambled to turn her phone off and hid it under her thigh for good measure before covering up with a smile. "Lunch." She wished she'd told Cô Nga about Jade in the very beginning.

Cô Nga eyed the plate of eggrolls on the table. "Eggrolls again? Five days in a row already. You're going to clog your heart to death."

Esme shrugged uncomfortably. Heart clogging was the whole point, though she hoped it didn't kill her. If she could manage high cholesterol and chest pain, she might be able to meet Phil Jackson as a patient. That was far better than calling him and hanging up when the call went to voice mail.

"Well, you're still young. You should eat all the bad stuff while you can," Cô Nga said as she slid into the seat on the opposite side of the table. "Talk to me. How are you two? You seem happy to me."

A smile spread helplessly across Esme's lips. "I've never been this happy in my life. I hope I make Anh Khải—"

The bells jangled on the door, and Khải stepped inside, looking like he was about to rob the place in all his stealthy black clothes. Her heart jumped with giddiness, and she ran to him. He closed his arms around her immediately.

"Why are you here?" she asked. "Are you hungry? Thirsty? I can get you something."

His response was a kiss that made her blood go warm and thick. "We had an off-site meeting today, and it finished early. I don't need anything."

"You come to see your woman, but not your mother. I see how it is," Cô Nga said.

There was a bite to her voice, and both Esme and Khải shriveled inward. It was true. Khải disliked visiting his mom because she always sent him on errands. He'd come just for Esme.

Knowing not to surprise-touch him, she grabbed his sleeve and ran her fingers down to his palm, and he held her hand tight.

His mom sighed. "These two kids. Here, here, come sit." She waved them toward the booth, and after they sat down, she pointed at Esme's plate of eggrolls. "She's been eating these all week. Do you have something to tell me?"

Khải considered the eggrolls, accompanying greens, and small cup of fish sauce with a blank stare. "She likes your eggrolls? They're the best in town."

"They're the best in all of California," Cô Nga corrected before she switched her attention to Esme. "This is how women eat when they're pregnant. Do I have a grandbaby on the way?"

Esme's jaw dropped as both mother and son turned to face her. Khải looked like he was about to have the heart attack Esme had been aiming for. "No, I'm not pregnant, I swear."

"Are you sure?" Cô Nga asked with narrowed eyes. "You're tired all the time."

"I'm sure," she said. She was tired because she stayed up all night studying. And fooling around with Khải.

Khải released a relieved breath, but an uncomfortable brew of emotions swarmed in Esme's belly. She wasn't pregnant, but there *was* a baby.

Tell them now, a voice commanded inside her head. Now was the perfect time.

"I don't mean to pressure you, but the summer is almost over," Cô Nga said as she focused on Khải and patiently folded her hands on the table. "It's time for you two to start thinking about the future."

Esme's heart lurched about her chest as she watched the muscles in Khải's jaw work.

What was he thinking? He couldn't want her to leave. Not after this perfect month together. But did he want her badly enough to marry her?

"I still have that reception room reserved for August eighth. If she doesn't marry you, she leaves on August ninth. What will it be? A wedding or a trip to the airport? Tell me your decision at your cousin Michael's wedding this weekend, so I have time to arrange things," Cô Nga said. "I'll let you two kids talk, ha? Maybe go for a walk. It's nice out, and there aren't any customers right now." His mom slid out of the booth and disappeared through the swaying double doors that led to the kitchens.

Before he could say anything, Esme got to her feet, untied the dark green apron from her waist, and picked up her phone. "I want to go outside." Mostly, she wanted to delay this conversation. She was terrified of what he'd say.

Khải followed her out of the dark restaurant and into the sun, and she held her phone to her chest as she walked blindly down the sidewalk that bordered the busy street. The air smelled of exhaust and concrete, almost like home. Was she going back soon?

She hated this. She didn't want her life—and her child's—to depend so much on someone else's choices. For the thousandth time since she'd come here, she wished she really was Esme in Accounting, that classy woman who didn't need anyone and had nothing to fear.

"Why are you walking so fast?" he asked.

She slowed down and sent him an apologetic look. "Sorry, Anh."

He shoved his hands in his pockets as he walked, eyes on the passing traffic. "We're supposed to be talking about the future."

"We don't have to." She wasn't ready for this conversation. She tightened her grip on her phone, but that didn't stop her hands from shaking.

After a second, she realized it was her phone. Someone was calling her. She glanced down at the screen.

Doctor Dad.

Panic shocked through her, making her palms prick and her face go cold. "My dad." She held her phone out to Khải.

He shook his head and widened his eyes. "Why are you giving it to me? Answer it. Hurry, before he hangs up."

She reached a finger toward the answer button, but she couldn't bring herself to hit it. "What if he's mad at me for calling too much? What if he thinks I'm a scammer? He'll say all I want is a green card and his money. It's true, I want a different life, but I also—"

Khải snatched the phone from her and hit the button himself, followed by the speaker button. Then he held the phone out for her to talk.

She covered her mouth. She couldn't speak. She couldn't even move. Sky and earth, what did she do now? Could she hang up? She wanted to hang up.

"Hello?" a voice said, deep, kind, nice. *Her dad.* "I've missed a few calls from this number. Is this about the package I keep missing delivery of? I'd really like to get my hands on it. The name's Phil Jackson."

Khải looked from her to the phone and back again, quietly telling her to talk.

"Hello?" her dad asked again. "Is this the courier service?"

Somehow, she found her voice and said in her best English, "H-hi. I am not the courier service."

"Oh, okay. So . . . why do you keep calling me?"

"I, um, I think . . ." She gulped down a deep breath of air. "My name is Esmeralda, and I think you are my dad."

There was a long pause before he said, "Wow. Let me sit down." Another long pause. She imagined him walking across his office in the hospital and sitting at his desk. "Okay. Tell me everything. Start at the beginning, with your mom."

"Trần Thúy Linh. You met her twenty-four years ago during a business trip, but you left before—"

"Wait, wait, hold on a second. Where was this business trip?"

An uneasy feeling shivered through her. "Việt Nam."

He cleared his throat. "I feel bad saying this, but I've never been there. I think . . ." He cleared his throat again. "You have the wrong person."

Her heart fell. Her stomach fell. Everything fell, and her hopes shattered on the concrete sidewalk. "Oh."

"I'm sure you're absolutely lovely, and now that I'm somewhat over the shock, I would love to have another daughter. But I'm not your dad. I'm so sorry—what was your name again?"

"Esmeralda," she replied.

"I'm so sorry, Esmeralda," he said, sounding like he was giving one patient in a long line of patients bad news. "Can I help in any way?"

"No, thank— Wait, yes. He went to Cal Berkeley. Like you. Do you know a Phil who went to Việt Nam twenty-four years ago?"

"Oh, gosh." The man—Phil—released a long breath. "I . . . *maybe*? But his name isn't Phil, it's *Gleaves*. So, no. I'm so sorry, Evange—Esmer—Esmeralda."

"Thank you . . . Phil. For your time," she said.

"No problem. Good luck. Good-bye."

The line went dead, and she stood there, watching as the cars zipped past and the traffic lights changed colors. Green, yellow, red, back to green.

Khải wrapped her in a tight hug, and she broke apart. She smothered her face against his chest, drenching his shirt with her tears, but he didn't complain. He continued holding her for what felt like ages.

When she finally calmed down and pulled away, he brushed the wet hairs from her face. He didn't have to say a single thing. She saw everything in his achingly sad eyes, and it comforted her more than words could have.

"I thought he was the one." Her voice came out much smaller than she'd hoped.

"Why?"

"I had a feeling." She placed her hand over her gut.

"Feelings can be very inaccurate. To get all the facts, I'd recommend going over the list again and calling each of them," he said. "I can help if you want."

With how much he hated phone calls, that seemed an enormous thing to offer, and she kissed him as her heart overflowed. "I'll call them. Thank you." A car turned into the parking lot and pulled into the spot right next to Khải's Porsche—a customer. "I should go back. We can talk about that other thing . . . later."

He nodded. "Okay."

They walked back to the restaurant hand in hand, and after a quick hug and kiss, she escaped inside. *Later* would come all too soon, but she was glad it wasn't now.

Khai walked back to his car and got inside, but he didn't start the engine. He couldn't stop thinking about what she'd said.

He'll say all I want is a green card and his money. It is true, I want a different life, but . . .

It was shocking he hadn't seen it earlier. *That* was her primary objective for this entire trip: a different life. Not a romantic relationship. It made perfect sense to him. If he were in her shoes, he would have done the same thing, except he wouldn't have focused so much effort on one marriage candidate—him. He would have done much more dating to increase his chances of success. Why hadn't she? Because she thought she'd find her dad and gain citizenship that way?

That *was* the best option. If she found her dad, she would automatically be granted citizenship, and she wouldn't need to marry anyone to do it. The process would probably be expedited then, too. But if she couldn't find her dad . . .

He fished his phone out and Googled "United States citizenship through marriage." According to the search results, the government granted green cards three years after marriage to an American citizen.

Khai was an American.

If that was all she needed—and it did look that way—he could marry her. He could have this beyond the summer. His head spun as he envisioned it. Him and her, together, sex and TV and sharing a bed and her smiles and laughter, without end.

No, that didn't seem right. That would be taking advantage of her. A green card wasn't worth a life sentence, but three years were required.

Three years with Esme.

The force of his wanting grew so intense his skin flashed hot. Compared to the three measly weeks he'd thought he had left, three years was a luxurious amount of time. He could give his Esme addiction *three entire years* of free rein, and then set her free to find love. Win-win.

But only if she didn't find her dad. With his mom wanting an answer by this Saturday, however, Esme was running out of time.

That decided it. If Esme didn't locate her dad this week, Khai was proposing.

CHAPTER TWENTY-ONE

Early Saturday evening, Esme was pulling her black dress over her head when her phone buzzed with an incoming call. She yanked the dress all the way down and leapt to pick up her phone.

Unknown caller.

She hit the talk button. "Hello?"

"Uh, hi, this is Phil Turner. I got your message?" a man said. "What is this about?"

She took a deep breath so her nerves had time to settle and repeated lines that had become familiar over the past week as she'd gone through her list of Phils one by one. "Hi, my name is Esmeralda. Have you been to Việt Nam?"

"Yeah, sure I have. If this is a free vacation or something, I'm not—"

"I am looking for someone who was there twenty-four years ago," she said.

"Oh. Yeah . . ." There was a long, drawn-out whistling sound like he was searching his memory. "No. My first time was Hanoi in early 2000."

She sighed as disappointment weighed on her. That meant there was only one Phil left, and there was no guarantee he was the One True Phil. If he hadn't been to Việt Nam either, that left her back where she'd begun.

"You are not the right person," she said. "Thank you for calling back."

"Sure, no problem. Good luck. I hope you find him. Bye."

He hung up, and Esme carefully set her phone down on the desk. The last Phil on the list was a Schumacher, or Shoo-mock-er, as Khải pronounced it. She tried the surname on—Esmeralda Schumacher—and frowned. That would take some getting used to, though she liked the meaning, shoemaker. There were a lot of feet in this world.

That reminded her she needed to wear torture heels all night again. She stepped into the offending shoes, picked up a handful of cheap jewelry, and gazed at herself in the floor-length mirror inside the bathroom. She held the sparkly necklace up to her throat but decided against it and put it down. Once she'd finished putting on the earrings, a bracelet, and makeup, a new woman stared back at her from the mirror.

She'd gotten it right this time. She looked classy like Khải's sister, and it gave her a much-needed boost of confidence.

Tonight was the night. She was going to tell him about Jade, and if he didn't seem completely overwhelmed, she was going to propose.

Just the thought of it made her hands tremble, and she rushed to the sink in case she vomited. As she was breathing away her nausea, Khải stepped into the bathroom, looking like a secret service body-guard in his black tuxedo.

"I can't stand these things." He twisted the ends of the bow tie around, looped them, and dropped his hands in exasperation.

"I know how." Glad for the distraction, she undid the mess he'd made and calmly tied his bow tie for him. "All done."

"Thank you," he said as he shook out his arms and took a breath like he was preparing himself for battle.

She smiled and smoothed her hands down his lapels, pleased by how he looked in the well-fitted suit. "You're wel— It's not here." She pressed her palms to the area where she thought his inner coat pockets were.

His forehead wrinkled. "What isn't?"

"The book you always bring."

He searched her face. "Are you telling me to bring one?"

"No," she said quickly. "Well, if you want." She shrugged. She'd much rather he talk to her, especially tonight when she was so nervous, but if he truly hated weddings that much, she didn't want to torture him.

He smiled. "Come on, then. It's an hour to Santa Cruz, and I don't want to be late."

She followed him out of the house and down the driveway to the curb, where he parked his car. Instead of getting in right away, Khải scowled at the white splats decorating the roof and windshield.

"This is statistically unlikely. It's not like I park under a tree," he said.

Esme's lips wanted to smirk, and she kept them straight with effort. "The birds are telling you to park in the garage. There's room in there. Just move the motorcycle to the side."

Then she bit the inside of her lip. Things had gotten so easy between them she'd forgotten this was a sore topic. Her stomach tensed as she watched him, not knowing how he'd react. Would he get angry like the day she'd gone to 99 Ranch?

After a brief pause, he said, "I don't like parking in the garage."

"Why?"

He blinked, and his face creased in thought. "Why?"

"What is the reason?" she asked, because it didn't make any sense to her.

"Because the motorcycle's in there," he said in a clipped voice before he went to open the passenger door for her.

Esme got into the car and watched as he shut her door, walked around to the other side, and lowered himself into his seat. He started the car and pulled onto the street like the conversation was finished. But it wasn't.

"If you don't like the motorcycle, why do you—"

"I didn't say I don't like it," he said.

She exhaled a tight breath, even more confused now. "Then why—"

He glanced at her for a quick second before he returned his attention to the road, shifted gears, and sped past a convertible. "That's just how I like things. It's like you and . . . Why *do* you roll socks that way?"

She looked down and spun the sparkly bracelet on her wrist. "You kept ignoring me. I did it to make you think of me."

"So you don't roll yours that way?"

"No," she said with a laugh.

He tilted his head to the side. "It worked."

She grinned. "I know."

Even though he didn't turn to look at her, his lips curved as he continued driving, and a comfortable silence followed. She watched the office buildings as they passed by, awed by their shiny exteriors and manicured lawns.

"That one is mine." Khải pointed at a building that had blue glass walls and large white letters on the top that read *DMSoft*.

She sat up straighter in her seat and inspected it with interest. "Which floor has your office?"

"The top. I share it with others."

"Like a boss," she said with a teasing smile, imagining him crammed in a tiny closet while the important people had all the windows.

He aimed a funny smile at her. "Something like that."

"Lots of the Phils are bosses. One thought I was his employee," she said for lack of anything better to say.

An unusual stillness settled over Khải before he asked, "Did you hear back from the last two?"

"One of them."

"It was a no?"

She pressed her lips together and nodded. "Do I look like a Schumacher?"

He considered her pensively before focusing on the road again. "Possibly."

"Maybe these are good for shoemaking," she said, holding her hands out and grimacing at them. "So ugly."

"What do you mean?"

She flashed an uncomfortable smile at him and crossed her arms to hide her hands, but he held his palm out.

"Let me see," he said.

"You're driving."

He pulled on her arm until she relented. Instead of inspecting her hand, however, he brought her fist to his mouth and kissed her knuckles. "I don't care what these hands do as long as they're yours."

It was silly—he was no poet—but his words made her eyes sting with tears. When he put his hand back on the gearshift, she rested hers on top of his. It wasn't a pretty hand by any means, but it *was* small compared to his. Did people think they made a good-looking couple?

She relaxed against her seat and watched him on and off for the rest of the drive, recognizing the emotion bursting in her heart. It had been creeping up on her, growing bigger every day, and there was no denying it now. When you felt this way about someone, you didn't keep secrets from them. No matter how scared she was, she was telling him everything tonight.

Attending a wedding in a tuxedo and bare feet was a first for Khai. He couldn't shake the feeling he was missing something—his shoes—but Esme appeared charmed. She dug her toes into the sand like a kid as they walked hand in hand across the beach toward the white folding chairs and wedding altar arranged before the water. She wore that same shapeless black dress again, but she was still so pretty she scrambled his brain. It was her smile. She was happy. All was right in the world.

"Only twenty people?" she asked.

There was a brief pause as he shifted his focus from her loveliness to her words. "Yeah, they wanted it small. Stella doesn't like crowds." Just like him. "Do you like big weddings?" He'd give Esme an enormous wedding if she wanted, but something like this was more his style. With less sand.

"Small or big, anything is good." Esme lifted her shoulders in an indifferent way, but then her eyes sparkled as she said, "The flowers, dress, and cake are the fun part."

He nodded and immediately committed those items to memory. If she agreed to marry him, they'd go to town on flowers, dresses, and cake. Flowers by the truckload. Couture wedding gown. Ten cakes, a hundred, for all he cared. As long as she said yes. Dammit, his stomach was all knotted up.

"They don't need to be like this," she added with a smile. "These look expensive." She pointed to the giant bouquets of white roses, orchids, and lilies decorating the outskirts of the seating area. "Your cousin spent a lot of money on these."

He scanned the flowers and things. "I guess so."

"I can arrange flowers myself. I know how." But then she bit her lip and brushed the long hair away from her face. "I can make my dress, too. I don't know how to make cake, but I can learn." Her green eyes met his, looking vulnerable. "I can make everything nice—but not expensive."

He didn't know what to say to that. She didn't have to make everything herself unless she wanted to. He didn't care if the wedding was expensive. It wasn't like he planned to get married over and over. Just once was enough. He would never want anyone other than Esme. His addiction was very specific.

"Here, here, Precious Girl and my son," his mom said, coming toward them in a black *aó dài* with bright blue flowers along the front. Without the added height of shoes, the white silk pants accompanying her dress dragged in the sand, and she yanked at them impatiently. "I never thought I'd go to a wedding without shoes. It's a different experience. Do you two have news for me?"

Esme's hand tightened on his, and she glanced at him for a second before she averted her eyes. "Not yet, Cô Nga. We still need to talk."

"I was thinking after dinner would be a good time," he told Esme. Esme nodded and flashed a small smile at him. "That sounds good."

His mom considered their joined hands thoughtfully. "Do what you need, but before you leave the wedding, you two need to talk to me."

"We will, Cô Nga," Esme said.

His mom nodded, appeased. "Enjoy the wedding, ha?" With that she went to chat with his sister, aunts, and cousins.

Khai and Esme were wandering toward the seats when Michael

appeared, clasped Khai's hand, and gave him a one-armed hug. He looked like he'd walked off a runway in his three-piece tux, even without shoes on.

"So glad you made it," Michael said. He smiled, but his motions were abrupt and jumpy, his breathing tight. He had to be nervous. Like Khai was. Except Michael's woman had already said yes. What was there for him to be nervous about?

"Are you okay?" Khai asked.

"Yeah, I'm great. Did I tell you I'm glad you made it? Because I am. Stella really likes you." Michael's gaze landed on Esme, and his lips curved into a crooked grin. "You must be Esme. Happy to finally meet you." He shook Esme's hand, and she grinned back with a dazed expression.

Great, she was falling under Michael's spell even though he was getting married within the hour. Damn Michael and his cursed good looks.

"Happy to meet *you*. Stella is a lucky woman," Esme said, beaming her fantastic Esmeness at him and speaking English to everyone but Khai.

Michael tried to smile but it turned into a gulp for air as he shook out his hands and squared his shoulders. "Thanks for saying that. I've never been this nervous. I'm so lost over her if she doesn't show up, I'm going to . . ." His words trailed off as he focused on a group of silhouettes in the distance, and his face went lovesick. He squeezed Khai's shoulder without looking at him. "You guys have a seat. It's starting."

Everyone hurried to sit, and the talking settled down. Esme practically vibrated with excitement. "Is Stella really pretty? Your cousin is so . . ." A dreamy look took over her face, and Khai was certain she'd say *handsome*. What she said instead was worse. "He's so *in love*."

Love. Khai's guts tied themselves in a big knot, and he forcibly reminded himself he was doing the right thing. She wanted a green card. He could get her one. This marriage would benefit both of them—for three years.

A guitar started playing a cover of a pop song, and Khai watched the ceremony with careful attention. If all went well, he'd be doing this soon. The wedding party walked down the aisle in pairs comprised of Michael's sisters, Quan, and a bunch of Michael's friends. Stella appeared in a gauzy white gown, which Michael had to have designed. When her dad gave her a teary smile, she smiled back and kissed his temple before taking his arm and heading toward the altar, where Michael waited, watching her with that lovesick look from before multiplied by a thousand. His eyes were even reddened like he was on the verge of tears. As Stella crossed the sand, her gaze never wavered from him. Whatever Michael felt for her, she reciprocated fully.

Girl loves boy loves girl.

As the two lovers exchanged vows and kissed, the sun dove into the horizon, and the sky blazed over the ocean. It was a magical moment. The camera flashed numerous times, a dozen cell phones glowed, no babies cried. The people in their small crowd wiped at their tears, Esme included, and Khai felt like an impostor at life.

Until Esme squeezed his hand to get his attention, pressed a surprise kiss to his lips, and then smiled at him. If they weren't in public, he would have yanked her close and kissed her until she melted. He knew how to do that now. As it was, he simply devoured her with his eyes, wanting her with the full force of his out-of-control addiction, but judging from the way her pupils dilated, she didn't mind.

He was leaning toward her to kiss her despite everything when everyone stood up to watch as Michael and Stella strode past. Staff from the nearby hotel guided them to a garden for a relaxed cocktail hour. He and Esme shared a Sex on the Beach while everyone ate

hors d'oeuvres and chitchatted. She had absolutely no alcohol tolerance, and after only a few sips she was leaning into him and giving
him the look that experience had taught him meant *take me to bed
and have your way with me*. That look was one of the best things in
the whole fucking world.

He was determined to have it for the next three years.

After cocktails, their party went to an outdoor seating area beneath a tent composed of wooden beams, white semitransparent
fabric, and golden Christmas lights. As the Asian fusion dinner and
speeches carried on, he rehearsed his proposal in his head. The logic
was sound and sure to appeal to her. She was going to say yes. It
wouldn't make sense not to.

When everyone was finishing their cake and mint chocolate chip
ice cream, Khai grabbed Esme's hand. "Walk with me?"

She ate one last bite of cake, pulled the tines of the fork from between her luscious lips, and set the utensil on her plate. "Okay."

They left the tent and strolled along the beach at a comfortable
pace, their hands clasped tight and their feet sinking into the sand.
The moon was nearly full and cast a silvery light upon the water, and
the air smelled of salt and sea and kelp. Once they were a suitable
distance away, he slowed to a stop.

It was time. Fuck, he was quaking inside. He'd never asked a girl
out. He'd never wanted to. And now he was proposing.

"Do you hear it?" Esme asked.

"What?"

"The music."

He perked his ears, and then he heard it. Soft guitar strains
flowed on the breeze, coming from the tent. He recognized it as De-
bussy's "Clair de Lune." "They're dancing."

She smiled, looped her arms around his neck, and started to sway
back and forth. "We are, too."

"You are. I don't know how."

"You just move like this," she said with a laugh.

He felt distinctly absurd, but he followed along and moved with her. And then somehow he stopped feeling absurd. It was just the two of them here, just the moon, just the ocean and the sand and music and two hearts beating.

And she was smiling.

He crushed his lips to that smile, stealing it, and when his tongue swept into her mouth, the tastes of fruit, vanilla, and champagne made his head spin. He'd never have cake again and not think of her, never drink champagne and not think of her. Every success of his life would taste like Esme. He couldn't help running his hands over her body, trying to find a way to all his favorite places, but this sack of a dress made it almost impossible.

When he made a frustrated sound, she laughed, kissed him one last time, and pulled away, wiping at the lipstick on his mouth. "We need to talk."

"You're right." He took a deep breath to clear the lust from his mind and gathered her hands in his. The sooner he proposed, the sooner he'd be done, and the closer he'd be to marrying her.

"Esme—"

"Anh Khải—"

He hesitated, surprised by the trembling of her hands. Unlike him, she really did shake when she was nervous, and he brushed his thumbs over her knuckles, hoping to soothe her. "You can go first if you want."

With a lift of her chin, she said, "Okay, me first."

She licked her lips and adjusted her hands so she could hold him as he held her. Several times, she started to speak but stopped before any words came out.

"Do you want me to go first, then?" he asked.

"No, I can." She sucked in another breath and chewed on her bottom lip before she said, "When I first came here, I had reasons to marry you. Lots of reasons. And I got close to you for those reasons. But then . . ." Her eyes met his. "Then I got to know you." Her fingers tightened around his. "And I got close because I *wanted* to be close. A lot of times, I forget my reasons. Because I'm happy. With you. *You* make me happy."

Khai's chest filled, and his heart raced, and he couldn't help smiling. There were an infinite number of reasons to exist on this earth, but that seemed the most important of them all—making Esme happy.

"I'm glad," he said.

"Maybe it's too fast, maybe it's not smart, but . . ." She smiled slowly, her eyes soft and liquid in the moonlight, and said in clear English, "I love you."

His lungs stopped breathing. His heart stopped beating.

Esme loved him.

Warmth bubbled over him in overwhelming waves. What had he done that she loved him? He'd do it a million more times. He brought her hands to his mouth and breathed a kiss to her knuckles. He couldn't speak, had no clue what to say.

Looking beautiful beyond compare with the moon and the stars and the water behind her, a teasing smile curved over her mouth, and she asked, "Do you love me? Maybe just a little?"

He went cold.

Not that question. Why had she asked *that* question?

He could give her every *thing* she wanted, a green card, real diamonds, his body, but love?

Stone hearts didn't love.

He didn't want to answer the question. All of him rebelled against it.

But he made himself admit the truth. "I don't."

She blinked and shook her head before she smiled again. "You love me *more* than a little."

"No, Esme." He stepped back and let go of her. "I'm sorry . . . but I don't love you a lot or a little. I don't love you at all."

I can't.

Her face went slack, her eyes wide, watery. "Not at all?" she whispered.

"I don't love you." His entire being hurt like it was imploding. "I never will."

"This isn't funny," she said.

"I'm not joking. I'm completely serious."

She didn't say a single word. She just stared at him as fat tears spilled down her face. He wanted to take his words back. He wanted to erase her sadness. He'd do almost anything to make her smile again.

But he couldn't lie about this. She's asked him the question, and she deserved to know the answer.

I don't love you. I never will.

Esme's heart broke apart, and the jagged pieces stabbed at her from the inside. At the same time, shame doused her; heavy, suffocating shame. She knew why he couldn't love her. She could go to school, change her clothes, and change her speech, but she could never change where she'd come from. The bottom of the bottom. So poor she couldn't afford to finish high school, so different even other poor people looked down on her, so low she couldn't climb free, not in Việt Nam. With all he'd done for her, she'd thought he saw beyond the things she couldn't change and valued her for who she was inside. But he didn't. According to his words, he never would.

Backing away from him, she said, "I'm sorry to bother you. I'll go."

He shook his head, his expression focused yet unreadable. "You don't bother me."

A laugh bordering on hysterical escaped her lips. "I don't understand." She turned to run, but he stopped her with a firm grip on her arm.

"We're not done yet."

She dragged in a breath and braced herself for the worst, almost afraid to look at him for fear of what he'd say.

"We should get married."

Her body sagged in confusion. "What?"

"I wouldn't mind you staying with me long enough to get your naturalization papers. After that, we could have a quick divorce. That would work out for both of us, I think," he said with a tight wrinkle of his lips. Maybe he meant it to be a smile.

She shook her head. She'd heard his words, but they didn't make any sense. "Why marry me if you don't love me?"

"I've gotten used to you being in my house and in my bed and—"

At the mention of his bed, fierce heat flooded her face, and she ducked her head. *The sex.* He wanted more sex. Of course he did. He'd been a virgin before this, and they were really good together. But she couldn't do it when it was making love for her and just sex for him.

"No." She brushed his hand off her arm and stepped back. "I can't marry you."

His forehead creased as he frowned. "I don't understand why."

"Because it will hurt too much." Because she loved him. If it was just a cold arrangement between strangers, maybe she could have done it. This marriage could do so much for Jade. But not if it destroyed her mother first.

Khải was not the solution. She had to keep looking and find another way.

He looked down at the ground. "I'm sorry."

Fresh hot tears cascaded down her face. She was sorry, too.

"Esme, don't cry. I—"

Without a word, she turned and stumbled across the sand back toward the wedding reception. She had to get away from here, and in order to do that, she needed her phone and money. She barged into the romantic tent and held her arms close to her body as she rushed past the couples slowly swaying in the sandy dance area, feeling like a trespasser.

There her purse was, slung over the corner of her chair. She looped the knockoff over her shoulder and tried her best to avoid eye contact with anyone.

"Are you okay, Esme?" Vy asked. She paused in the middle of mixing sugar into a cup of tea. Her hair was perfect, her makeup perfect, her black dress perfect, because she'd been born into this.

Esme forced a bright smile and nodded. Khải entered the far side of the tent, scanning the crowd with a frown like he was looking for something. His gaze locked on her. She couldn't hear what he said, but she knew it was her name.

He walked in her direction, and panic shot through her. She had to get away. All these people thought she'd reached above herself by chasing Khải. She didn't want to be there when they learned Khải agreed with them.

She raced away from the table. And smacked into something firm. Looking up, she saw Quân's face.

"Hey, going somewhere in a hurry?" he asked with his characteristic good cheer.

"Sorry, I—" She glanced over her shoulder and found Khải

striding toward her with a determined gait. *No.* "Please, let me go. *Please?*"

"What's going on? Are you two fighting?" Quân asked.

Her vision went blurry as she shook her head. "Not fighting." Khải was coming closer. She sidestepped Quân and hurried off. As she slipped outside, she saw Quân stop Khải, talking to him with a concerned look on his face.

She sprinted over a long stretch of sand, feeling the coarse grains rub her feet raw, and eventually found pavement. She didn't know where she was going, but it was away and that was good enough for now.

Her phone rang and rang, but she ignored it and kept running blindly, from him and from this horrible shame. When she couldn't stand the ringing anymore, she stopped, dug her phone out of her purse, and turned it off.

As she stood there, lungs burning, mouth dry, feet possibly bleeding, she realized she had no idea where she was. Somehow, she'd ended up on a quiet street lined with little beach homes and tall palm trees.

There was no Khải, no Cô Nga, no Mom, no Grandma, no Jade, no one. Just Esme.

And she had nowhere to go. There was a great big world all around, and none of it was hers.

Where did you go when you had nowhere?

K hai wandered around the beach for what felt like hours, but he couldn't find Esme. She'd vanished into the night.

He tried calling her again, but it went straight to voice mail.

The worst feeling crept over his skin. The air was cool, but he couldn't stop sweating. He yanked his bow tie loose, clawed at his hair, and tore his coat off. He almost chucked it into the surf, but he remembered the velvet box inside his coat pocket. That belonged to Esme. Well, it would once he had the opportunity to give it to her.

How could she just leave like this?

Quan jogged toward him from the opposite end of the beach. "I couldn't find her down there. Did you see her anywhere?"

What a frustrating question. If he'd seen her, he wouldn't be standing here alone. "No."

Quan scrubbed at his buzzed head. "What the fuck happened between you two? Why'd she run?"

Khai kicked at the sand. "I suggested we get married."

Even in the darkness, Khai could see his brother's eyes widen. "Wow, okay. I'm surprised she wasn't happy about that. I thought she was really into you."

Khai's grip on his bunched-up tux coat tightened so much the fabric squeaked. "She is. Well, she *was*. She told me she's in love with me tonight." He still hardly believed it.

Quan gave him a weighted look. "And?"

Khai ignored the question and started walking toward the street. Maybe she was sitting on a bench over there, waiting for him. Maybe she'd gotten over her momentary anger, thought things over, and wanted to change her answer.

"And what, Khai?" Quan insisted, falling in step beside him.

He tucked his jacket under his arm and stuffed his hands in his pockets. "I told her the truth."

"Which is . . . ?"

He walked faster, leaving the sand for the pavement, and stared at the late evening Santa Cruz street. There was a bench next to a lonely streetlight, but it was empty. He peered at the parking lot where his car was. No signs of life.

She was nowhere to be seen.

Quan grabbed his arm with a firm hold. "Khai, what did you tell her? Why was she crying?"

He tried to swallow. It didn't work the first try, or the second, but he remembered how on the third attempt. "I told her I don't love her back."

"That's bullshit," Quan exploded. "What the fuck?"

"I said it because it's true," he said.

"You're crazy in love with her. Just look at you," Quan said, waving his hands at Khai like it was obvious.

"I. Am. Not," Khai bit out.

"The fuck you're not. You're an all-or-nothing guy, so we knew the first girl to catch your attention would be the one. Esme is your 'one,' Khai."

"I don't *have* a 'one.' I don't do relationships." He walked down the sidewalk a block, looking all around. Where was she?

Shit, was she safe? This didn't look like a shady area, but that wasn't any kind of guarantee. Adrenaline spiked, and his heart crashed against his ribs as he dug his phone out and tried her number again.

Straight to voice mail again.

Dammit.

"Why won't she pick up?" he muttered, more to himself than anyone.

Quan answered anyway. "She doesn't want to talk to you. You don't tell a girl you don't love her and then ask her to marry you. I don't know what you were thinking."

Khai crammed his phone back in his pocket impatiently. "She needs a green card. I can give her one. It's that simple. I even told her I'd be willing to give her a divorce as soon as everything was official. She should have been happy. She shouldn't have said no and run."

Instead of speaking right away, Quan exhaled and rubbed a hand over his face as he shook his head. *"Shiiiiit."*

At least they were in agreement about something. This situation was exactly shit.

"Why are you willing to do all that for her if you're not into relationships?" Quan asked with narrowed eyes.

Khai looked away from his brother and shrugged. "I'm used to her, and it's okay living together. Why not?"

Quan threw his hands up in the air. "Great reasons for marriage. I'm gonna go back to the wedding. If you hear from her, let me know."

As Quan stomped back to the wedding tent, Khai returned to his car and got inside. Her high heels lay on the passenger side at uneven angles, and he searched the interior of the car in excitement. Until he remembered she'd left them here before going in.

He drove around aimlessly, searching the streets, sidewalks, benches, and shop fronts for a woman in a loose black dress and no shoes. He didn't see her anywhere.

When he stopped in front of the same traffic light for the fourth time, he acknowledged it was time to give up. She had her phone and purse and knew how to take care of herself. If she didn't want to be found, there was no point in looking. Even so, he'd stay close just in case.

He pulled his car into a random parking spot by the beach, cranked the brake, and turned off the engine. Then he sat and waited, drumming his fingers on the steering wheel as he stared up at the darkened sky.

CHAPTER TWENTY-TWO

Bright light pooled on top of Esme's eyelids, and she winced and rubbed at her face, scattering little bottles from the minibar onto the floor. The TV was still on, and the hotel room's ceiling wouldn't stop spinning.

Or maybe she was the one spinning.

She pushed herself up, and bile surged up her throat as the room tilted. *Oh no.* She panic-ran to the bathroom, and her knees hit the cold tile just as she threw up in the toilet.

Over and over, until it felt like her eyes were exploding. When it finally stopped, she rinsed out her mouth and gazed blearily at her face in the mirror. She'd vomited so hard she'd left little red dots on her upper cheeks and around her eyes. On top of that, her hair was a tangled mess, she still wore the black dress from yesterday, and she smelled horrible. If her mom and grandma could see her now, they'd be so disappointed.

They'd tell her to crawl back to Khải's where it was safe, thank him for offering to marry her, and get the marriage certificate signed before he changed his mind. Jade needed him.

But a one-sided love would destroy Esme, not to mention set a horrid example for her daughter to follow. Esme was *not* going back.

She found her phone, located Phil Schumacher's phone number, and called him again. It rang several times before it disconnected without going to voice mail. So she called again. Halfway through the first ring, a recording played. "The person you are trying to reach is unavailable."

What did *that* mean?

She tried again. And again, halfway through the first ring, the message came on, "The person you are trying to reach is unavailable."

He must have blocked her number. He might be her dad, and he'd blocked her. It made her stomach drop and her pride hurt, but she told herself that was fine.

She didn't need him.

She didn't need anyone.

Maybe she was still drunk off minibar drinks, and maybe she was being overly emotional, but as she stood in that cheap motel room alone, truly alone, she swore she was going to do things by herself from here on out. She wasn't good enough for Khải or this mysterious Phil Schumacher, but she was good enough for herself.

She didn't need a man for anything. She only needed her own two hands. As she washed her hair and scrubbed the sand from the wedding off her feet in the plastic shower, a fire raged in her heart. She didn't know how, but she was going to prove her worth. She'd show everyone.

She spent the day setting up a new independent life. She took a bus to Milpitas and searched the area by Cô Nga's restaurant for apartments, found a place that offered monthlong leases and signed the contract, and went shopping for apartment supplies and new clothes. She'd rather walk around naked than ask Khải for her things. He could have them.

That night as she slept in a sleeping bag on the floor of her empty studio apartment, she dreamed Jade's father took her away, and she cried herself awake and huddled against the wall, listening to the creaking of the building and the cars passing by outside. As it always did, her fear gradually changed into guilt. If she'd given Jade to her father and his wife, right now Jade would have a complete family with a mom and a dad, not to mention an expensive house and servants. Because she *hadn't* given Jade up, her girl was stuck in a one-room shack while her mom carried on a separate life across the ocean. Would a better mother have given her baby away? Was it selfish to keep Jade? *Was* love enough?

Fierceness overtook her. Love would have to be enough. It was truly all she had.

When the sky lightened, she gave up on sleep and researched work visas on her phone. There had to be opportunities for someone like her in a place like this. She was very good at withstanding difficulty. But she read website after website, and they all said the same thing: She needed to have a college degree, twelve years of specialized work experience, or some impressive mixture of the two. She had work experience, but something told her toilet cleaning wasn't the kind of specialization they were talking about.

She was still struggling to accept this information when she walked into Cô Nga's restaurant later that morning.

"Oh, Precious Girl has arrived." Cô Nga ran to her and hugged her tight. "You had me so worried. Why did you leave without telling anyone anything, ha? Everyone was worried to death about you."

Slightly in shock, Esme hugged Cô Nga back. "I'm sorry." She hadn't thought anyone would care about her after she turned down Khải's proposal. She stepped away, forced a smile, and held her arms out. "You can see I'm fine."

"Khải looked everywhere for you. He said he called you many times. Why didn't you answer?" Cô Nga asked.

She focused on putting her purse in the regular spot by the cash register and keeping her breathing even. That was the only way to keep herself from falling apart. "I didn't have anything to say to him."

Cô Nga dismissed Esme's words with a wave of her hand. "How are you two going to work things out if you don't talk things over? Tell him what's wrong, and he'll fix it. It's only easy."

Esme's heart thudded, but thankfully, she'd cried enough these past couple of days that her eyes stayed dry now. "There's nothing to fix. We don't fit, Cô."

Her certainty must have been written all over her, because Cô Nga took one look at her, and her face went slack. "Are you sure?"

Esme nodded.

"Where have you been? Is it safe? Do you need money?" Cô Nga asked, patting Esme's cheek and squeezing her arms like she needed to reassure herself Esme was really there.

"I have everything I need, thank you. I'm staying at that place down the street, the one that rents rooms monthly. It's nice," Esme said with a bright smile. Compared to her house back home, it was luxurious. It wasn't hard to be nicer than her house, though.

"You're here."

She whipped around and found Khải standing in the doorway to the restaurant. He wore his regular secret agent uniform of black suit and shirt, but he looked different than usual. He looked tired. But still so beautiful he sent a sharp pang to her chest.

Desperate for a distraction, she grabbed the tray of sugar packets from the shelf and began adding the appropriate number of packets to the little boxes in the booths. "Hi, Khải."

"You didn't answer any of my calls," he said as he strode inside.

"Sorry." She could do this. She was going to maintain her composure. Three white packets of regular sugar. Two brown packets of Sugar in the Raw. Three yellow packets of—

He pulled her into his arms and held her tight. "I was worried about you."

For the longest time, he simply hugged her, and she let him. There were reasons why she shouldn't, but at the moment, she couldn't remember them. He felt so good, smelled so good, and her lonely self drank him in. Something unfamiliar prickled against her cheek, and she brushed her fingers over his face and leaned away to get a better view. What was this?

"You didn't shave—"

He kissed her, and sharp sensation arrowed straight to her heart. As soon as she softened against him, he deepened the kiss, taking her mouth with aching presses of his lips that made her dizzy. It was impossible not to respond when he kissed her like this, like he'd been worried sick about her, like he was passionately in love with her.

His mom coughed noisily. Esme broke the kiss and tried to step back, but Khải's arms tightened around her.

"Where have you been?" he asked.

"I got an apartment close by."

He went motionless. "You're . . . moving out?"

She hesitated for a second before nodding.

"I don't see why you can't stay with me. Like before. We don't have to—" He released a frustrated breath, looked out the front window, and grimaced. "This is not the best neighborhood."

His disdain for the area made her muscles stiffen. "It's fine." The people weren't as rich here, but that didn't mean they were bad. They were a lot like her, to be honest. She pushed against his chest, and he reluctantly let her go.

"It's really not fine. The crime stats in my neighborhood are lower. You should come back."

She shook her head. "I can't."

He raked a hand through his hair and took a half step toward her. "You were fine at my place until recently. Why can't—"

"Do you love me?" she asked softly, giving him a chance to change everything.

He clenched his jaw tight and clasped her hands in his. "I can keep you safe, and I can carry you when you're hurt, and I can . . ." His gaze dropped to her mouth. "I can kiss you like it's the first time *every* time. I can—I can . . ." His expression went determined. "I can work with you on the lawn. I can even get it professionally done. I can fix up the house for you. If you want. Whatever kind of wedding you want, I can—"

"Khải," she said firmly. "Do you love me?"

His eyes fell shut, and the fight leaked out of him. "No, I don't."

She blinked back tears, pulled her hands away from him, and continued packing the sugar boxes. Three pink packets. Three blue packets. She wasn't going to fall apart. She wasn't going to fall apart. "You should go. You will be late for work."

He took a long, uneven breath. "Good-bye, then."

She forced a smile. "Have a nice day."

He leaned forward like he had every intention of kissing her, and for a moment, she was going to let him. She could almost feel the softness of his lips on hers, almost taste him. She turned her face to the side at the last second, and after hesitating briefly, he backed away.

"Bye, Mom." He waved at Cô Nga.

And then he was gone.

Esme's shoulders slumped, and she watched his silver Porsche speed from the parking lot through blurred eyes. Sadness swelled and dragged, and she was vaguely amazed she managed to stay standing. Look how strong she was. She could handle this. He was just another man.

Cô Nga came and sat down in the booth, looking shell-shocked and defeated. "I don't understand when he's like this. He prefers you, I can tell. It's clear as daytime. Why did he say that? I don't know."

Saying nothing, Esme focused on the sugar packets. She stuffed one last packet into the black box, placed it against the wall next to the sriracha, hoisin, and chili sauce, and moved to the next booth. As she picked up the white sugar packets, however, wet droplets splashed onto the paper. She wiped it on her shirt and got out a new packet, but she got that one wet, too.

"Here, here, here." Cô Nga pulled her into a hug. "Here, here, Precious Girl."

Her control snapped, and hard sobs wracked her. She wasn't that strong, after all. "I'm sorry," Esme said. "I'm not your 'precious girl' anymore. I tried. But then I fell in love with him, and I can't be with him when it's like this. I'll break."

Everyone deserved to love and be loved back. *Everyone.* Even her.

Cô Nga rubbed Esme's back like she was shredding carrots. "Here, here, you'll always be my Precious Girl. Always."

Esme hugged her tighter before she swiped a sleeve over her face. "I would have liked to have you as my mother-in-law."

Cô Nga patted her cheek, watching her with sad, wise eyes. Then she got her phone out of her apron and held it as far away as possible as she squinted at the screen, selected a phone number to call, and put it on speaker.

After a series of rings, Quân picked up, asking in a distracted tone, "Hi, Mom, how are you?"

"You need to talk to your brother," she said.

"Does this have anything to do with Esme—Mỹ? Did you ever find her?"

Cô Nga nodded quickly even though Quân couldn't see. "Yeah, yeah, she's here."

"Oh good, that's great. I'll—" Background voices interrupted him, and there were muffled sounds like he'd covered the phone to speak to someone on his end. "Yeah, I have to go. I'll call him tonight."

"Not tonight. Now," Cô Nga insisted. "And if he doesn't answer, you need to go see him."

"I can't. I'm in New York pitching for the next stage of fund—"

Cô Nga spoke over her son. "Come home. This is *important*. He's your only brother and needs your help."

Quân released a slow breath. "Sometimes, he doesn't want my help."

"You have to try. He's your responsibility. Be better than that stinky father of yours."

There was a long silence on the phone before Quân said, "I'll take care of it. I really have to go. Bye, Mom."

The line went dead, and Cô Nga muttered to herself and stuck her phone back in her apron.

Esme grabbed a handful of sugar packets but hesitated before putting them in the box. "I don't know what Anh Quân can do, Cô Nga. He sounds busy." This drama between Esme and Khải didn't seem like it should take priority.

Cô Nga waved Esme's comment away. "You have to be tough with Quân like this. I know, I'm his mom. But he gets things done when I push him. You'll see."

"He seems to do well all by himself. He's a CEO, isn't he? That's an accomplishment." Esme couldn't imagine doing anything like that.

"It sounds good, but it's a small company. Nothing like Khải," Cô Nga said in a dismissive manner.

Again, Esme got the impression they weren't talking about the same Khải. Why did people make it sound like he was mega-successful when he wasn't? She shook her head and got to work. It didn't matter.

She had to mind her own business. There were three weeks left before she had to leave, and the clock was ticking.

In this country of empowered people, justice, and fairness, opportunities were there for everyone. Marriage and birth couldn't be the only ways to belong here. She didn't believe that.

There had to be something she could do to earn her place here, some way to prove herself. She had to keep looking.

Khai sat down in front of his desk in his office, and he honestly didn't remember driving here, walking into the building, or going up the elevator. He'd done it all on autopilot.

He'd been too busy adjusting to the knowledge that Esme was safe and unharmed. The previous day had passed in a white blur. Even though logic had told him she was most likely fine, horrible scenarios had possessed his mind nonstop, and he'd been a wreck, not sleeping, not eating, watching the news in case she showed up on a gurney in an ambulance.

Now that he knew she was okay, he finally relaxed and let himself contemplate the fact that she was not only refusing to marry him, but moving out early, too. Back there in the restaurant, he'd made the best case for staying with him that he could. And she'd turned him down—as she should have.

Just look at him now. He'd thought he'd go through a terrible withdrawal when Esme left him for good, but he was shocking himself with how fine he was. Everything was perfectly, perversely, anticlimactically *fine*. He wasn't sad or mad or depressed. He felt . . . nothing.

As he started his computer and watched the screen come to life, mundane work tasks lined up neatly in his head—emails, projects, important shit. He was like a fucking machine. Back online, ready for production.

When he opened his first email, however, it took him three tries before his cold fingers could type "Hi, Sidd" correctly (that would be Sidd Mathur, the *M* from *DMSoft*), and even then, he wasn't sure he'd spelled "Hi" right. Was it just an *H* and an *i*? That didn't seem like enough letters for such an important concept.

Whatever, he would plow through. People said he was smart. All he had to do was focus. He was good at focusing, too good sometimes. When he finally finished the email, he checked the clock and was floored to see he'd spent two entire hours on one short paragraph of text.

He sighed and lifted a hand toward his forehead to massage it—and accidentally poked himself in the eye. *Shit*. Now that he was paying attention, his head throbbed, his face hurt, and his limbs felt off, like they'd been taken from someone else and glued onto him. He was probably getting sick. It had been a while since the last time, so he was due something awful. Come to think of it, he hadn't had a flu shot in years.

He opened his desk drawer, got out the small bottle of ibuprofen he kept there, popped the lid off, and shook a couple of pills into his palm. At least, that was how he envisioned it in his mind. What really happened was he scattered pills all over himself, his desk, and the floor.

When he went to clean up the mess, pills crunched under his feet and knees and slipped out from between his fingers. By the time he'd gathered the majority of the pills back into their jar and accidentally pulverized the rest, he'd banged his elbow on his chair and hit his head on the desk.

He stepped into the hall, meaning to go to the kitchen for water, and he noticed the office was eerily empty. It was like working on Christmas.

That was when he remembered today they had an off-site company-wide team-building thing. *Fuuuuck.* His partner was going to give him shit for being antisocial again. When his phone started buzzing, he dug it out of his pocket and answered it without checking who it was.

"Yo, it's me. How are you doing?" asked a familiar voice that did *not* belong to his partner.

"Hi, Quan. Everything's . . ." He glanced at the pill bits all over the floor of his office, and look at that, one of his shoelaces had come undone. "Everything's fine. Why are you calling?"

"Mom says I need to fly back from New York to see you because it's an emergency. What's up?"

"There is no emergency."

"How's Esme?" Quan asked in a neutral tone.

"Fine."

Quan kept quiet and waited.

When Khai couldn't take it anymore, he said, "She's not coming back. She found an apartment by the restaurant that she likes better than my place."

"How are you with that?"

"Fine. I'm just . . . fine." And he wished he wasn't. If he could manage some manner of dramatic emotional upheaval and prove he was heartbroken at her loss—and therefore in love—he could keep her.

But nope. He was A-OK.

"Want me to come home early?" Quan asked. "We can do shit. I dunno, go pick up chicks at a tax convention or something."

"No, thanks." He didn't want to do anything that involved women for a long time, and the thought of "picking up chicks" made his headache worse, even though it meant he got to go to a tax convention.

"You sure?"

"Yeah."

"Okay then, but if you need anything, you can call me whenever. If I don't pick up, I'll call you back as soon as I can," Quan said.

"You don't need to tell me this. I already know." Quan was the most dependable thing in Khai's life.

"Just reminding you. Okay, I'm gonna let you go now. Bye, little brother."

"Bye."

As soon as the line went dead, he looked around the vacant office, took a step, and almost ended up facedown on the floor. Sighing, he went down on one knee and grabbed his laces, but he tried multiple times and the things wouldn't tie. What the fuck was wrong with him? He had to be coming down with the flu. Fed up with the entire process, he took his shoes off and carried them with him as he left the building and walked home. No way he was driving or going to a team-building thing like this.

The trek was long and hot and weird with no shoes on, and he was pretty sure people slowed down as they passed him. He didn't feel at all like a Terminator today, not one in good condition, anyway. When he reached his place, he was sweaty, dehydrated, and badly in need of a shower, but after the door swung open, he stood there, unable to enter.

His entire body resisted going inside. His head spun, his heart slammed, and his stomach twisted. The house was too dark, and the musty air made him want to throw up. It didn't make sense. He'd been in there just this morning. But he'd been too focused on possible Esme catastrophes to notice anything else.

He sat down on the concrete steps outside and smeared the sweat away from his clammy face. This flu really sucked. He was *exhausted*. He could sleep and sleep for ages. But he had to shower and air out the house first. That musty heaviness, whatever it was, had to go. Maybe one of Esme's fruits was decaying in the trash and there were mold spores floating everywhere.

Gritting his teeth, he got up, stepped inside, and tossed his shoes to the floor, not caring where they landed. He couldn't breathe. The air was thick and oppressive, all wrong.

Mold spores, mold spores.

He marched to the kitchen and yanked the trash out of the cabinet. Empty. What the hell? He searched the kitchen for other locations where fruit could be moldering away. None.

All surfaces were spotless. The only thing out of place was a half-filled water glass on the counter. Esme's. Warmth pricked over his cold skin in a sick wave. He didn't realize he was reaching for the glass until he saw his hand approaching, and he stopped himself before making contact. Curling his fingers into a fist, he backed away. He didn't want to put her glass in the dishwasher like he always did. He wanted it . . . right there.

This suffocating *air*. He hurried through the house, opening all the windows and doors, but it didn't help. His nausea got so bad he spent a few minutes hunched over the toilet, but he didn't throw up. Bed, he should just go to bed, but not when he was sweaty like this.

Somehow he got through a shower without wounding himself in the process and dressed in an inside-out sweater (to keep the seams off his skin) and workout shorts—he wanted layers, lots of layers, and was looking forward to his heavy blankets. But when it was time to get in bed, his limbs locked, and he couldn't do it.

It was official now. Esme was never going to sleep in this bed again.

No more naked Esme welcoming him close, inside her body, crying his name as she clung to him. No more Esme weight draped over him like a sloth in a tree, warm and soft and perfect. No more Esme smiles at night, in the morning, and every time he looked at her.

He yanked the comforter off the bed and carried it to the living room, where he wrapped the blanket around himself and collapsed onto the couch. Fuck, they'd had sex on this couch. On the green shag carpet, too. Everywhere. And there was another one of her half-filled cups on the coffee table. He couldn't escape her—he didn't even know if he wanted to—and his head felt like it was going to explode.

He covered his face with the blanket. And breathed in her Esme scent. At first, he expected his nausea to worsen, but his muscles relaxed instead. Heaven, sweet heaven. If he shut his eyes, he could almost imagine she was here, wrapping her arms around him, and sleep dragged him to a place where he didn't hurt anymore.

Thank fuck for the blanket. He was never washing it again.

K hai woke at odd intervals throughout the night and the next day: 12:34 A.M., 3:45 A.M., 6:07 A.M., 11:22 A.M., and then 2:09 P.M. That last time bothered him with its lack of logic, and he was scowling at his phone when Quan walked through the unlocked front door in jeans and an old black T-shirt.

Quan took in the shoes scattered on the ground, the opened windows, and Khai's blanket-clad form on the couch and asked,

"What's going on? Did you burn a pizza in the oven or something? Why are you venting the place out?"

Khai sat up, but the blood rushed from his head from the sudden movement, and he slumped against the back of the couch. "The air felt funny."

"You okay?"

He rubbed at his aching temples. "Shouldn't you be in New York pitching for your B-round financing?"

Quan toed his shoes off and crossed the room to press a hand against Khai's forehead. "I did the important stuff yesterday and rescheduled the rest. Was worried about you with the breakup and Andy's death anniversary coming up."

Khai pushed his brother's hand away. "It's just that flu that's going around. Go back to New York. I'm *fine*."

Shit, *death anniversary*. A cold sweat broke out over him, making his skin tingle as his heartbeat went erratic. He'd purposely blocked it from his mind because he hated those kinds of things, and this was the big one, the ten-year anniversary. There was going to be a ceremony, more monk chanting, and geysers of tears. His head throbbed on the verge of explosion.

"There *isn't* a flu going around. It's summertime." Quan frowned and stuck his hand back on Khai's forehead. "You don't have a fever."

"It's in the pre-fever stages, then." Khai mumbled the words because sound hurt now.

Quan sat down on the coffee table and searched his face like an astrologist reading the stars. When he shifted his position to get more comfortable, the water glass got in his way. He reached for it, but Khai stopped him.

"Don't."

Quan blinked and asked, "Why not?"

"I like it there."

Quan stared at the water glass before fixing his eyes on Khai with a look of dawning understanding. "Holy shit, it's *hers*, isn't it? Do you know how cute that is?" Rubbing at his jaw, he added, "Also maybe a little emotionally unstable. You're not being creepy, are you? Like stalking with binoculars and calling her at night to make sure she's sleeping alone?"

"What? No." But who the hell would she be sleeping with? If Quan meant another man, that was disturbing enough to warrant lengthy contemplation.

"Those weren't suggestions," Quan added. "Don't do that."

"I'm not being creepy," Khai said in exasperation.

Quan nodded, and after a stilted moment, he dug his phone from his pocket and held it up like he was snapping a picture.

"What are you *doing*?" Khai asked.

"Sending a picture of your beard to Vy. You look kinda like God-frey Gao right now."

Khai rolled his eyes and scratched at his face. How long had it been since he'd shaved? He couldn't remember. The past days were a mess of chaos in his mind.

"I'm not joking. Look at you," Quan said, holding up his phone with the snapshot of Khai on it. As far as Khai was concerned, he looked less like a movie star and more like a drug addict, but what did he know?

Just then, message boxes from Vy flashed on the screen.

Oh momma.

Tell him to keep it.

Rawr.

Khai grimaced and rubbed at the back of his neck. "Not sure if I like my sister *rawr*ing at me."

Quan laughed before his expression went serious. "Only Esme can, right?"

Khai thought that over for a few seconds before nodding once. Attraction, sex, lust, and wanting all orbited around one focal point for him. The focal point was Esme.

"I've been thinking about what you said at Michael's wedding, about how you're not in love, and I dunno. Maybe you're not, but this . . ." Quan motioned at the open windows, the cup collecting dust on the table, and Khai's couch-ridden form before resting his elbows on his knees and leaning toward him. "This is you being sad, Khai."

He frowned at his brother. What bullshit was this? "I'm not sad. I have the flu."

Quan stretched his head from side to side until his neck audibly popped. "You know you've been like this before, right? It's a predictable pattern with you."

"Yes, I've had the flu before."

"I'm talking about being heartbroken," Quan said, his eyes delving into Khai's in an uncomfortable way.

Khai's body stiffened. "I'm not. I—"

"Do you remember when Mom and Dad separated when we were little?" Quan asked quietly.

"A little. They were together, and then one day they weren't. It was fine." He shrugged.

"Except you weren't fine. You stopped talking, and you got so clumsy you had to stay home from school for two weeks." An ironic smile touched Quan's mouth. "I remember because there was no one to take care of you, so I had to stay home, too. I made us ramen in the microwave, and you were upset because there was no poached egg like when Mom cooks it."

"I don't remember any of that." And what he did remember was neutral and colorless, flat. He'd been told to give his dad one last hug before he left town for good. He remembered hugging a person who used to be everything and feeling . . . nothing.

"Maybe you were too young. How about . . . after Andy's funeral. Do you remember that?"

An irritated sensation scratched up Khai's back, and he kicked his blanket off, suddenly needing to be free. He wanted to brush his teeth and shower, shut all the windows, and maybe put that cup in the dishwasher. Wait, no, he wasn't ready to put the cup away yet. "Yeah, I remember. I was fine." Too fine. "Can we not talk about this?"

"Why?"

"There's no point. I wasn't heartbroken then, and I'm not now." Stone hearts didn't break. They were too hard. "I'm like a Terminator with logic programming and no feelings." He stretched his lips into a plastic smile.

Quan rolled his eyes. "What a load of shit. Are you going to say you don't love at all? I *know* you love me."

Khai tilted his head to the side. He'd never thought about that before.

"There is literally nothing you can say to make me believe you don't," Quan said with absolute confidence. "Go ahead. Try."

"I hardly ever do things with you, and we don't have a bunch of similar interests, and—"

"And you never forget my birthday, and you always share your food with me even when it's your favorite, and I know anytime I need something, I can count on you, no matter what," Quan finished.

"Well . . . yeah." Those were hard rules in Khai's universe.

"That's brother love. We just don't say it because we're tough and shit, but yeah, I love you, too." Quan punched him on the shoulder. "And why the fuck are you wearing a sweater in late July?"

Khai rubbed his shoulder. "I told you. I have the flu."

"You don't have the flu. This is how your heart breaks. It's like you hurt too much for your brain to process, and then your body shuts down, too. You were a lot like this after Andy. Even down to the one sock."

Khai looked at his feet and was surprised to see he only wore one sock. "Maybe it came off in my sleep." He dug through the blanket, but it wasn't there.

"Or you forgot it. After Andy, you were so out of it, we were all afraid you'd accidentally kill yourself by walking in front of a bus or forgetting to eat."

Khai shook his head and scratched at his beard. "That doesn't sound like me."

Quan laughed. "No, it doesn't. That's why we were all so worried, and you seemed off ever since then. These past couple months are the happiest I've seen you in a long time, to be honest."

Khai gritted his teeth. He hadn't been *happy*. He'd been in an Esme high. There was a difference, though at the moment, his mind wasn't clear enough to figure out what it was. Frustrated, he pulled off his one sock and tossed it on the floor. There, now he was symmetrical. But a lone sock lay on the floor, completely out of place.

Quan considered Khai for several long seconds before saying, "Are you ready for the death anniversary next weekend? Talking about him might help. You never do."

Khai fixed his attention on the sock on the floor. "I did. At Sara's wedding."

Quan released a heavy exhalation. "Yeah, I heard about that. I should have been there with you."

"It's not your fault when I hurt people," Khai said.

"It's not yours, either."

Khai shook his head at his brother's insensible logic and focused on the sock again. He should pick it up, find its mate, and stick them in the laundry together. It was distinctly infuriating imagining his socks journeying through the house separately. They were designed to be together.

Unlike Khai. He was meant to be a lone sock. Lone socks had a place in this world, too. Not everyone had two feet.

"When's the last time you ate?" Quan asked.

Khai lifted a shoulder. He couldn't remember. "It's okay. I'm not hungry."

"Well, I am. You're going to eat with me." Quan got up and padded into the kitchen. The fridge opened, plates clattered, silverware clanked, and the microwave hummed and beeped. Soon, they were eating together on the couch as Quan flipped through TV channels until he found a program where ticker symbols scrolled along the bottom.

Khai hadn't brushed his teeth, showered, or shaved, and he was fairly certain he was a psychopath, but sitting there with Quan, things seemed better. Eating with his brother and watching TV while sick felt familiar, and fuzzy memories flickered in his mind.

Maybe he really had been in this same position before, but as for the rest of it, the brokenhearted stuff, he couldn't bring himself to believe it.

CHAPTER TWENTY-THREE

Early the next week, when Angelika went to take the GED exam, Esme went, too. She didn't need a GED and had no one to impress, and a high school diploma wasn't going to help with her work. But the cost hadn't been horrible, and she'd done all this studying. She told herself she did it to set an example for Jade.

But deep inside, she knew she did it for herself, too.

Unconsciously, she'd been studying for it this entire time.

Usually, she couldn't do things because the opportunity wasn't there, and the worry persisted that maybe she couldn't because she just wasn't good enough. Maybe all rich people were rich because they deserved it. Maybe she was poor because she, too, deserved it. But now the opportunity was right here, and she wanted to see.

What happened when you gave someone an opportunity?

Later that week, she still hadn't figured out how to solve her visa problem, and the determined fire in her heart had banked. When she got her transcript in her email inbox, she opened it with resignation.

The contents put goose bumps on her head. She checked the

name three times to make sure they hadn't made a mistake and sent it to the wrong person, but no, the name was unmistakably Esmeralda Tran.

Under every category, it read: *PASS GED College Ready + Credit.* She'd achieved perfect scores across the board.

Did this mean she was smart?

It *did.* The proof was right here on her phone. Her heart burst with pride—in herself, for a change. Well, she wasn't *very* smart. Just a little smart. Most people graduated from high school here. But that was more than she'd ever dared to dream of. This country girl had a high school diploma.

This was important. This meant something big. But her mind was too busy with this explosive happiness to grasp it all.

Her phone buzzed a few times, and when she looked at the screen, she saw she'd received text messages from Angelika.

I passed!

We're celebrating at the boba shop by school.

Come!!!!!!!

Why not? She wanted to share her news, but it was the wrong time to call home, and talking to Khải was out.

She punched in a quick response, checked her spelling twice, and sent it. Congratulations! See you there. :)

After she finished closing down the restaurant, she untied her apron from her waist, put it away, and waved good-bye to Cô Nga. It took three minutes to cross the street and walk to the bubble-tea shop, and when she stepped inside, the humidity wrapped around her like a blanket. Small flat-screen TVs were mounted on the walls by different groupings of tables. One played a Taiwanese drama. One played a football game. The one by the small group of Esme's classmates played a golf game.

Esme waved at everyone, ordered and paid for a plain black tea with milk and pearls, and helped herself to the seat next to Angelika. The space across from her was taken by Miss Q, who was wearing jeans, a relaxed button-down shirt, and, of course, a scarf. Stylish as ever.

"I knew you would pass," Miss Q said with a wide smile.

"Of course she passed." Angelika flipped her hand like it was a foregone conclusion, and Esme grinned.

"I passed, thank you. Congratulations to you, too. Congratulations to everyone."

The other seats at the table were occupied by three male classmates, Juan, Javier, and John, and they congratulated her back before they got up.

"We have to go, but glad to see you," Juan said. "Time for college now, eh?"

She blinked in shock. The idea had never occurred to her. *"Maybe."* She grinned in unexpected excitement before reality caught up with her, and the smile drooped off her lips as she waved at the men. "Bye."

"Why the look?" Miss Q asked once the guys had left the shop.

"I can't go to college."

"Why?" Miss Q and Angelika asked at the same time.

Esme flinched. "Because I have to go back to Việt Nam on August ninth." And there was no way she could afford to go to school back home. They needed her income too much, and that didn't factor in the bribes she'd need to pay to move her paperwork and get accepted anywhere good.

"What kind of visa do you have?" Miss Q asked.

Esme looked down at her ugly fingers on the table. "Tourist visa."

"Me, too." Angelika covered Esme's hand with her own and squeezed. Something sparkly caught Esme's attention, but Angelika pulled her hand out of sight before Esme could take a closer look.

"There are other kinds of visas, you know," Miss Q pointed out. "If you get accepted by a college or university here, they'll grant you a student visa. They'll even let you bring your family here for the duration. After you get a degree, you could try for a work visa."

The air punched out of Esme's lungs. "Could *I* get accepted to a college or university here?"

Her GED scores flashed in her mind's eye. *PASS GED College Ready + Credit.*

"Of course you could. Were your scores good?" Miss Q asked.

She nodded, trying to keep the smile off her face and failing, and showed Miss Q her transcript on her phone. "Thank you for teaching me." She'd earned each of those scores by herself. They were *hers.*

And maybe they were the key to belonging here.

Miss Q grinned and kept on grinning and her eyes sparkled with unshed tears. "The pleasure is mine."

Excitement bubbled in Esme's blood like champagne right after they popped the cork. If what Miss Q was saying was true, she actually *could* become a real accountant. Or maybe something else. She could be *anything*. She could be sophisticated and educated someday and hold her chin up—even in front of Khải.

Except there was one problem. "How much is college?" she asked hesitantly.

"It depends on the school. Anywhere from ten thousand dollars a year to fifty thousand for undergraduates, but there are loan programs and scholarships," Miss Q said.

Tension stole through Esme's muscles. Ten thousand American dollars was more than she'd made in her whole lifetime. If a job here wasn't guaranteed, she didn't know if she dared to take out a loan like that once, let alone four times. But if she could keep working at Cô Nga's, she could probably manage. It would be tight, but that wouldn't be anything new.

She was mentally doing the math, figuring out how many shifts she could take and subtracting the costs of rent, food, and tuition, when Miss Q added, "In your case, you'd have to get a scholarship because you're not allowed to work on a student visa, but I know schools nearby that offer them, even to international students. With your GED scores and personal experience, you have a chance, Esme. I'm going to contact the people I know and see if they'll consider you as a special case."

Esme's lips moved without making sound. She understood the individual meanings of the words spoken, but she was in too much shock to interpret their overall message. She knew about failure and struggling to earn her way. Generosity of this magnitude didn't make sense to her.

"Keep your eyes open for my email, okay? It could come any day. If I send you an application, fill it out and send it to me right away. I'm going to go call my friends now. Good-bye, you two." Miss Q charged out of the boba shop like she was on a mission, going so fast Esme didn't even have time to thank her.

Could Miss Q really help Esme get a scholarship? That would be . . . amazing. And everything. It was, she realized, her very last option.

Experience told her to check her enthusiasm, but Miss Q believed in her, and she really had passed the GED with perfect scores. If she could do that, just think of all the other things she could do if she had the chance. This was real. This might actually happen. And her hope grew out of control.

Originally, she'd envisioned herself marrying Khải and continuing life as a waitress. That was great, wasn't it? She'd give Jade a wonderful future that way, and she'd be with Khải. Maybe they'd make more babies.

But now, a new dream formed in her heart, one she'd never dared to encourage but wanted with breathless intensity: *doing* something she was passionate about, *changing* this world for the better, being *more*. She didn't even know what she was good at, but if she could explore and learn . . .

One of the workers at the shop handed Esme her milk tea, and she thanked him and drew the sweetened tea and chewy pearls into her mouth through the large straw. The TV flashed to a close-up of a golf player, and the DMSoft logo on his hat looked familiar.

After a second, she remembered that was where Khải worked. On the top floor, in a closet. It had to be a big company if they sponsored golf tournaments. Good for Khải. Maybe if he worked hard, they'd promote him, and someday he could redo his yard.

"What happened to your boyfriend?" Angelika asked, breaking the silence.

Esme's hands tightened around her milk tea. "No more boyfriend. Not *ever* boyfriend." They'd just been . . . housemates who slept together.

Now that she was gone, she hoped he was climbing the walls with sexual frustration. She hoped he thought of her when he pleasured himself. Because he'd be doing a lot of that from now on.

Unless he met someone new.

Her hackles rose as she imagined Khải with another woman, kissing her the way Esme liked, caressing her the way Esme needed, letting her touch him the way only Esme ever had. Would he trust another woman with his body now that Esme had "initiated" him? She supposed she should feel proud if that was the case, but it just made her want to claw this imaginary woman's face like an angry jungle cat.

She shook her head to clear it of the violent thoughts, and found Angelika watching her with sad understanding.

"He was a good catch," Angelika said. "My fiancé, he is sixty. And gone all the time for business." She looked down at her dazzling engagement ring. That was what Esme had noticed earlier. Angelika had gotten engaged without saying anything. "His children hate me. They are older than I am."

"In time, they will see," Esme said.

Angelika looked down at her left hand, fisted it, and dropped it below the table. "I do not think so. They keep telling me to go back to Russia, and they are convincing him to get the vasectomy—you know, so he cannot have more babies? I am afraid this will end in divorce. Or not happen at all."

"Why do they—"

"To protect the money when he dies," Angelika said bitterly. "I agreed to sign a contract before the wedding, so if we divorce, I do not get anything. But that is not enough for them. I always wanted a family."

"Does he . . . love you?" Esme asked.

A soft smile spread over Angelika's lips. "Yeah, he does. And I love him."

Esme squeezed her friend's arm. "Then you two will be fine." Unlike Esme and Khải.

Angelika smiled before her expression went thoughtful. "A scholarship sounds good, but have you thought of dating other people?"

Esme shook her head.

Angelika sent her an impatient look. "It is just dating, Esmeralda."

"Dating has kissing and touching and . . ." She couldn't bring herself to say *sex*. The thought of being with another man so soon made her skin crawl. A different woman would be out romancing every desperate man she could find—she had Jade to think about, after all—but Esme couldn't make herself do it. She was probably naïve for thinking this way, but if she married, it had to be a *real* marriage. She didn't have the heart to take advantage of anyone or hurt them. That meant she had to fall out of love first. "I am not ready."

Angelika's lips thinned, but she eventually nodded. "I hope you get that scholarship. I don't want you to leave. You are my only friend here."

Esme told herself to prepare for disappointment. But her heart wouldn't listen. She had this dream now, and she'd never wanted anything so much. She clasped Angelika's hand, and her friend squeezed back.

"Me, too," Esme said. "Me, too."

CHAPTER TWENTY-FOUR

Khai had done this before. He could do it today. He was mostly over his flu. Shoes off, sock-clad feet on hardwood, the fog of incense, the heavy floral scent emanating from the numerous white bouquets, and there, on the far side of the main room, an altar with a large golden statue of Buddha sitting on a lotus blossom.

He strode past the family and friends dressed mostly in gray robes, sitting cross-legged on the rugs on the floor, and approached the altar. One of the monks up there handed him a stick of incense, and Khai accepted it awkwardly. He didn't know what the hell to do with it. This was his mom's scene, not his. He stabbed it into the giant bowl of rice with the other incense and considered the photograph in front of the statue. Andy standing next to his blue Honda motorcycle.

Andy wore the same smartass grin he flashed every time he delivered a great comeback. He always had a comeback, always. Sometimes, he even thought up things to say in advance, so he'd be ready when the occasion came. Not like Khai, who either froze up when people teased him or didn't realize he was being teased in the first place.

He touched his fingertips to the picture, and the coldness of the glass surprised him. He didn't usually spend time contemplating philosophical questions about life and humanity, but right now, as he stared at his cousin's likeness in paper and resin, he wondered what made a person a person. Was it something mystical like a soul? Something scientific like neural connections in the brain? Or something simpler, like the ability to make someone miss you ten years after you'd died?

He recognized the dull emptiness inside of him as missing someone. He missed Andy. And he missed Esme. But that wasn't the same as being heartbroken. Quan was wrong about that.

When she stepped into the pagoda and set her shoes by the front door with all the other pairs, his entire body froze.

Esme.

She wore the same shapeless black dress from before, and for a confused moment, it felt like she'd walked straight from Michael's wedding here. But two weeks had passed. Logically, Khai knew that.

Her eyes met his. Her expression was tense at first, but after a moment, her lips curved slightly. It wasn't her usual brain-scrambling smile, but it was still a smile. Sharp needles of sensation pricked his skin from head to toe, and he dragged air into his lungs with effort.

She padded barefoot around all the people on the rugs and stopped next to him by the statue and Andy's picture. "I came to help with the food after," she said in a low tone.

The monk handed her a stick of incense, and she inclined her head and thanked him before pressing the incense between her palms and bowing to the statue the way Khai should have. After she stuck the incense in the rice bowl, she considered the photograph of

Andy, touched the motorcycle, and gazed at Khai with an unreadable expression on her face.

"It was his?" she asked.

He didn't think he could speak, so he nodded. The motorcycle had been Andy's most prized possession, and Dì Mai had given it to Khai, saying Andy would have wanted him to have it. His mom had been angry at first, but when Khai didn't ride it, she'd forgotten about it.

Most of the time, Khai forgot about it, too, and that was what he preferred. He automatically pushed the motorcycle and accompanying memories to the back of his mind and focused on Esme. Her skin was paler than normal, and she'd lost weight, but she was still unmistakably Esme. No one else had eyes that specific shade of green. *So pretty.* The need to hold her became a visceral ache in his muscles and bones, but she stepped away before he could act.

She padded around the sitting area and sat on the edge apart from everyone. His mom waved at him from where she sat with Dì Mai, Sara, Quan, Vy, Michael, and other family members, but he walked past them and seated himself next to Esme.

"Why are you— You should sit with family," Esme said with a deep frown.

A metal bowl rang, signaling the ceremony was beginning, and he was grateful. He didn't know how to explain himself. He just needed to be at her side.

A skinny bespectacled man in gold robes and Buddhist rosary beads launched into a speech on loss and time healing all wounds, and Khai tuned the words out. He couldn't breathe. It was like someone had him in an invisible choke hold. He pulled at the collar of his shirt, but he hadn't worn a tie and the top buttons weren't fastened. He shouldn't feel this way.

Cameras flashed now and then, and videographers filmed the speech as the crowd listened in rapt attention. His aunt had invited a celebrity monk from Southern California to the pagoda, and it was a big honor to have him speak about Andy. Khai, however, wished he'd stop. Every time he heard his cousin's name, this suffocating sensation worsened.

It was like Sara's wedding, except his eyes were burning and his skin was tingling, like blood was rushing back after circulation had been cut off. What the fuck was happening?

The metal bowl rang again, and countless off-key voices sang incomprehensible words. Incense, chanting, somber faces, Andy. He'd experienced all of this before, but it was different this time. He'd had time to absorb and process. A lot of time.

And now barriers in his mind fell, swamping him in confusion. The emptiness inside of him expanded. The *missing* grew until it overwhelmed him. Andy memories flooded his head, a childhood together, school together, and that last night when he'd waited and waited for Andy to show up. And he never did. Khai's throat knotted, his lungs hurt, his skin flushed hot.

A small hand pressed on his jacket sleeve and traveled down the length of his arm to rest over his knuckles. He clasped Esme's hand tight, and she gazed at him like she understood. But how could she possibly, when he didn't?

"Come on," she whispered. "Let's go outside."

He got up, distracting their celebrity speaker midsentence, and his mom aimed a disapproving scowl at him. Esme ignored everyone and tugged on his hand until he followed her out to the pagoda's koi pond.

"Sit, Khải, you look bad." She directed him to a stone bench that overlooked the water. He sat, and she brushed the hair from his clammy forehead with cool, soft fingers. "You need water."

When she tried to pull away, he wrapped his arms around her waist and held her close. "Don't go."

"Okay," she said, and she urged him to rest his cheek against her chest. Her fingers smoothed through his hair and along his scruffy jaw.

He breathed her in. She smelled slightly different than she used to, like she'd changed laundry detergents, but he found the comforting feminine scent underneath it all. *Her* scent. The scent of woman and clean skin and Esme.

The ash of incense slowly faded from his senses, and he let everything slip away but her. The sick feeling receded. He could breathe again. People began to walk by, a few at first, but gradually more. Still, he didn't let her go. He needed her touch, her smell, the steady beating of her heart, *her*.

"Mỹ," his mom said, making Esme stiffen against him. "Come help me with—oh, never mind. I'll have Quân help me." His mom's footsteps quickly retreated.

Esme ran her fingers through his hair before asking, "We have eggrolls here. Want some?"

"Not hungry." It would take something catastrophic to lure him away from her right now. He was like a wounded beast who'd found a respite from the pain of his injuries. "Unless you want them?"

She laughed a little. "No, I ate too many already." She brushed her fingers across his scratchy cheek.

He hadn't thought he'd ever have this again, and he let his eyelids fall shut as he soaked up her touch. She was better than sunlight and fresh air.

Time passed, he didn't know how much, and his mom came back and said, "You two should go. Khải, take Mỹ home for me, ha?"

"Cô, I can help clean up." Esme pulled away from him, and he bit back a protest. He wanted to grab her arms and wrap her back around him like a scarf. "There are a lot of containers and—"

"No, no, no, it's all taken care of. People are leaving now. Go home," his mom said, waving dismissively at them. "You'll drive her, ha, Khải?"

Esme's mouth opened like she wanted to speak, and he quickly said, "Yeah, I'll do it."

"Good, good." His mom hurried away.

He got up from the bench and took a deep breath. His head pulsed, but he hadn't felt this good in days. "Let's go, then."

"Are you better? We can wait," she said.

"Yeah, I'm better." A bit achy and bruised inside, but improved. Pretty much the way he felt when he'd been sick for days and his fever finally broke. Except he'd never spiked a fever.

As they walked to his car, he was intensely conscious of the respectful distance between them. She kept her fingers laced together, and the set of her shoulders was tense as she focused on the path ahead. Just two weeks ago, they would have held hands. Just two weeks ago, she'd been in love with him.

Was two weeks enough time to fall out of love with someone?

It made him a greedy bastard, but he wanted her love. He wanted to be her "one," the recipient of her smiles, the *reason* for her smiles, her drug. She was his.

After all of this, it was clear he didn't have the flu. He'd been going through withdrawal, and it was much worse than he'd originally imagined. He had to find a way to make her stay.

They piled into his car, and he started the ignition and rested his fingers on the wheel. "Where do you live now?"

She looked down at her tightly clasped hands. "The month-to-month place by the restaurant."

His gut twisted, and an unpleasant sensation spilled over his skin. "That is not a very good part of town."

"It's good enough for me."

No, it wasn't.

Gritting his teeth, he left the pagoda in San Jose and headed to her place via the 880N. He sped through flat territory with drab office buildings and storage lots and pulled up to a small gray apartment complex tucked behind a beat-up strip mall. On the way from his car to her apartment, his shoes crunched over shattered glass from a broken beer bottle, and they passed a stray shopping cart lying on its side.

He hit the lock button on his key fob just in case and scanned the area for bored kids who might be interested in keying his car or slashing his tires. None, thankfully. His house wasn't great, but at least he didn't have to worry about vandalism.

When she stopped in front of a door on the ground floor of the building, his displeasure grew. *Not safe.* It would be so easy for someone to break in. She had a lot of character, but that wasn't enough to protect her against someone bigger, stronger, and possibly armed. His hands started sweating at the idea of some asshole breaking through one of her windows and coming inside to—

"Do you want to come in?" she asked, peering over her shoulder at him from just inside her open doorway. "You don't look good."

At his silent nod, she opened the door wide and let him in. It was a plain studio apartment with brown carpet, a sleeping bag on the floor with a pile of textbooks next to it, a mostly empty closet, and a teeny linoleum kitchen.

She'd left him for this.

He hated everything about it.

"Thirsty?" Without waiting for him to reply, she hurried to the kitchen, filled a disposable cup from the tap, and brought it to him.

He drank down the water, grimacing at the hard taste, and handed the cup back to her. She stepped toward the kitchen, clearly planning to put it away or in the garbage or something, and he took advantage of the opportunity to gather her in his arms, pressing her close, her chest to his. She gasped, and the plastic cup fell forgotten to the ugly carpet.

"Marry me," he said.

She drew in a sharp breath, and her green eyes searched his face. "Why?"

He shook his head. He didn't know how to say this. It felt too big. At the same time, it didn't feel like enough. "I've *missed* you." So badly his body had broken down. "I need to know you're safe and happy. And I want you close. With me."

Her hands balled up against his chest like they did when she was fighting against touching him, and he covered them with his and worked on the fingers until they unfurled.

"Come back with me and marry me."

"Khải . . ." She bit her lip.

Acting on instinct and desperation, he angled her head back and kissed her. She softened against him like always and pressed herself close, and his body hardened in a euphoric rush. The wild idea crossed his mind that if he kissed and touched her right, he might muddle her senses to the point where she said yes by accident. And *hell yes*, he would hold her to it.

"Marry me."

Khải's kiss. Khải's touch. His hands sweeping over her body, demanding, possessive, making her melt. She'd tried to stay away from him, but his intense sorrow during the death anniversary had worried her. She hadn't known how to be there for him, but *this*, she knew exactly what to do with this. He needed, so she gave.

He said it again. "Marry me."

It was probably wishful thinking, but she heard *I love you* in his words. Each proposal seduced her more. The cool fabric of her sleeping bag met her back, and he covered her with his body. A rough palm slid under her dress, up her thigh, and cupped her between her legs. Knowing fingers stroked her, and she drenched the fabric of her underwear.

"Marry me," he whispered against her lips.

"Khải—"

Before she could finish speaking, he pushed her dress up above her breasts and feasted on her, making sharp pleasure shock from her nipples straight between her thighs. His hand slipped into her panties, and slick fingertips rubbed her *there*, taking away her ability to think. What had she been about to say? She couldn't remember. She was lost in desire—hers and his. He'd never been this out of control, this urgent.

He kissed his way down her body with hungry licks and small nips and bites, and goose bumps shivered over her with each prickle of his beard on her rib cage, her tummy, her hips. That was new, but she liked it. He yanked her panties off impatiently and fastened his mouth on her sex, and she clenched hard and tight.

His repeated proposal echoed in her head. He'd turned to her in his time of need and let her in. He loved her, she *felt* it, and the knowledge propelled her straight over the edge with a startled moan.

He glanced up at her in surprise. "I only licked you once."

"*Khải*," she whined, threading her fingers into his hair and directing him back where she wanted him. He couldn't stop, not yet. If he stopped, she'd—

A wide grin stretched over his lips before he sucked her back into his mouth, and the convulsions tore through her. She rocked against his face, over and over until the aftershocks spaced out, and then he was gathering her close and pressing kisses to her temple, her cheek, her jaw.

"Marry me," he said in a gravelly voice.

She heard it again. *I love you.*

He sought out her lips and stroked his tongue deep as he gripped her hips and pressed her against his hardness. "Say yes."

Her body softened in readiness. Yes, she wanted him. Yes, she loved him. Yes, she wanted to marry him. She cupped the generous bulge between his legs and demanded, "Say you love me." She had to hear him say it. She deserved to hear it.

He ground his hips against her hand as a hoarse sound escaped his throat.

She eased his zipper open, captured his firm length in her palm, and kissed his swollen mouth softly. "Say it one time. Just one time." Once would be enough.

His lungs gusted as he stared deep into her eyes. "I missed you."

She stroked him, running her hand to the base of his sex and back to the tip. "And?"

He swallowed loudly. "I want you."

She wrapped a leg around his hip and touched the head of his sex to her wet folds. *This* would get him to say it. "And?"

He shuddered, and his eyes went dark. "I need you."

"And?" Her throat swelled as disappointment threatened. *Say it, just say it.* Why wouldn't he say it?

Regret swept across his face, and she jerked away from him and sat up, pulling her dress down so it covered her nakedness. He hadn't let her in, after all. She'd been making love to him again when it was just sex to him, and it made her feel horrible and cheap and small. She wanted to run away, but this was *her* apartment. She'd paid for this place with her own hard-earned money.

"You should go," she said, proud the words came out even.

Growling her name, he got up and raked his fingers through his hair in frustration. His arousal stood out proud and eager, and the sight was enough to make her sex ache with wanting.

She hugged her arms tight to her chest and turned away from him. "Please shut the door behind you."

There was a long pause before a loud zipping sound broke the silence. She heard feet pad across the carpet, heard him lean down to put his shoes on, and then the door squeaked as it opened and shut.

When the engine of his car rumbled to life, she locked the door, went into the bathroom, and cranked on the hot water in the shower. It was her turn to wash him off and leave him unsatisfied. She refused to cry. If he didn't love her, someone else would. She wasn't going to settle for a one-sided love. Not in this lifetime. Not ever.

Once she'd scrubbed her skin bright red, she climbed out of the shower, dressed, and checked her email. There it was. An email from Miss Q. A local community college was considering her. That sounded perfect. She gathered up her things and went to the school library, so she could fill out the application and send it out as soon as possible.

She couldn't have Khải, but she didn't need him. She was going to earn her way all by herself, and that was a billion times better.

CHAPTER TWENTY-FIVE

*H*e should have lied.

Khai mentally kicked himself on the way home. *I*, *love*, and *you* were just words, and it wasn't like he'd never lied before. He'd told his aunt Dì Anh he liked the blended aloe vera juice she made. He didn't. He wasn't even sure it was edible. It was slimy and gave him cramps every time.

If he lied, he could have Esme for three years. He needed those three years. Desperately. He swore he wouldn't keep her permanently. He wouldn't do that to her. Three years only. He should practice saying the words, turn the car around, and go lie to her right away. It wasn't too late.

"I." He cleared his throat and tried for the second word, but it wouldn't come out. After driving for a while, he gripped the gear shift tighter and said, "*Love*, dammit. Love, love, love."

Fuck, his heart was pounding, and sweat stood out on his skin, and he felt absolutely absurd. It wasn't going to work if he had to say the words five minutes apart.

He forced himself to say, "I love. I love. I love. *I love.*"

Alarms rang in his head. *Lies.* Sweat beaded on his upper lip and trickled down his neck, and blue sparks floated over his field of vision.

Okay, he had to stop or he'd get in a car accident. He'd practice later.

When he got home, however, Quan's black Ducati was parked in Khai's regular spot at the curb. And the garage was open.

What. The. Fuck.

He screeched into the driveway, cranked the emergency brake, and turned the key in the ignition before jumping out of his car.

"What are you doing?" he asked as he stomped toward the garage, where Quan stood next to Andy's motorcycle. He'd tossed the tarp off and put the black helmet on the seat.

"It's time you got rid of this cheap-ass bike," Quan said, giving him a steady stare.

Khai fisted his hands as his muscles went rigid. "No."

"You're ready now."

"No."

"Okay, then ride it," Quan said.

"No." Khai stalked over to the bike and reached for the key in the ignition.

Before he could yank it out, Quan grabbed his wrist tightly and met his gaze head on. "I know why you're pushing her away even though you love her."

"I. Don't. Love. Her," he said through his teeth.

Quan's jaw dropped. "How can you say that? You were *there* today. You were the one holding on to her like you were falling apart, and she was the one keeping you together. She was exactly what you needed. Because you love her, and she loves you back, you shit."

He repeated himself, "I. Don't. Lo—"

"You *do*," Quan said. "But you've got weird shit going on in your head. Do you feel responsible for Andy or something? Guilty? You're afraid of losing her, so you push her away? What is it? Figure it out today because she's leaving in a week, and you'll regret it forever."

Khai shook his head as his brain hiccuped. That wasn't right. That didn't make sense. That wasn't him.

And fuck, there was only one week left.

"Why won't you ride the damned bike?" Quan asked.

Khai looked at the wall. "You're 5.5 times more likely to get in a fatal accident on a motorcycle than a car."

"That's still only a 0.07 percent chance. We have a higher chance of dying from Mom's cooking."

Khai blinked. "You remember the exact number?"

Quan rolled his eyes and threw his hands in the air. "Yeah, I can read, and I remember shit. I'm actually kind of smart."

"Riding a motorcycle isn't smart."

Quan aimed a pointed stare at him. "Sometimes the things people do and believe don't make sense. I feel most alive when I might die. And you, you're convinced you don't feel, and the responsible thing is to avoid people."

"That's the way things are," Khai said.

"No, it's bullshit. Where was Andy heading when he got hit by that semi?"

Khai looked down at the deep scratches on the motorcycle. Those had happened the night of the accident. "He was coming to see me."

"Why?"

Khai tilted his head as his chest hollowed out and caved inward. "Because I asked him to. I wanted to hang out."

Shit, this awful feeling was guilt. He had a name for it now.

"And have you once in the past ten years invited anyone to come see you?" Quan asked.

Khai shook his head. "But that's because I don't need people around. I don't get lonely."

"The guy who invited Andy over because he didn't want to be alone doesn't get lonely?" Quan asked. "How's that flu going for you? Did you ever get a fever?"

Khai stared at his brother mutinously. He didn't want to talk about the fever he'd never had.

Quan arched an eyebrow. "So are you gonna tell her now?"

"Tell her what?"

"That you're embarrassingly in love with her, that's what," Quan said in an exasperated tone.

"How many times do I have to tell you *I'm not in love with her*?"

Quan rubbed at his head for a moment before he took a bracing breath and considered Khai with renewed patience. "How do you know?"

Khai blinked. "How do I know I'm not in love?"

"Yeah, how do you know you're not in love?"

"I know because I can't love." He'd gone over this already, and he didn't like repeating himself.

"So, like, you don't think about her ever?" Quan asked.

"No, I do."

"And you don't care about her? Like if she's sad, you don't give a shit?"

"No, I care," Khai said.

"And you wouldn't take a bullet for her?" Quan asked.

"No, I would. But you would, too. That's the right thing to do."

"You don't like being with her more than other people? You could trade her for someone else with no regrets?"

Khai scowled at his brother, not liking how he was manipulating the questions. "No, I like being with her a lot, and I wouldn't trade her for anyone else."

Quan gave him a deadpan look. "I bet the sex is super shitty."

"It's none of your business what it's like." Memories from less than an hour ago played in his mind, Esme coming against his mouth, moaning his name, rubbing his cock over her wet sex. "But it's not shitty."

"Lucky bastard," Quan muttered. "I hope you realize when you say all those things about someone, it means you've got it bad for them."

Khai stepped away from the motorcycle, abandoning the keys to Quan. "I really don't." Love and addiction were different things.

"Oh, come on, Khai," Quan exploded.

"I'm going to take a shower. After you've decided what you're doing with the motorcycle, please shut the garage."

He escaped into his house through the garage entrance. Once inside, he took his shoes off, carried them to the front door, and sat down on the couch, propping his elbows on his knees and burying his face in his palms. Through the hard slamming of his heart, he heard the garage door shut and Quan's Ducati roar to life. The loud engine sound receded and disappeared altogether.

Alone again.

He wasn't lonely, though. He liked this.

Like wasn't the right word. He was accustomed to this. Well, he used to be. Until Esme came along.

On Monday, Esme got an email from Miss Q saying the community college had received her test scores, and her application was under expedited review per her recommendation.

It was really happening. She had a chance of getting a college education and changing her life for good. All on her own merits. Hope grew to gigantic proportions, and that dream of being someone possessed her. She wanted it for herself and for her baby. How wonderful would it be to *show* Jade what she was capable of *by example*.

The days after that passed in an anxious haze, where she switched back and forth between extreme confidence and deep despair. She found the contact information for an immigration attorney who could—hopefully—help her bring Jade and her family here during the duration of her studies, but she didn't call him. She'd only call if she got the scholarship.

On Wednesday, her apron buzzed while she was taking an order, and she *knew* that was the email. She was too busy to check, but the email hung heavy in the back of her mind as she worked through the lunch rush. As she ran orders back to the kitchen, her blood hummed with excitement. It was a full scholarship, and she was on her way to being Esme in Accounting for real and taking care of her family all by herself. As she carried food trays out to the tables, her heart dropped. It was a rejection, and she was going to go home with little to show for her time here.

Back and forth. Back and forth.

By the time the last customer left, tucking a fantastic twenty-dollar tip under his empty water glass before winking at her, she was all nerves. Instead of pulling her phone out right away, she cleared the tables and wiped them down.

With each swipe of wet dish towel on tabletop, she prepared herself for the upcoming news. If it was good, she was going to call her mom right away, thank Miss Q, and schedule an appointment with the immigration attorney. If it was bad, it was okay. There were good sides to her life back home, and she would keep her eyes open for other opportunities.

But didn't "Esmeralda Tran, college student" have a nice ring to it? She would be such a good college student. She'd study like she had this summer. She'd earn every scholarship dollar, and later, she'd make something of herself.

When the last table was clean, she pulled her phone out of her apron, sat in her regular booth, and typed her passcode into the phone with trembling fingers. Her inbox contained one new email from the community college with the subject title "Regarding Your Scholarship Application." The preview of the text read, "Dear Ms. Tran, Your application has been thoroughly reviewed by . . ."

Was that good or not? It could go either way from there.

Her heart raced, blood rushed to her head, and her mouth went dry. She was afraid to open it and read more. Maybe she should . . . delete the email. *She'd* be in control of her failure then, instead of these people who didn't know her. They were judging her based on some test scores and a handful of essays she'd written in an afternoon. That wasn't enough to measure the value of a person.

She cleared that nonsense out of her head and scolded herself for being a coward. She had to look. This could be everything to her, her family, and her girl. After taking a deep breath and sending a prayer to the sky, Buddha, and Jesus, too, she opened the email.

Dear Ms. Tran,

Your application has been thoroughly reviewed by staff at Santa Clara Community College.

Our international student scholarship sees extremely high competition every year and as such can only be awarded to the most exemplary students with proven academic potential.

While we commend you on your performance on the GED exam, after careful review of your application, we regret to tell

*you we cannot offer you this scholarship. We wish you luck in
your future endeavors.*

Respectfully,
Santa Clara Community College

She breathed inward. And kept breathing inward. Her eyes
blurred over, and her face burned hot, and her lungs threatened to
burst. When she exhaled, she lost more than air. She exhaled her
dreams and her hopes, and her body crumpled upon itself.

Droplets splashed against the freshly wiped tabletop, and she let
them fall. She'd been evaluated, deemed to have little to no worth,
and discarded. This kept happening to her. Again and again and
again. And she was so tired now. So tired.

How did you change your life when you were trapped like this?
Her history didn't define her. Her origins didn't define her. At least,
they shouldn't. She could be more, if she had a chance.

But people didn't *see* who she was inside. They didn't *know*. And
she had no way to show them without an opportunity.

The bells on the door jingled, and she looked up in time to see
Quân stride to her table. He wore a motorcycle jacket over a designer
T-shirt and jeans and dominated the restaurant with his large body
and larger presence.

He took one look at her, and his face creased with concern. "Oh
hell, what's wrong?" He glanced toward the kitchen. "Was it my
mom? Did she yell at you? I'll talk to her." He headed that way, and
she hurried to swipe an arm over her face.

"No, no, it was not Cô." She took a ragged breath and got to her
feet. Pushing a smile onto her lips, she asked, "Want anything? Water? Coffee? Coca-Cola?"

"No, I'm good. You should sit. You look . . ." He shook his head without finishing, ushered her back into the booth, and took the seat across from her. "What happened?" When she didn't respond right away, he asked, "Something with Khai? I kind of thought you two would get back together this week. I had a talk with him."

She pushed a practiced smile onto her lips and shook her head. "No, we are not together." She fingered the edges of her phone—more accurately *Khải's* phone, since she was going to give it back to him before she left.

"He hasn't called you or anything?" Quân asked.

She thinned her lips. "No." Would she have picked up if he had? She knew he wasn't going to tell her what she wanted to hear, but then, she couldn't help worrying about him either. The ceremony on Sunday had shaken him up in a way she'd never seen before. "How is he?"

Quân stretched his head from side to side and rubbed the back of his tattooed neck. "That's the big question, isn't it? No one knows. I don't think *he* knows."

She didn't know what to say to that, so she looked down at her phone.

"Why the tears?" he asked, sounding so *nice* she almost started crying again.

"Some news. I knew it was bad, but I had the hope anyway, and then . . ." She shrugged.

"News about what?"

"Scholarship, to go to college here. I did not get it." She tried as hard as she could to keep her tone light and even, but her voice wobbled at the end anyway.

"That was your plan? To get a scholarship and student visa?" he asked.

She nodded and pasted a determined smile on her face, bracing herself in case he laughed at her like the people at the community college probably had.

"Khai loves you, you know," he said instead.

She stiffened like lightning had struck her, and her heart skipped one beat, two beats. "He told you that?"

"No," he said with a twist of his lips. "He didn't tell me that. Well, not with words. But I can tell. You know he's autistic, right?"

That word. She remembered hearing it before. "Yes, he told me."

He searched her face. "Do you know what it means?"

She fidgeted with her phone uncomfortably. To be honest, she hadn't thought about it much. "I thought maybe the touching. There is a way to do it."

"That's part of it, but there's more. His mind is different—no, it's not a sickness. The way he thinks and also the way he processes emotions are not like most people."

That gave her pause. Yes, he was different, but his differences weren't unpassable obstacles. At least, she hadn't found them to be. To her, Khải was just Khải, and she accepted him the way he was.

The thing she still hadn't been able to accept was the fact that he didn't love her, that he didn't accept *her*.

As if he could read her mind, Quân said, "Khai loves you. He just hasn't figured it out yet."

She had difficulty believing that. Love wasn't complicated. You either felt it or you didn't. There was nothing to "figure out."

Quân's gaze turned penetrating, and he asked, "Do you want to find out once and for all if he does? I know how."

Her pride told her to say no, she'd given him enough chances. But her heart had to know. Feeling vulnerable, she said, "Yes, how?"

He looked her directly in the eyes and said, "If it doesn't work, you'll end up married to me. Willing to gamble?"

CHAPTER TWENTY-SIX

K hai stared at the Evite on his phone in a dazed stupor. He had to
be dreaming—no, not dreaming, nightmaring. This couldn't be
real.

YOU'RE CORDIALLY INVITED TO

Esmeralda and Quan's Wedding

Saturday, August 8th
11:00 a.m.–3:00 p.m.
San Francisco, CA

PLEASE RSVP BY AUGUST 7TH

Who the hell sent their invitations out the same week as their
wedding? No one, that was who. He was probably still in bed, hugging Esme's pillow close because it smelled like her. The scent had
been fading, and he didn't know what he'd do when it was gone

altogether. Start cuddling up with the dirty laundry she'd left behind maybe.

His phone buzzed with an incoming call as he stared at the Evite.
Quan mobile.

He hit the talk button immediately. "I just got your Evite."

Quan laughed, the fucker.

"It's not funny," Khai said, but his relief was almost dizzying. It
was just a practical joke.

"It wasn't meant to be," Quan said. "We're really getting married
Saturday."

His brother's words hit Khai like a punch in the gut, and he sank
down onto his couch. Esme's glass on the coffee table caught his eye.
There was only a tiny amount of water left inside. It would probably
dry out around the same time she married his traitor of a brother.

"You're really getting married?" he asked.

"That's the plan, yeah."

"To Esme." *His* Esme.

"It's either that or watch her leave on Sunday," Quan said. "This
is mostly to get her a green card, but I *do* like her. I'm looking at it as
a trial period. Who knows, maybe it'll work out, and we'll make a
go of it."

That gut-punched feeling worsened, and Khai gripped the edge
of the couch with his free hand and squeezed until his knuckles
turned white.

"Unless you're going to do it," Quan added.

"I already asked her."

"You know what you have to do if you want her to say yes."

"I. Don't. Love. Her," he gritted out. Why did people keep pushing him on this? It wasn't like he *enjoyed* saying he didn't love her.
He *wanted* to love her. He just . . . didn't.

"Did you get rid of that bike yet?" Quan asked in a casual tone.

Khai's muscles tightened until the blood vessels on his arm bulged. "No."

"Maybe you should go do that." Khai opened his mouth to argue, but before he could get a word out, Quan said, "I gotta go, but you're coming Saturday, right?"

"Yeah," Khai said.

"Great. See you then."

The line disconnected, and the gravity in the room pulled him down further.

This wasn't just a dance or a night. This was marriage. Esme was marrying Quan. She'd be sharing his apartment with him, maybe even his bed because of the nightmares, smiling at him every day, filling his silence, reading his accounting books.

She would fall in love with Quan. If she could fall for Khai, she'd *definitely* fall for Quan. And Quan would love her back. Quan would be excellent to her.

Fuck, he didn't want his brother to be excellent to Esme.

He pressed his palms to his eye sockets until his eyes hurt, but then he let his hands drop away, and he was staring at her glass again. There was only a millimeter or two of water left, and when it was dry, the likelihood of her filling it was basically zero.

What should he do? He couldn't let her go, and he couldn't marry her. But he couldn't let her marry Quan, either. None of the available options were acceptable.

He clenched his jaw and shot to his feet. That meant he had to find another option. And he knew just the one.

Tomorrow was the big day, and Khải hadn't called or tried to see Esme even once.

If he was willing to let her marry his brother, he couldn't be jealous.

Quân was wrong.

Just as she thought of him, Quân strode into the restaurant. Her chest constricted when she saw the large garment bag thrown over his shoulder.

She could guess what that was, and it made her palms sweat.

He set it down on the table and aimed a lopsided smile at her. "Vy borrowed this for you."

Esme wiped her hands on her apron. After looking at him to confirm it was okay, she reached for the zipper and pulled it down.

Gauzy folds of cloth spilled out of the bag, and she gasped and covered her mouth. It was Sara's ten-thousand-dollar Vera Wang gown.

Quân chuckled at her reaction. "It turns out booking wedding venues last minute is pretty nuts. You kinda have to take what you can get, and what I got was San Francisco City Hall—the couple who reserved it had some massive breakup and canceled yesterday. You're going to want to dress up."

"It is nice?"

"Yeah, pretty nice," Quân said with another laugh.

She pulled her hands away from the dress and wiped her palms over her apron again. She knew he'd mentioned marrying her if Khải didn't figure out his feelings, but he couldn't mean it. Why would he want to marry her? He didn't know anything about her.

With a wrinkle of her lips, she zipped the garment bag back up. "You should cancel the wedding and return this to Sara. Anh Khải did not call me. Don't waste your money."

"Can't. I already paid for city hall, and your family are on their way, remember?" His eyes gleamed as he aimed a clever smile at her, distracting her from the spark of desperate joy that came when she thought of seeing her girl after so long. "Besides, if you look happy because I'm spoiling you, he'll get even more jealous."

"More?" A bad taste filled her mouth. It was clear that he wasn't jealous *at all*.

Quân stepped close and tilted his head as he looked at her. "He's totally jealous over you. You know that, right?"

She stared at him without answering.

"I meant it when I said I'd marry you," Quân said. "It'd just be a temporary thing, anyway. I'll do my thing, and you'll do yours. Separate rooms. We can divorce when the time comes."

"But . . ." She shook her head in bemusement. "*Why* help me?"

A sad smile stretched over his lips. "Because I'm his big brother, and I need to make things right." Then his smile warmed and reached his eyes. "And I like you and want to see you make it. It's a small thing for me to do, but it means a lot to you, right?"

The breath seeped out of her, and all she could say was, *"Yes."* It was everything to her.

He pushed the dress back toward her. "Really, it's not a big deal to me, and my mom loves having you help at the restaurant. I don't see any downside to this."

Tension built up inside. She had to tell him. He deserved to know. She stared down at the garment bag, unsure if she should pull it closer or push it away. It depended on how he reacted to what she was going to say. "I have a little girl. Jade. She was home. In Việt Nam. Khải . . ." She bit her lip and ran her finger along the zipper. "He does not know about her."

When a long moment of silence passed, she peeked up and found Quân smiling at her. She saw no judgment in his eyes. "I like kids."

"You do?" she said on an exhaled breath.

"Sure."

"D-does Anh Khải?"

He thought about it for a second before saying, "I think he'd like *your* kid."

"Do you still want to marry?" she made herself ask. Sweat misted her skin, but she continued, "I want her to come live with me—with us. And my *má* and *ngoại*."

"Yeah," he said with a laugh. "Let's do it. The more the merrier, right? It actually doesn't matter much to me. I'm hardly home."

Her throat choked up, and she swiped the moisture from her eyes with the back of her arm as her body weakened with relief. "Then I am happy and grateful to marry you. But we do not need a nice wedding." Honestly, she wanted a cheap one. She was going to owe Quân for the rest of her life, and she didn't want to add an expensive wedding to her tab.

He shook his head at her. "I can see you worrying. Don't."

"But—"

"It's really fine, Esme." And this time, there was a hard edge to his tone and expression.

She nodded. "Okay, no worrying." But that was a lie.

Marrying Quân was the solution to all her problems. Once she married him, she could apply to schools as a legal resident and work for her tuition. She wouldn't need a scholarship in order to pursue her new dream.

But a large part of her still hoped Khải would intervene, and worried that he wouldn't. Her future, even an empowered one, wasn't perfect unless he was in it. And not as her brother-in-law.

CHAPTER TWENTY-SEVEN

Today was the day.

Khai had done everything humanly possible to find a way out of this mess. He'd spent money, pulled strings, found encouraging leads—if he bought a racehorse, he could say Esme was a horse trainer and get her a special visa that way—but he needed more time. He was out of time.

The wedding started in an hour.

He'd changed into his tux and was ready to go, but he couldn't bring himself to get into his car. That old playground song kept looping in his head. *Esme and Quan sitting in a tree, K-I-S-S-I-N-G...*

He'd lose his fucking mind if he saw Esme and Quan kiss. She was *his* to kiss, his to have and to hold, his to—

His to what?

He couldn't stand looking at the now-empty glass on his coffee table, so he fled. He didn't have a destination in mind, but of course, he ended up there.

In the garage.

He pressed the garage button, and as light filled the dark space, he advanced toward the bike. Dust particles sparkled in the sunlight like fireflies, and he breathed the old mustiness and gasoline-on-concrete smell into his lungs. For a moment, he shut his eyes, letting the scent take him back to a different time.

He yanked the tarp off the motorcycle and ran his fingers over one of the black handles. Bumpy texture, the grooves that fingers had worn into the rubber, cold, lifeless. It was always this way. Always disappointing. Just like when he'd walked it home after Esme took it to the store.

He ran his fingertips over the deep scratches on the side. He half expected to find blood in there, but his fingers met nothing but rough metal. Against the odds, this was all the motorcycle had to show for its collision with a four-ton semitruck. Andy hadn't been so lucky.

He'd been that 0.07 out of 100 who ended up in a fatal motorcycle accident. Because of Khai.

Khai had asked him to come over. Maybe *asked* wasn't the right word. He'd said something along the lines of, "Come over. Let's do stuff."

There'd been grumbling about summer school homework, and Khai had told him to bring it and they'd do it together. More like Khai would just do Andy's homework for him, but Khai didn't care as long as Andy was there.

"See you soon," Andy had said.

The drive from Andy's parents' place in Santa Clara to Khai's mom's place in East Palo Alto was about twenty-five minutes if you took Central Expressway, and Andy always did. He said the trees made him feel like a badass.

But twenty-five minutes had passed. Thirty. Forty. An hour. And still no Andy. Khai had paced back and forth, aggravated and impatient, sick, and he'd flipped through the pages of every book he could find until the corners were permanently upturned like ski slopes. When the phone had rung hours later, an incomprehensible *knowing* had claimed him. He hadn't picked it up. He'd stood still, rooted to the floor as his mom answered the phone. When she'd gone pale and sank against the counter, she'd confirmed his suspicion.

"Andy's dead."

Khai's head had gone quiet and crystal calm. No feelings, no pain, no more sick worry, just pure logic. In that moment, a pattern had arisen. Two points made a line, and you could extrapolate the slope and direction from there. His dad had left their family for a new one. Andy had died.

Bad things happened when he cared about people. But did he really care about them? Not if you compared his apparent level of caring to other people's.

He was pulling the motorcycle helmet over his head and straddling the bike before he realized what he was doing. A turn of the key in the ignition. The deafening roar of the engine.

He shot out of the garage and sped down the street.

He didn't plan to, but his hands guided him to Central Expressway. To the soaring pines. Sunlight in a cloudless sky. The pressure of the wind on his body. How many times had Andy experienced this? Hundreds maybe. Before everything had changed, Khai had planned to get a bike so they could do this together. In a way, they were doing it together now. The engine drowned out the crashing of his heart, but he felt it inside. He felt everything. Exuberance, fear, excitement, sorrow. *Most alive when you might die.*

He reached the place where three lanes merged into two, and a choking heat swelled over him. His lungs hurt, his muscles ached, his eyes stung. He brought the motorcycle to a skidding halt on the left shoulder and stumbled away, kicking up rocks and debris until he could brace himself against a pine tree.

This was the place. Andy had died right here. But there was no more caution tape, no more deep gouges on the road, none of that stuff. Sun, rain, and ten years of time had eroded the site of the accident, so it looked like anyplace. Just like time had dulled his emotions to the point where his brain could process them. It wasn't too much.

But it was a lot. It was the death anniversary all over again. But now there was no Esme, and he was alone with this sadness. It dragged and crushed, swallowing him. He tore his helmet off so he could breathe, but the hot air suffocated him instead. He raked at his hair and rubbed at his face.

And when he lowered his hand, his fingers came away wet. For a second, he thought it was blood, but the shiny fluid shone clear in the daylight.

Tears.

Not because of dust in his eyes or frustration or physical pain. These were sad tears for Andy. Ten years late.

He shook his head at himself. That took "delayed reaction" to an extreme. But he was an extreme kind of person.

His heart wasn't made of stone, after all. It just wasn't like everyone else's. Even without the tears, he'd know. He recognized he'd been deluding himself for a while. Quan was right.

It was easier to keep people at arm's length when it was for their own good instead of his. That way, he got to be a hero instead of a coward.

But now, he didn't care if he was a hero or a coward. All he wanted was to be Esme's.

When he checked his watch, he was dismayed to see it was 10:22 A.M. He'd been wasting time with an emotional episode—him, emotional—and the wedding started in thirty-eight minutes. He was going to be late, especially because it was impossible to find parking in San Francisco.

For a car.

A motorcycle, however . . .

He swiped his sleeve across his face, pulled his helmet back on, revved the engine, and exploded onto the streets. Central Expressway W, 85N, 101N. He'd never ridden a motorcycle on the freeway, and it was terrifying and exhilarating. There were no layers between him and the cars speeding at seventy, eighty, ninety miles an hour.

Most alive when you might die, indeed. He would have attempted a hundred miles per hour just for the hell of it, but he didn't want to willfully push himself into that 0.07 percent.

Once he reached the long stretch of the trip, he mentally tackled the problem at hand: He had a wedding to stop.

And there was only one thing that would make Esme change her mind. Only one thing she wanted to hear.

Three small words.

And the last time he'd tried to say them, he'd almost gotten himself into a car accident. He might as well practice now since he was living on the edge.

"I . . ." He tried to get the next word out, but his mind and body stubbornly resisted. Ten years of training were difficult to undo in such a short period of time. He forced the word out. "Love."

His heart jumped and started sprinting as fast as the motorcycle.

"I. Love." He took a heavy breath and plowed ahead with determination. "*I* love. I *love*. *I love*. I love, I love, I love." The wind stole most of the sound, but he still felt ridiculous talking to himself.

Until he added the last word.

"Esme." Everything softened inside of him. "I love Esme."

That felt good. That felt *right*.

He hoped he wasn't too late.

CHAPTER TWENTY-EIGHT

The minute hand on the clock ticked onto the six. Ten thirty A.M. and still no Khải.

Esme hugged her hands over her stomach and stared at her reflection again. The bride in the mirror looked sophisticated and beautiful—a ten-thousand-dollar Vera Wang dress would do that to anyone—and pale as death.

Khải wasn't going to stop the wedding. She had to marry his brother.

She'd told herself a thousand times he wouldn't come, and yet, the reality of it still crushed her like a mountain. Tears threatened to spill and ruin her makeup, and she quickly blinked them away. She told herself to be happy. Any other girl back home would say this was a dream come true. Handsome husband, designer gown, city hall, extravagant floral bouquets, tons of guests, and on top of all that, she and her family would be able to stay. They'd have that new shiny life they'd hardly dared to hope for. She could follow her dreams and be a proper role model for her daughter.

But it was the *wrong* handsome husband. Quân was great, but he wasn't Khải. He hadn't rushed to see her at the doctor's office or carried her to the car afterward. He hadn't kissed her like she was everything. He didn't reserve his best smiles for her only.

Without Khải, this wedding felt like a farce, but she was going to go through with it anyway. She'd told Quân everything, laid her secrets and flaws bare, and he still wanted her to have this opportunity. The government didn't care about her, the schools didn't, the scholarship organizations didn't, but this one person did, and sometimes one person could make a world of difference. She was going to do everything in her power to make sure he didn't regret helping her. She was going to make a difference to this world.

She squared her shoulders and lifted her chin, feeling determination burn deep within. She wasn't impressive in any way you could see or measure, but she had that fire. She *felt* it. That was her worth. That was her value. She would fight for her loved ones. And she would fight for herself. Because she mattered. The fire inside of her mattered. It could achieve and accomplish. People might look down on her, but she was making her way with as much integrity as she could with limited options. The woman in the mirror wore a wedding gown and high heels, but her eyes shone with the confidence and drive of a warrior.

If that wasn't classy, she didn't know what was.

"*Má.*"

Esme turned away from the mirror just as a small body launched itself at her. Little arms wrapped around her waist, and her heart burst with incandescence. She hefted her girl up and hugged her tight, pressing their cheeks together like she always did, and that enormous love bloomed inside of her. Baby smell, baby-soft skin, little body—well, not as little now.

"Here my girl is."

A little face snuggled close, and over her girl's shoulder, Esme saw her mom and grandma walk into the room.

They'd just arrived from Việt Nam yesterday and had to be exhausted and jet-lagged, but they'd both dressed in their fanciest *áo dài* and were grinning from ear to ear with excitement. Her mom even wore makeup. Esme had never seen her so beautiful, and suddenly, she was glad Quân had decided to have such an extravagant wedding. Weddings were as much for families as they were for the bride and groom, maybe more.

"Already, let your mom go. You'll ruin her dress," her mom said as she urged Jade to climb down. Then she hugged Esme tight, and Esme couldn't help catching the light smell of fish sauce from her mother's clothes and hair and grinning. Esme had to be half Americanized now if she detected that scent. She didn't mind it, though.

Her mom pulled away and sighed with maternal pride as she looked at Esme in her gown. "Girl is sublimely beautiful."

"Truly beautiful." Her grandma hugged her briefly, an extraordinary display of affection since older generations didn't generally hug, and Esme caught the smell of more fish sauce. Instead of worrying about venting out the room, she breathed the smell deep into her lungs. It reminded her of home. She was a country girl, after all. Her origins didn't define her, but they were a part of her. She refused to be ashamed of them.

"Má looks like a fairy," Jade said in awe before her forehead wrinkled. "Will Cậu Quân be my dad after this?"

Esme sighed and brushed her fingers over her girl's soft cheek. "I don't know. Maybe. But don't get your hopes up, okay? Cậu Quân is just marrying me to help us. It's not a real marriage. Do you understand?"

Jade's expression turned solemn. "I understand."

"This place is too nice for it not to be a real marriage," her mom insisted, looking at the fancy crown molding and furniture. "So clean, so big, *air conditioning*. He has good intentions, Mỹ à."

Esme didn't have the energy to explain, so she sighed and lifted her shoulders. The four of them settled onto the couches, Jade right next to her mommy, and caught up on the gossip from home as the minutes ticked by on the clock.

Esme grew antsier with each passing second until finally she hugged Jade close and shut her eyes, too distracted to concentrate on the talking.

A knock sounded, and Quân cracked the door open, walked inside, and shut the door behind him. He nodded at her grandma and mom and winked at Jade before focusing on Esme, looking dangerously handsome in his suit and tattoos. Maybe he appeared a little dazed, too. Esme had never looked so stunning, and she knew it.

Recovering, he said, "It's time." He shrugged his shoulders to adjust his suit coat. "He's not here, so let's do this."

"Are you sure?" Esme asked.

"Absolutely. Are you?"

Esme stood up, brushed her skirts off, took a big breath, and nodded. "Yes. Thank you. For everything."

His eyes met hers and crinkled at the edges as he smiled. "Of course." He opened the door and led Esme and her family into the hallway, where an older man in a suit waited with an elaborate bouquet of white roses in his hands. "This is my uncle. He's going to walk you down the aisle."

The man smiled and bowed his head at everyone, murmuring polite greetings.

"No, I'll walk her down," her mom said before she grabbed Esme's hand and squeezed. "I've been both her mom and her dad since she was little. I should do it."

Quân smiled in surprise. "Okay, then. Bác will let you know

when it's time to walk. See you there." He nodded at her once and ushered her grandma and Jade toward the ceremony location, leaving Esme and her mom there in the hallway with his uncle.

She took shallow breaths and flashed a tight smile at her mom and Quân's uncle as she battled a rising sense of panic. She was doing the right thing; she knew it. But her heart didn't care. It wanted what it wanted, and that was not Quân or a fake marriage. Her heart wanted Khải, forever.

Loud footsteps echoed down the marble hall, and for a second, her hopes rose. Maybe he'd come after all.

But the footsteps faded before anyone appeared, and Esme's hopes plummeted again.

A cello started playing somewhere in the distance, and Quân's uncle said, "This way."

He handed Esme the bouquet, and her hands went numb. Loud silence filled her head.

It was time.

Her mom hooked arms with her, smiled with encouragement, and guided her to follow Quân's uncle. The building echoed as high-heeled shoes clicked over the marble, *click-click, click-click, click-click*. They entered the rotunda, where the ceremony was to take place at the bottom of the grandest staircase she'd ever seen. A domed ivory-colored ceiling arched several stories above with intricate artwork of angels—or perhaps naked people. Either way, they had to be cold.

Rows and rows of guests, flowers, a cellist, a handsome groom waiting for her at the altar. It should have made her happy. It didn't.

She clutched her bouquet tighter, lifted her chin, and prepared to walk down the center aisle between the seated guests.

"Sir, you can't go in here. There's a wedding taking place. Sir—"

A commotion behind her had her whipping around as her heart sang with anticipation.

But it wasn't Khải.

It was an older man, a familiar-looking man, even though she was certain she'd never met him before.

Average height, a bit of a belly, khaki pants, a light-blue button-down shirt, and a navy-blue sports coat. Short hair that was more salt than pepper. And eyes that could be any color from this distance. If she was being honest, they looked brown.

Her heart stopped beating.

Did he have truck-driver hands?

"Is it you?" he asked, but he wasn't looking at Esme. "Linh?"

Esme's mom gasped and covered her mouth.

The man stepped forward, his movements slow like he was in a trance. "I got the strangest voice mail yesterday. Someone asking for a Phil who knew a Linh in Vietnam twenty-four years ago. He said Phil's daughter was getting married in San Francisco's City Hall today, and she needed her father."

He searched Esme's face before focusing beside her again, and her mom gripped Esme's arm like it was the only thing keeping her upright.

"I didn't know for sure. I thought chances were low. I came anyway," the man said as he came closer yet, two meters away, one meter, and the light-green shade of his eyes took the breath from Esme's lungs. "I took the next flight out, a red-eye, from New York City."

"Y-you live in New York?" her mom asked, using the only English Esme had ever heard her speak.

"Alone—I live alone in New York." He cleared his throat before continuing. "I came back. For you. I looked for you everywhere. You were nowhere. But now, I think I know why. She's"—his gaze switched back to Esme—"mine?"

Her mom pushed on Esme until she stepped toward him, and Esme said, "Schumacher? Is that your name? Phil Schumacher?"

Puzzled creases darkened his brow. "Phil Schuma— No, I'm not a Schumacher. My name is Gleaves. Gleaves Philander. I went by Phil until I grew into Gleaves," he said with an apologetic smile before his eyes widened with horror. "That's why you couldn't find me? All you knew was Phil. You've been looking for a Philip."

"Do we want to postpone the wedding and talk about this somewhere in private?" Quân asked as he stalked down the aisle toward their small group.

Before anyone could answer, there was another commotion behind them. "Sir, there's a wedding—"

"I'm here for the wedding," a familiar voice said, and Khải burst into the room, looking out of sorts with his hair standing up in all directions and his chest billowing on heavy breaths like he'd run here. He took one look at Esme, and his eyes went dreamy.

"You're late," Quân said.

Without taking his eyes away from Esme, Khải said, "There was traffic, but it helped that I rode the motorcycle here. I went around the stopped cars."

"About time," Quân said.

But Khải didn't acknowledge his brother. He was watching Esme like he usually did, with complete, undivided attention. "I'm sorry I'm late—with riding the bike and coming here."

She shook her head. Once she'd seen the photograph of his cousin next to the motorcycle, everything had clicked into place. "No need for sorry. I understand you."

Khải swallowed and stepped toward her, stretched his fingers out, relaxed them, stretched them out again. "Is the wedding over already? There was something I needed to say."

"No, it is not over." Esme's hands shook, so she tightened them on her bouquet. He was here. He'd come. He had something important to say.

Her hope grew so big she didn't know how her body held it.

His shoulders sagged in relief before he noticed the other wedding crasher next to him. "Who are you?"

The man—very possibly her *dad*—fumbled for words for a moment before he said, "I'm Gleaves."

Khải nodded like everything was perfectly normal. "You must be the right Phil, then. Glad you made it."

"You're the one who left the voice message," Gleaves said.

"You never called me back."

"I hopped on the next plane out."

"That's good—" Whatever Khải would have said next was interrupted when Jade ran down the aisle and latched onto Esme's skirts.

"He's Cậu Khải," Jade said.

Khải's jaw dropped, and he stared at Jade. "There's a tiny Esme."

Esme's heart slammed hard as she glanced from Khải to Gleaves and back. Both men looked dumbfounded. "Her name is Jade. She is mine."

Jade huddled closer.

Khải's eyes met hers. "You never told me."

"Cô Nga said you did not want a family, and I was afraid, and—" She bit her lip. She didn't have any more arguments than that.

What had he come here to say? Had this news changed things?

She lifted her chin. If he thought she was unclassy for having a baby so young, he didn't deserve her or Jade.

He surprised her by crouching down, considering Jade, and holding his hand out like they were acquaintances meeting for business.

Jade glanced at Esme for a second before she eased toward Khải. After looking at him for a long while, she shook his hand like a little grown-up.

Neither said a single word, but Esme got the feeling they understood each other perfectly.

When Khải straightened, he glanced around, looking at Gleaves, Jade, Quân, and finally Esme's mom. Inclining his head at her, he said, "*Chào, Cô.*"

Her mom narrowed her eyes at him. "Already, what important thing do you have to say? We have a lot of people here waiting for the wedding to start."

At that moment, Esme became horribly conscious of the attention focused on them, hundreds of curious eyes. "Má, let's go somewhere private. He can say it there, and—"

"No, here, where everyone can see," her mom demanded in a steely voice, standing up to him despite the gigantic gap in their wealth and education levels. "My daughter was good to you, and you broke her heart. What do you have to say?"

He flinched and let his gaze roam over the crowd, and Esme knew he hated their attention as much as she did. Eventually, however, he focused on her again, stepped forward, and spoke.

"*Anh yêu em.*"

She drew in a silent breath and covered her mouth, too shocked to speak, to do anything. Even in her wildest dreams, he told her in English.

He took another step toward her, and another, until they were a mere arm's length apart. Looking at her like she was everything, he said, "I love you. I told myself I didn't. Because I was afraid to lose someone again, and I doubted myself, and I wanted only the best for you. But the feeling has gotten too big to deny. My heart works in a different way, but it's yours. You're my one."

He motioned toward Gleaves and Quân, and both men stood up straighter.

"You have options now. You don't have to marry if you don't want to. Now that we've found your dad, your paperwork will be easy—well, easier. But if you *do* want to marry . . ." He breathed in deeply and fell to one knee. "Marry *me*. And not just for three years, but for keeps." He patted at his pockets and grimaced. "I forgot your ring, but I swear I got you one. It's nice. You can probably cut windows with it if—" He cleared his throat and looked at her with melting softness. "Will you marry me? If you still love me?"

Her heart filled and filled and filled until her eyes blurred over with tears. "I will always love you."

"Is that a yes?" he asked.

She handed the bouquet to her mom and pulled him to his feet. "I do not have to, but, yes, I will marry you."

His biggest grin stretched over his face, with dimples, and before all the wedding guests, he drew her close and kissed her like the first time. Lips to lips, hearts melting together, no distance between them, not even an arm's length.

EPILOGUE

Four years later

The sun beat down on Khai as he sat on the bleachers in Stanford University's outdoor stadium, waiting as students in gowns and square hats marched across the stage far below. Jade had been excited an hour ago, but now she occupied herself by reading from a chapter book with some manner of magical she-warrior on the cover. From time to time, Khai's mom dug slices of peeled Asian pear from her purse and handed them to her, and Jade absently gobbled them down as her eyes scanned the words on the page at a greedy clip.

"My Ngoc Tran, summa cum laude," the announcer called out.

Khai and their entire row of family jumped to their feet and cheered. During the naturalization process, she'd chosen to use her Vietnamese name on all official documents. He was the only one who called her Esme now, and he liked that.

Esme waved at them from the stage, and when she blew a kiss in their direction, Khai knew it was just for him. Jade didn't like kisses anymore—he missed it a little if he was being honest—but she was more interesting to talk to now.

After all the students' names had been called out, they went to meet Esme at a prearranged spot on campus. The second she saw them, she split from her friends and ran to hug and kiss him.

"I'm all done," she said, grinning in a way that still scrambled his brain after four years with her.

"Not really," he said. "You still have approximately six years before you get your PhD in international finance." The way she explained it, she wanted to solve the big problems in this world, and they all revolved around money.

She playfully punched his shoulder. "Done for now."

"Is that when you're finally going to marry him?" her dad asked. "After graduate school?"

Her mom squeezed her recently married husband's arm. "Don't pressure her. School first, marry after."

Gleaves made a grumbly sound, but he nodded.

Khai's mom, however, barged in and said, "Why no pressure? She made such a beautiful baby. It is a waste not to make more."

All three grandparents nodded and mumbled in agreement, and Jade rolled her eyes. "I'm nice, too, and hardworking and a lot of other things."

Esme went to hug her girl. "Yes, you are. You make Mommy proud."

"I'm proud of *you*, Mommy," Jade said, earning a teary smile from her mom.

As Khai watched mother and daughter, he recognized *he* was the proud one. Four years ago, he'd thought he had too many women in his life to have room for another, but he'd been wrong. He'd had just enough room for two more, and his heart, he found, was very far from being made of stone.

He wrapped his arms around them and kissed Esme's temple. "I'm proud of both of you."

Esme smiled and asked Jade, "What do you think? Are you ready for Mommy to marry Cậu Khải?"

Jade danced in place. "Really? This summer? The drive-through wedding in Las Vegas?"

Khai laughed. "You sound more excited than your mom."

"Then you can adopt me, and you'll officially be my dad," Jade said.

Khai's chest swelled, and not once did he tell himself it was a heat flash or a health problem. He knew exactly what it was.

When he looked at Esme, her green eyes softened, and she ran her fingers over his jaw. "Look at that smile and those dimples. You must love us a lot."

"More than a lot. Are you sure you want to do it this summer? I can wait as long as you want."

He'd already put Esme and Jade in his will, though they didn't know—about the will itself or all the money they'd be inheriting from him because he had no idea what to do with it. That stuff wasn't important.

All that mattered was that they'd be taken care of if something happened to him. Not that they needed him at all. Esme was a force to be reckoned with.

"I'm ready," Esme said. Then her lips curved. "And I want to see Elvis."

He laughed. "No one in Vegas is the real Elvis."

Eyes sparkling, she said, "I know. But maybe they feel like Elvis inside. That's the important part."

He brought their foreheads together as he laughed again. "You're definitely stranger than I am."

"No way."

He grinned.

She grinned back. *"Em yêu anh."*

Without hesitation, he replied, *"Anh yêu em."*

The words wrapped around and around them, drawing them together.

Em yêu anh yêu em.

Girl loves boy loves girl.

THE END

AUTHOR'S NOTE

Most of my childhood memories of my mom involve her sleeping. Either I'd stayed up late and managed to catch her coming home from work and climbing into bed, or I was sneaking into her bedroom in the morning before school and digging through her purse for lunch money, trying my best not to wake her because I knew she'd worked ridiculous hours the day before and would do it all over again this day. She wasn't the kind of mother that I saw on TV or that my classmates had, but while our interactions were short and far in between, they were enough for me to understand I was loved and she was proud of me.

I was certainly proud of her (and will always be). My mom is a legend in my family. Hers is a classic American dream story. At the end of the Vietnam War, she and my four older siblings (ages three through seven), my grandma, and a handful of other relatives fled to the United States as war refugees. With no money, no connections, broken English, an eighth-grade education, and no help from the men in her life, she was able to work her way into owning not one, not two, not three, but *four* successful restaurants in Minnesota. She was and is my hero, my idol, and my role model. She made me believe I could do anything if I tried hard enough.

But as much as I admire and love her, I didn't actually *know* her very well. Not as a person. I didn't have a deep understanding of what drove her, what her fears and vulnerabilities were. Like most of the people in my life, she always tried to shield me from the bad, leaving me with bright eyes and little concept of how difficult it truly was to make her way in this country. That changed when I wrote this book.

I'm ashamed to say, however, that when I first set out to write *The Bride Test*, Esme—this character who shares so much in common with my mom—was not the heroine. She was the unwanted third leg of a love triangle, a woman from Vietnam whom Khai's mom had arranged for him to marry even though his heart was elsewhere. I figured the story would be deliciously angsty and maybe a little amusing. Despite communication issues and a culture clash, Khai would feel obligated to help this woman, but in the end, he'd find a way to be with his true love, someone American-born.

A funny thing happened as I tried to write that story. Esme kept outshining the character who was meant to be Khai's true love. Esme was brave, and she was fighting for a new life for herself and her loved ones in every way she could. She had reasons, she had depth, but she also had a striking vulnerability. All of her "drawbacks" were not due to her character. They were things beyond her control: her origin, her education level, her lack of wealth, the language she spoke—things that shouldn't matter when determining the value of a person (if that can even be done). It was impossible not to love her. After the first chapter, I stopped writing.

I asked myself why I'd automatically decided my heroine had to be "Westernized." Why couldn't she have an accent, have less education, and be culturally awkward? The person I respect most in the entire world is just like that. After careful self-analysis, I realized I'd been subconsciously trying to make my work socially acceptable, which was completely *un*acceptable to me as the daughter of an immigrant. The book had to be reconceptualized. Not only did Esme deserve center stage, but I *needed* to tell her story. For me. And for my mom.

But when I restarted the drafting process with a fresh concept and new heroine, I ran into more roadblocks, *tougher* roadblocks. I'm not an immigrant. I have an Ivy League education. I've never experienced true poverty. What do I know about this kind of immigrant experience? I began to research in earnest, hoping I could find what I needed in books and video like I always had in the past.

For interested parties, here are some of the resources I read/watched for greater insights into the Vietnamese immigrant experience:

1. *The Unwanted* by Kien Nguyen
2. *Inside Out & Back Again* by Thanhha Lai
3. *It's a Living: Work and Life in Vietnam Today* edited by Gerard Sasges
4. *Mai's America*, a documentary by Marlo Poras

These resources, while wonderful, were insufficient for my purposes. What I needed was a window into the heart of a magnificent Vietnamese woman, someone who had left everything behind, started over in a new world, and succeeded despite the challenges. It would also help if this woman knew what it was like to love an autistic man with issues of his own. Like my father. This was when the conversations started between my mom and me.

For the first time, she opened up and gave me both sides of her stories, not just the bright sides. For example, I'd always known she grew up poor, but she'd never gone into detail. Now she told me about the kind of poverty that still gives her goose bumps when she thinks back. I would share these stories, as I think they provide an amazing contrast to the present and illustrate just how far she's come—they make me *prouder* of her—but to my mom, these stories are a source of terrible shame, even decades later as a successful businesswoman. She told me about the time an American officer offered to adopt her as a little girl and send her home to the States—surely that had to be better for her than being poor in Vietnam—but when her dad found out, he'd cried and cried. I'd heard the story about how my family members escaped to the United States and were taken in by a host family in Minnesota, but I never knew that their refugee plane originally landed in Camp Pendleton, California. No one ever told me that they had to leave for a refugee camp in Nebraska because a violent civilian crowd threw things at them and yelled for the "chinks" to "go home." Through fresh tears, my mom told me about the blatant discrimination and sexism she faced in the workplace, about how she cried during her breaks but vowed to work even harder and prove herself. Because good work, she says, always speaks for itself. And so it did. And so it does.

Because of these conversations, I was able to give Esme a depth and soul that I wouldn't have otherwise. I hope that comes out in the reading. Most important, the conversations gave me my mom, the fuller, more authentic version of her, and now I love her even more, respect her even more. I'm grateful for all those hours spent talking to her and so proud to share the essence of her with readers through Esme.

Sincerely,
Helen

THE
Bride
TEST

HELEN HOANG

DISCUSSION QUESTIONS

1. Khải grew up in America, while Mỹ was born and raised in a small village in Vietnam. What cultural differences can you see and how do you think this affects who they are now?

2. In the beginning of the book, Khải's mother is in Vietnam to search for a wife for Khải. Do you think it's wrong of his mother to meddle and interfere in his personal life, or is this justified as an act of love?

3. Prior to reading this book, how would you have imagined an autistic man? How does Khải compare to this vision?

4. Throughout the book, Khải is adamant about not having feelings, thus creating a chasm between him and everyone else. When do you see a breakthrough in this way of thinking? How does Mỹ help with this?

5. Khải memorizes a set of rules that his sister made him that lists what he should do when he's with a girl (page 37). Do you agree with this list?

6. Though Mỹ originally goes to America with the purpose of seducing Khải, a lot of her time is spent going to night school and working at Cô Nga's restaurant. This reflects the hard work that immigrants go through to build a life in the U.S. Can you or anyone you know relate to this?

7. Mỹ lies to Khải about her occupation and tells him that she's an accountant. She does this because she's embarrassed by her station in life but also to feel some sort of connection to him. Should she have just told him the truth from the beginning or do you think her lie helps bring them together at least a little?

8. As adamant as Khải is about not loving Mỹ, he does things for her that show how much he does care about her, such as carrying her and helping to find her father. What other ways does he show he loves her?

9. At the end of the book, Khải tells Mỹ he loves her in Vietnamese. What is the significance of this?

Photo by Eric Kieu

Helen Hoang is that shy person who never talks. Until she does. And then the worst things fly out of her mouth. She read her first romance novel in eighth grade and has been addicted ever since. In 2016, she was diagnosed with autism spectrum disorder in line with what was previously known as Asperger's syndrome. Her journey inspired *The Kiss Quotient*. She currently lives in San Diego, California, with her husband, two kids, and a pet fish.

CONNECT ONLINE

helenhoang.com
facebook.com/hhoangwrites
instagram.com/hhoangwrites
twitter.com/hhoangwrites

Ready to find
your next great read?

Let us help.

Visit prh.com/nextread